Items should be returned on or before the last date
shown below. Items not already requested by other
borrowers may be renewed in person, in writing or by
telephone. To renew, please quote the number on the
barcode label. To renew online a PIN is required.
This can be requested at your local library.
Renew online @ **www.dublincitypubliclibraries.ie**
Fines charged for overdue items will include postage
incurred in recovery. Damage to or loss of items will
be charged to the borrower.

Leabharlanna Poiblí Chathair Bhaile Átha Cliath
Dublin City Public Libraries

Dublin City
Baile Átha Cliath

Date Due	Date Due	Date Due
1 0 AUG 2009		
0 4 DEC 2009		
2 3 MAR 2011		
8 DEC 2012		
2 7 JAN 2014		
2 0 OCT 2017		

THE FANTASTICAL FEATS OF FINN MACCOUL

THE FANTASTICAL FEATS
OF
FINN MACCOUL

Edited and retold by
NORAH MONTGOMERIE

Illustrated by Paul Rumsey

BIRLINN

First published in 2009 by
Birlinn Limited
West Newington House
10 Newington Road
Edinburgh
EH9 1QS

www.birlinn.co.uk

ISBN: 978-1-84158-817-9

Set in Adobe Jenson and Silvus at Birlinn
Printed and bound in Great Britain by Bell & Bain Ltd., Glasgow

Contents

PREFACE

NORAH Montgomerie was my Grandmother. This collection of folk tales was initially accepted for publication in the 1970s, following a number of successful children's story books and other folk and fairy tale collections, including *The Well At World's End, To Read and to Tell* and *More Stories To Read and to Tell.*

Due to prevailing economic conditions at the time (the reason in the letter at least) the publisher pulled out of the deal in 1979, leaving this collection as yet unavailable to the public. This made Norah very unhappy, as she sincerely believed not only in the power of these tales but also in their inherent value. Before she died I promised her that I would try and get this collection the public recognition I know she felt it deserved.

Ingunn and I have tried, in re-editing this collection, to recreate the original volume from a large number of disparate sources. We have included acknowledgments and references where we have found them, and apologise now if there are those who may have been inadvertently overlooked. May we extend our thanks from her to those people now.

The order of the tales is the order set by Norah, and we would not dream of changing that in any way. There is a logical sequence to the tales, starting from the naming of Finn and ending on the Isle of Skye, where it is rumoured he is buried. Many versions exist in draft form of each of the tales, but we have tried to use where possible those versions which were corrected and accepted as final.

I am only sorry that Norah could not see this collection being published. We hope in publishing it posthumously we will do a little to keep her work alive, and allow the people for whom these tales were told to at least gain access to them.

Julian Brooks, Oxford, 2009

ACKNOWLEDGEMENTS

Acknowledgements are made to Kenneth Hurlstone Jackson and Routledge & Kegan Paul Ltd, for permission to reprint 'The Hill of Howth' from *A Celtic Miscellany*, Kenneth Hurlstone Jackson, 1951, 1971.

And my sincere thanks to Professor Jackson for answering queries, and also to the Edinburgh and Scottish Libraries in Edinburgh for their courtesy and patience.

Norah Montgomerie

Introduction

HE CELTS fascinate us, and it would be surprising if they did not. They have left such strange and mysterious evidence of their ancient culture. Although usually connected with Ireland, Wales and the West Highlands of Scotland, the Celts once swept through Europe, leaving a trail of carved, sculptured and standing stones; and magical traces like the White Horse of Uffington and the Giant of Cerne Abbas, in Dorset.

The Celts of antiquity originally had affinities with the Indo-European warrior groups that overran the Indus Valley civilisations, a millennium or so before the Celts, as we know them, emerged from the Salzkammergut centre of salt and copper mines at Halstatt, in Upper Austria, about 800 BC. Salt was, of course, of great importance to the Celts. The wealth it created produced an exchange of materials and ideas from the outside world, and development followed. This was confirmed by the great variety of materials imported from Greece, Etruria, and Rome, found in the huge Celtic cemetery excavated at Halstatt in the last century.

From 800 BC to 500 BC, there was an important technological change taking place in Europe. Iron was replacing bronze in the making of tools and weapons. Although bronze continued to be used by the most skilled Celtic craftsmen, it was evident that iron was more durable, and that those who used it would gain technological and military superiority and power over their rivals. 'They shook all empires but they founded none,' said the German historian, Mommsen.

This may account for the fact that the Celts became famous as great warriors as well as great hunters; and that the SMITH and the SWORD assumed power and supernatural importance in their mythology. This mythology is full of strange gods and stranger happenings, with the grim tradition and custom of beheading and collecting human heads, which they displayed on spikes at the entrance of their strongholds. The Celts venerated the human head, and their temples were decorated with the heads of their enemies, and they even had niches for the human skulls, which were preserved as trophies. So it was natural that their heroes should be warriors; and the most popular of them was Finn MacCoul, Lord of the Fian. 'The origin of the French nation goes back to the Celts…', as Prof. Hubert says.

Finn MacCoul led bands of warriors, called the Fianna, who lived apart from and were independent of normal society. Fian, Fianna, means a kind of Vassal, suggesting that they were conscripted from a subject population. Their leaders (Finn was the most outstanding) had no territorial lordship – they moved from place to place, and supported themselves by hunting (they are hunters when they're not fighters). Finn is no aristocratic hero – he is a folk hero – crafty as well as brave, vindictive as well as generous. Membership of the Fianna was exclusive. Acceptance was gained only by successfully undergoing initiatory ordeals as proof of excellence of courage, prowess and exceptional dexterity. In spite of this, many of the tales reveal members of a Fian as true folk heroes, resorting to cunning and supernatural powers to get them out of tight corners.

The sagas came out of the folk and to a large extent were developed by the folk. It also entered the Courts of Ireland, when they had grown tired of the tales of northern heroes and wanted a saga of their own, and so Finn became a national hero-guardian of the high Kings of Ireland.

J.F. Campbell, in Volume IV of his *Popular Tales of the West Highlands*, describes the Fianna as: 'Irish militia, raised in the ninth century under the command of Finn MacCoul, who was appointed by provincial kings of Ireland, General in Chief, with several commanders under him, the most eminent of whom was Diarmid, his nephew. This force consisted of 7,000 men in times of peace, and 21,000 in time of war. They were maintained for the purpose of repelling the

Danes and the Norwegians (the Lochlanners of the tales) whose frequent incursions and bloody invasions had desolated the country for years.'

This may or may not be actual history; what interests us are the legends that have grown up about these men, who were not only warriors, but also great hunters, herdsmen and fishermen. And we are amazed at the freedom and mobility with which they moved about the length and breadth of the land, and sailed the oceans, in pursuit of their quarry or enemies. According to tradition, Finn and the Fianna were generally represented as Irish heroes. The scene is often laid in Ireland, but there are hundreds of places in Scotland in which some of their exploits took place, and there are many mountains, straits and lochs bearing their names in all parts of Scotland.

Finn himself was never a god, nor was he ever called a king of any country. He was sometimes called the King of the Fianna, and was said to be the strongest among them. He was also a poet and practised the art as a protection against his hereditary enemies of the house of Morna, who had been responsible for his father's death. He was a seer as well as a warrior. According to some legends, he acquired the power of prophecy by dipping his finger into the broth of the flesh of the Salmon of Wisdom, which he was cooking. He had a tooth of knowledge, and by touching it with his finger, he could foretell the future. (Could this belief be connected with the origin of the term 'wisdom' teeth?)

Finn had a wooden whistle, called the 'Wooden Crier,' and a hammer called the 'Ord Fianna'. If he blew the whistle three times, or struck the hammer three times, in both cases it would be heard by any member of a Fian, 'across the four quarters of the Universe', and they would go at once to Finn's aid in an emergency. Most prized of all Finn's possessions was his sword, the famous Mac an Luin, or 'White Sword of Light,' which had been forged by the Smith of the White Glen to fit his hand and no others.

There are similarities between Finn and the Welsh hero, Gweynn ap Nudd, and with the British hero, Arthur. All defend their territories against the foreign invader and overcome dreadful monsters. They are all hunters and can invade the supernatural world. Each has a special sword.

If Finn is much more primitive than Arthur, it may be because he has not been romanticised by a literary genius like Sir Thomas Malory, despite the efforts of Macpherson. There are parallels in some stories, especially that of Diarmid and Gráinne. Legends about them circulated among the common people before they were accepted by the Christian Church in Ireland, and eventually by the literati of the twelfth, fifteenth and eighteenth centuries. As a rule, the spread of a national heroic tradition is mainly determined by political considerations; thus the spread of Arthurian romance throughout Europe coincides with the establishment of an Angevin empire, the centre of which was England.

These tales of Finn MacCoul and other Celtic heroes are often variants of tales common to all Celtic, Aryan, and indeed, most races. They are essentially mythic, that is they involve the supernatural, and are made up from incidents common to the mythopoetic stage of story telling that all peoples pass through.

Nutt believed in the evolutionist theory of folklore rather than the diffusionist theory, and is quoted as saying: 'No other Aryan civilization has developed itself so independently of the two great influences: Hellenic and Hebriac, which have moulded the modern world: nowhere else in the course of development less perplexed by cross-currents; nowhere can the great issues be kept more steadily in view.' (Alfred Nutt, *Celtic Myth and Saga* Archaeological Review, II (1889) p. 137.) He concluded that modern Celtic folklore did retain ideas held by primitive Celts.

Not only are the incidents common to all such stories, but so are the pattern and ritualistic method of telling them, for example, the 'triad' pattern in which there are always three sons, three kings, three daughters, and three attempts before there is success in overcoming terrible obstacles (third time lucky?). The duration of time is usually a year and a day, or seven years. But the deer, with his antlers, and the salmon, are special to Celtic folklore.

Another characteristic pattern in these stories is the 'Run'. Runs are stereotyped descriptive passages, which are common to all orally preserved myths or tales. They serve to assist the narrator's memory, and act as a framework within which he fits the incidents. Celtic storytelling is very rich in the variety and number of runs incorporated, as is the Greek mythology of Homer. The chief characteristic of these runs is the accumulation of adjectives, which express minute shades of meaning. The collocation of words depends as much on their sound as on their meaning; so a literal translation from the Gaelic into English is bound to lose some of this, and read as sheer nonsense. These runs fall into several types, according to the incidents/occasions they describe. (Runs were employed in the long hero tales by storytellers, to involve/impress their audience and to afford a rest to the narrator's memory.) Sometimes the language of the runs is obscure or corrupt. Some of these passages or runs are so fine that it may be they were composed in the first place by early bards or poets. Certainly some are the essence of poetry. In these tales there are runs to describe 'resting on a hill', 'wrestling', 'storms', 'sailing on the sea' and 'casting of spells' etc. Apart from assisting the narrator's memory they create a sense of participation on the part of the listener, who enjoys anticipating the passages. All 'live' entertainers know the value of this, and anyone who has told stories to children knows their delight in repetition and the formal pattern of a story. Children are merely small men and women. To deny ritual completely is to cut off some basic part of ourselves, and we do so at our peril.

One character who puzzles some people these days is the 'Big Lad', the wandering gillie or servant, who turns up in so many stories, seeking service with the hero. It has been suggested that he could be the hero's 'alter-ego', the spirit that demands attention, and who, once the hero has taken him into his service, drives the hero on to overcome impossible difficulties and undertake dangerous quests, which companions think unnecessary or even ludicrous. Most of us have come across such 'Big Lads', but only heroes take them on.

Most sources for the tales about Finn and the Fianna are in Irish or published in Ireland. All are interesting, but I have not used any of them. Instead I have gone to the Scottish collections, which I know well and have always found refreshingly direct. They are the oral records, as told in Gaelic by untutored fishermen, crofters, blacksmiths, tailors, over one hundred years ago to a group of devoted men who lived beside them, most of them ministers of the Church, in the Highlands and Islands of Western Scotland. They are to be found in the *Popular Tales of the West Highlands*, collected and translated into English from the Gaelic by J.F. Campbell, and published in four volumes by Alexander Gardener of Paisley between 1890 and 1892. Also in the less-known *Waifs and Strays of Celtic Tradition*, where in five volumes are the collections of stories translated by D. MacInnes, John Gregerson Campbell and J. Macdougall, published by the Folk Lore Society and David Nutt of London between 1890 and 1895, under the directorship of Lord Archibald Campbell.

We owe special gratitude to all nineteenth century collectors who carefully gathered songs, ballads and folk tales, wrote them down in their beautiful long-hand in little notebooks, and eventually found enthusiastic publishers to capture them for us in print. But they had their difficulties, as the Rev. J.F. Campbell pointed out in 1890:

'Certain persons were so zealous in the cause of TRUTH, that they assured a simple old man who had repeated a number of stories to one of my collectors, that he would have to substantiate every word he had uttered, or suffer punishment for telling falsehoods. I found him in great perturbation, evidently expecting that I had arrived to call him to account, and I had some trouble in setting his mind at rest. He repeatedly assured me that he had only told what others had told him.'

Perhaps this is why the best oral storytellers are now the tinkers and travelling folk. The School of Scottish Studies in Edinburgh has collectors recording them on tape.

These days, it is not the religious folk who are critical of the way these tales are told, but some of the academics, who seem to prefer to keep them safely in university archives, rather than have them circulating in more popular form, available to the folk to whom they belong.

The excellent work being done by members of the School of Scottish Studies must never be forgotten; and anyone wanting to hear the folk tales that are still being told by the travelling folk, can obtain permission to listen to their tapes.

I have only selected the stories about Finn MacCoul and other Celtic heroes from the aforementioned collections of nearly two hundred tales. I have edited them lightly, to make them more readable to more people. I have tried to do so with the admiration and affection I feel for those nineteenth-century collectors. If I have whetted appetites, there is a list of sources at the end of this book, and I include some clues to the chief characters and more unusual words. But for a deeper understanding of the background of Celtic mythology, there is nothing as revealing as the standing and sculptured stones of Britain and Ireland and, more comfortably, in the National Museums and the little collection in a church hall in Meigle, Perthshire. These carvings are full of interesting symbols, as are the tales. Once upon a time they evoked instant recognition and understanding. We can still respond to their meaning once we have found the clues.

Norah Montgomerie, Edinburgh 1978

The Hill of Howth

DELIGHTFUL to be on the Hill of Howth,
very sweet to be above its white sea;
the perfect fertile hill, home of ships,
the vine-grown pleasant warlike peak.

The peak where Finn and the Fianna used to be,
the peak where were drinking-horns and cups,
the peak where bold O'Duinn brought Gráinne
one day in stress of pursuit.

The peak bright-knolled beyond all hills,
with its hill-top round and green and rugged;
the hill full of swordsmen, full of wild garlic, and trees,
the many-coloured peak, full of beasts, wooded.

The peak that is loveliest throughout the land of Ireland,
the bright peak above the sea of gulls,
it is a hard step for me to leave it,
lovely Hill of delightful Howth.

Irish, author unknown, fourteenth century, translated by Kenneth H. Jackson.
From Kenneth Hurlstone Jackson, *A Celtic Miscellany*,
Routledge & Kegan Paul, 1951.

PROLOGUE

THERE was a king over Ireland for whom the taxes laid on him by the Lochlanners or Scandinavians, were most grievous. These invaders came to his kingdom in summer and at harvest, to feed themselves on his crops and stock. They were strong brave men; eating and spoiling as much food as the Scots and Irish were preserving for another year.

The King of Ireland sent for his counsellor, and told him all that was in his mind. He said he wanted to find a way to stop the invaders from robbing him. His counsellor told him that this could not be achieved in a moment, but that it could be rectified in time. He told the king how this could be done, saying:

'You must marry a hundred of your strongest and biggest men to a hundred of your strongest women. The first generation of their union must marry each other, also the second generation. Then you can let the third generation face the invaders, and drive them from your shores.'

This was done. When the third generation came to maturity, they went to Scotland, with Cumhal at their head. They began to rout all invaders and drive them back to their own land.

Cumhal made himself King of Scotland, and he would allow no Lochlanners nor Irish into Scotland. This grieved the King of Lochlann, and he tried to make friends with Cumhal. The three kings of Lochlann, Scotland and Ireland made a treaty of conciliation; and arranged a great feast for all their men, so that there could be friendship between them.

At the same time, there was a plot between the King of Lochlann and the King of Ireland to kill Cumhal, King of Scotland. But Cumhal was very powerful, and there was no way of putting him to death, unless he could be slain by his own sword.

The Naming of Finn

FINN'S father was Cumhal, an Irish chief of high standing but driven from leadership by other chiefs. Once, after a battle, Cumhal entered the house of the Ulster Smith, and asked for a drink. The Smith's daughter gave him a drink in a vessel which had nine pipes. The water had to be sucked out of one pipe, while the fingers were kept over the others.

While he was drinking, the water spouted from one of the pipes and the Smith's daughter laughed. Cumhal threw aside the dish, and stayed that night in the Smith's house.

Returning to the battle, Cumhal was wounded and lay trampled underfoot. There he was slain by one of the enemy, a fisherman called Black Arcai. This man had found him and had offered to take him to safety if Cumhal would exchange swords with him. But when Black Arcai got hold of Cumhal's sword, he thrust it into Cumhal's back, and killed him.

The news of Cumhal's death was spread abroad, and there was a story that a son of Cumhal would avenge his death, and would one day take over the leadership lost on the death of Cumhal. The enemy heard this and made a decree that every male child born in the next nine months must be slain.

Now the Smith's daughter became heavy, fruitful and speckled. At last, the time of her confinement drew near. A woman, called Speedy Foot, helped the midwife, and when a baby boy was born, she hid him out of sight. The second child to be born a few minutes after, was a twin girl. Speedy Foot smuggled the boy out of the house, and hid him, and so saved his life.

She went with the boy to the best Joiner-smith in Ulster, and asked him to make her a secret house in a tree. He made it so well it was impossible to detect, and looked like all the other trees.

'If there is no one who knows this secret but the two of us,' said Speedy Foot, 'it is safer if there is only one of us.'

And she struck off his head.

Speedy Foot and the boy lived in this tree house till the boy grew into a strong stripling of a lad. She taught him all manner of skills and he could swim, leap and run faster than most boys of his age.

All the boy needed now was a name. Speedy Foot took him to a loch where the children of his father's enemies were playing in the water. She told him to avenge his father's death. He dived into the loch, and every child near him he held under the water.

He was seen by people on the shore, who cried out:

'Who is that fair one who is drowning the children?'

'There you have your name,' cried Speedy Foot. 'Your name from now on shall be Finn!'

This is how the son of Cumhal got his name, Finn, which means 'fair'. When the enemies of his father chased after him, Speedy Foot took hold of him, slung him on her back, and fled with him into the Ulster Woods. Then, growing tired, she put him down. At once, Finn grasped her legs, slung her over his shoulder, and carried her through the woods, heedless of her cries, and mindless of anything but escape from his pursuers. When he got out of the wood, there was a loch before him, but he found there was nothing left of Speedy Foot but her shanks. These he threw into the loch, which is called Loch Lurgan, the Loch of the Shanks, to this day.

Finn went on his way with hunger tormenting him. He came to a river where a man was fishing, and he asked the man to catch a fish for him. The man agreed and caught a salmon. Now, the salmon is a royal fish, and the man refused to give it up. He cast his rod again, but again it was a salmon and again he refused to give it up. This happened three times. The fourth fish he gave to Finn.

'You can roast it,' said the fisherman, 'but if you allow the salmon to burn, and a spot of its skin to bubble and rise, your head will be used as a shinty ball.'

Finn roasted the salmon over a fire he had kindled, but after a while a spot of the fish's skin began to bubble and rise. He put his finger on the spot to keep it from rising further, but the fish was very hot and burnt his finger, which he put into his mouth to relieve the pain. At that moment he knew, as if by magic, that the fisherman was Black Arcai, the man who had killed his father, Cumhal – and how he had killed him.

'That is the death I shall give you,' he vowed.

And so, when Black Arcai's back was turned, Finn took his sword, which really was Cumhal's sword, and cut off his head.

Finn went on his way alone till he met the Ulster Smith who asked him who he was.

'I'm a good servant in search of a master,' said Finn.

The Smith engaged Finn for a year and a day, and his wages were to be a sword that would fit his hand alone. The Smith had never had a lad who could ply the hammer as well as Finn, and was pleased for him to stay.

Finn knew, by putting his finger on his tooth of knowledge, that his mother was in the house. And when she saw him, she said that one third of her hearing had been restored at the very sight of him, but she warned him to take no payment from the Smith, her father, only a sword that would fit his hand and no other's.

At the end of a year and a day, the Smith told Finn to go to a pile of swords and choose one for himself. Every sword Finn tried, he shook, and it broke into tiny pieces. The Smith made a heavier sword, but the same thing happened.

'Who are you, that a sword will not fit you, which would fit any other? Curses on you! I wish I had never seen you!'

The Smith said he would have to stay up all night to make a sword for him. Finn's mother told him that the sword would have to be tempered in the blood of a man or a dog, and that she would know when that moment arrived and the sword was ready to be tempered. It was at that moment that Finn must take a dog and throw it in at the smithy door. Finn did this, and the Smith killed the dog with the sword as he tempered it.

Finn entered the smithy and took the sword. It was called Mac an Luin, the Sword of Light, and would be with Finn till his death. He tried it and it suited him perfectly. Then he struck off the Smith's head, and when he came out of the smithy, he took leave of his mother and went on his way.

He went in search of his father's men. At last he found them in a cave by the shore. Their hair and their beards were overgrown, their clothes were tattered and held together with seven pins and seven skewers, and they lived on shellfish and anything they could find without hunting.

There was a prophecy among them that Cumhal's son would come sometime. An old man among them challenged Finn with being Cumhal's son, saying:

'I know you, for one-third of my strength and eyesight has returned to me at the sight of you, but do not reveal yourself to the others all at once, for they'll devour you with joy and kindness. Rather reveal yourself to them one at a time.'

One at a time they saw him and knew he was Finn MacCoul, and they were filled with joy and hope once more. Finn cut their hair and their beards with his Mac an Luin; then they washed themselves, whetted their swords and bent their bows, and made Finn their leader, and became the first members of the Fianna. Together they took back Cumhal's kingdom from the enemies.

How Finn Kept the Children of the
Big Hero of the Ship

ONE day, Finn and his men were on the Hunting-hill and they killed a great number of deer. They were tired after the chase, so they sat down to rest on a pleasant knoll, at the back of the wind, in the face of the sun, where they could see everyone, and no one could see them.

While they were sitting in that place, Finn looked towards the sea, and saw a ship making straight for the haven beneath them. When the ship came to land, a Big Young Hero leaped out on to the shore, seized her by the bows, and drew her up seven lengths onto the green grass.

Then, he ascended the hillside, leaping over the hollows and slanting the knolls, till he reached the spot on which Finn and his men were sitting.

He saluted Finn frankly, energetically, fluently; and Finn saluted him in the same way, then asked him where he had come from and what he was wanting. He told Finn that he had come through night-watching and tempest of sea; because he was losing his children, and he had been told that there was not a man in the world who could keep his children for him but Finn, King of the Fianna. And he said to Finn:

'I lay on you crosses and spells and seven fairy fetters of travelling and straying, that you shall be with me before you eat food, drink a draught or close an eye in sleep.'

Having said this, the Big Hero turned away from them and went down the hill the way he had come up it. He reached his ship, placed his shoulder against her bow, and put her out. He leaped into her, and departed in the direction he had come, until they lost sight of him.

Finn was now under great heaviness of mind because of the vows and spells that had been laid on him. He must fulfil them or travel onwards till he died. He did not know where he should go or what he should do. He said farewell to his men, and descended the hillside to the shore. He could go no farther the way the Big Hero had gone, so he walked along the shore. He had not gone far when he saw seven men coming to meet him. When he reached them he asked the first of them what he was good at.

'I am a good Carpenter,' said the man.

Finn asked him how good he was at carpentry. The man said that, with three strokes of his axe, he could make a large, complete ship of the alder tree yonder.

'You are good enough,' said Finn, 'you may pass by.'

Then he asked the second man what he could do, and he said he was a good Tracker.

'How good are you?' said Finn.

'I can track the wild duck over the crests of nine waves within nine days,' said the man.

'You are good enough,' said Finn, 'and you may pass by.'

Then he asked the third man what he could do, and he said that he was a good Gripper.

'How good are you?' said Finn.

'Once I have got a grip on something I will not let go till my two arms come from my shoulders or until what I am holding comes away with me.'

'You are good enough,' said Finn, 'and you may pass.'

Then he asked the fourth man what he could do, and he said he was a good Climber.

'How good are you?' said Finn.

'I could climb on a filament of silk to a star if you could tie it there,' said the man.

'You are good enough, you may pass by.'

Finn then asked the fifth man what he could do, and he said that he was a good Thief.

'How good are you?' said Finn.

'I can steal an egg from the heron while her two eyes are looking at me,' said the man.

'You are good enough,' said Finn. 'you may pass by.'

Finn then asked the sixth man what he could do, and he said he was good at listening.

'How good are you?' said Finn.

'I can hear what people are saying at the extremity of the Uttermost World,' said the man.

'You are good enough,' said Finn. 'you may pass by.'

Finn then asked the seventh man what he could do, and he said he was a good Marksman.

'How good are you? said Finn.

'I can hit an egg as far away in the sky as a bowstring or bow can carry an arrow,' said the man.

'That is good enough for me, you may pass,' said Finn.

All this gave Finn great encouragement. He turned round and said to the Carpenter:

'Prove your skill!'

The Carpenter went over to the alder stock, struck it with his axe three times, and, as he had said, the ship was ready.

When Finn saw the ship, he ordered his men to put her out. They did this, and went on board her, and Finn with them.

Finn now ordered the Tracker to go to the bow and prove himself. At the same time he told the Tracker that a Big Young Hero had left that haven in his own ship the day before, and that he wanted to follow the Big Hero to wherever he now was. Finn himself went to steer the ship, and they sailed away.

The Tracker was telling Finn to keep the ship that way and this way. They sailed a long way without seeing land, but they kept their course until evening was approaching. In the gloaming they noticed that land was ahead of them, and they made straight for it. When they reached the shore, they leapt to land and drew up the ship.

They noticed a fine large house above the beach, in the glen. They made their way to the house, and when they were nearing it they saw the Big Young Hero coming to meet them. He ran towards them and put his arms about Finn's neck, and said:

'Dearest of all men in the world, you have come!'

'If I had been your dearest of all men, you would not have left me as you did,' said Finn.

'Oh, it was not without a way of coming that I left you,' said the Young Hero. 'Did I not send a company of seven men to meet you?'

When they reached his house, the Young Hero told Finn and his men to go in. They accepted the invitation and found an abundance of meat and drink there.

After they had quenched their thirst and satisfied their hunger, the Young Hero came in and said to Finn:

'Six years from this night, my wife was in childbed, and a son was born to me. As soon as the child came into the world, a Hand came in at the chimney, and took the child away in the hollow of its palm. Three years from this night, the same thing happened again. Tonight my wife is again in childbed. I was told that you, Finn MacCoul, were the only man in the world who can keep my children for me. I have courage now that I have found you.'

Finn and his men were tired and sleepy. Finn told the men that they were to stretch themselves on the floor of the room where the child was to be born, and that he would sit up and keep watch. They did as he instructed them, and he sat beside the fire.

At last Finn was overcome with sleep, but he had a bar of iron in the fire, which as his eyes began to close with sleep, he would thrust into the palm of his hand, and that kept him awake.

About midnight, the Hero's wife was delivered of a son. As soon as the child

came into the world, the Hand came in at the chimney. Finn called on the Gripper to get up. The Gripper sprang to his feet, and took hold of the Hand, and pulled it in to the eyebrows at the chimney.

The Hand gave a pull on the Gripper and pulled him up to his two shoulders. The Gripper gave another pull on the Hand, and brought it in to the neck. The Hand gave a pull on the Gripper, and brought him up to his very middle. The Gripper gave a pull on the Hand, and pulled it in over the two armpits. The Hand gave a pull on the Gripper, and pulled him up to the smalls of his feet. Then the Gripper gave a brave pull on the Hand, and it came right out of its shoulder. When it fell on the floor, the pulling of seven geldings was in it. But the giant outside, whose arm it was, quickly put in his other hand, and took away the child in the hollow of his hand.

They were all very sorrowful that they had lost the child, but Finn said:

'We shall not yield to this. We will go after the Hand before the sun rises on a dwelling tomorrow.'

At break of dawn, Finn and the men turned out, and went down to the beach where they had left the ship. They launched the ship and leapt on board. The Tracker went to the bow, and Finn went to steer her. They departed, and now and again the Tracker would cry to Finn to keep the ship in that direction or to keep her in this direction. They sailed a long distance without seeing anything before them except the great sea.

At the going down of the sun, Finn noticed a black spot on the ocean ahead of them. He thought it was too small for an island and too big for a bird, but he made straight for it. In the darkening of the night they reached it. It was a rock, and a castle, thatched with eel-skins, was perched on top of it.

They landed on the rock. They looked about the castle, but saw neither window nor door where they could get in. At last they noticed that the door was on the roof of the castle. They did not know how they would get to it, because the thatch of eel-skin was so slippery. But the Climber said:

'Let me go, I'll not be long climbing it!'

He sprang towards the castle, and in an instant was on the roof. He looked in at the door and, after taking particular notice of everything inside, he climbed down to where the others were waiting.

Finn asked him what he had seen. He said he had seen the giant lying on a bed, a silk covering over him and a satin cover under him, with his hand outstretched and an infant asleep in the hollow of it.

On the floor he saw two boys playing shinty with sticks of gold and a silver ball. There was a large deerhound bitch lying beside the fire suckling her two pups. Then Finn said:

'I do not know how we shall get all the children out.'

'If I get in,' said the Thief, 'I'll not be long getting the children out safely.'

'Climb on my back,' said the Climber, 'I'll take you up to the door.' The Thief did this and he got into the castle.

Instantly he began to prove his skill. The first thing he did was put out the infant; then he put out the two boys. He stole the silk covering from over the giant and the satin covering from under him, and put them out as well. He put out the two gold shinty sticks and the silver ball. He stole the two pups suckling the deerhound bitch beside the fire. These were the most valuable things he could see inside the castle. He left the giant asleep, and returned to the ship.

Finn put the three children and all the things the Thief had stolen into the ship with the help of his men, and sailed away. They sailed but a short distance, when the Listener stood up and said:

'I am hearing him! I am hearing him!'

'What are you hearing?' said Finn.

'The giant has just wakened!' said the Listener, 'and has missed everything that was stolen from him. He is in great wrath, sending away the deerhound bitch, telling her that if she does not go after us he will go himself. But it is the bitch that is coming.'

Soon, when they looked behind them, they saw the deerhound bitch swimming towards them. She was cleaving the sea on both sides of her in red sparks of fire. They were seized with fear, and did not know what they should do. Finn considered, and told them to throw out one of the pups; for when the bitch saw her pup drowning, she would surely rescue it and return to the castle with it.

They threw out the pup and, as Finn had said, it happened; the bitch rescued her pup and returned to the castle with it. This relieved them for the time being.

Shortly after, the Listener got up trembling, and said:

'I am hearing him! I am hearing him!'

'What are you hearing now?' said Finn.

'The giant is again sending out the bitch, but since she'll not go, he is coming himself!'

When they heard that, their eyes were always looking behind them. At last they saw him coming, and the great sea had not reached his haunches. They were seized with fear, for they did not know what they should do. Then Finn remembered his tooth of knowledge. He put his finger under it, and learned that the giant was immortal, except for a mole in the hollow of his hand. The Marksman stood up and said:

'If I can get one look at that mole, I will have him!'

The giant came walking through the sea, to the side of the ship. He lifted his hand to seize the top of the mast and sink the ship. But when the giant's hand was stretched up to grasp the mast, the Marksman saw the mole. He fired an arrow at it. The arrow struck the mole, the giant's death-spot, and he fell dead, into the sea.

Now they were all happy, for there was nothing to make them afraid. They put about, and sailed back to the castle. The Thief stole the pup again, and they took it along with the pup they already had. Then they returned to the Young Hero. When they reached the haven, they leaped out and drew the ship up on dry land.

Finn went with the three children of the Young Hero, and everything he and his men had taken from the castle, to the house of the Young Hero. He went to

meet them, and when he saw his children, he went down on his knees to Finn and said:

'What reward can I give you, Finn, king of the Fianna?'

Finn said he wanted nothing but his choice of the two pups they had taken from the castle. The Young Hero said he could have them and a great deal more if he asked for it. But Finn wanted nothing but the pup. The pup was Bran, who became Finn's companion in many a fight. The other pup, who was Bran's brother, was left with the Young Hero, and he was the Grey Dog.

The Young Hero took Finn and his men into the house, and made for them a great and merry feast, which was kept up for a year and a day, and if the last day was not the best, it was not the worst.

That is how Finn kept the children of the Big Hero of the ship, and how Bran was found.

THE HERDING OF CRUACHAN

HE HERDSMAN of Cruachan had three sons, and when he became sick with a mortal illness, he sent for his eldest son. The son came, and his father said to him:

'My son, the reason why I have sent for you is because I am not likely to be long in this world, and I wish you to take the herding of Cruachan in my place.'

'I will not take it,' said his son, 'and I do not thank you for the offer of it.'

'Tell the elder of your two brothers to come here to speak with me,' said the father.

The second son came and said:

'Father, what do you want of me?'

'I want to know if you will take over the herding of Cruachan when I die?'

'I will not,' said the son, 'nor do I thank you for the offer of it.'

'Tell your young brother to come here,' said the father.

The youngest son came, and said:

'Father, what do you want of me today?'

'It appears that death is near me,' said his father.

'Then I will take over the herding of Cruachan for you, father.'

'When I die, and you have buried me, you shall set out for Cruachan. You will go round it once and you will go round it twice. You will sit on a pleasant, green-sided hill, on which the sun rises early and sets late. There will come to you a young, curly, brown-haired wizard-champion with a gold ball and a silver shinty stick, and he will say to you: "You must play shinty with me today, young son. You have lost Cruachan." You will then say to him: "Who will stop me?" And you will play together on that day; and he'll say: "Take your winnings!" And you'll say: "The reward I want is the best woman in your land." He'll then take you to his country and show you the most beautiful woman you've ever seen. But you will not choose her. You will see a small, untidy woman cleaning out the byre, and you'll say to the wizard-champion: "That is the woman I choose." He will give her to you, and you will marry her, and bring her home. She will tell you how to do everything. Farewell now, my son, and may Cruachan bring prosperity to you.'

The father died and was buried. Next day the youngest son set off to go round Cruachan. He went round it once, and he went round it twice. He sat down on a pleasant green-sided hill, on which the sun rose early and set late. The young, brown-haired wizard-champion came to him with a gold ball and a silver shinty stick, and said to him:

'You must play shinty with me today.'

'Who will stop me?' said the young herdsman.

They played shinty together that day keenly and hotly. At last, the young herdsman won; and the wizard-champion said:

'Now, name your winnings.'

'I want as my winnings the best woman in your land.'

The wizard-champion brought him the most beautiful woman he had ever seen, but he saw a small, untidy woman cleaning out the byre, and he pointed to her, and said:

'That is the woman I will have.'

She was brought to him, and he took her home and married her.

Next day he set off to go round Cruachan again, and he went round it once, and he went round it twice; then he sat down on a pleasant green-sided hill, on which the sun rose early and set late. The young, brown-haired wizard-champion came with a gold ball and a silver shinty stick, and said to him:

'Will you play shinty with me today, young son?'

'Who will stop me?' said the young herdsman.

They played that day keenly and hotly. The young herdsman of Cruachan won the game. Then the wizard-champion said to him:

'Take the reward of your win.'

'The reward I want is the best filly in your land.'

The wizard-champion took him to see the most beautiful fillies he had ever seen, but then he saw a shaggy dun filly.

'That is the filly I will have,' said he. And he took the shaggy dun filly and went home with her.

His wife met him, and said:

'How did you fare today?'

'I won the game!'

On the next day, he set out to go round Cruachan. He went round it once, he went round it twice, and then he sat down on a pleasant green hill, on which the sun rose early and set late. The young, brown-haired wizard-champion came and said to him:

'Must you play with me today?'

'Who can say that I must not?' said the young herdsman.

That day they played hotly and keenly. The young herdsman lost the game, and he said to the wizard-champion:

'Take your reward!'

'The reward I ask for,' said the wizard-champion, 'is that you get for me the White Sword of Light, which the King of Sorcha has.'

The young herdsman went home that evening, and when he reached his house, neither his wife nor his shaggy dun filly was to be found. The giant, King of Sorcha, had come and stolen them away.

He passed that night alone in his house, and went to bed. In the morning he made his breakfast, and set off to search for his wife and the filly. He baked a bannock to take with him, and went on his way.

He went on for a long time, till the soles of his feet were blistered and his cheeks were sunken. The yellow-headed birds were going to rest at the roots of the bushes and the tops of the thickets, and the dark clouds of night were coming and the clouds of day were departing. Far away, he saw a house, but although it was far away, he did not take long to reach it. He went in, and sat down at the upper end of the house. No one was there, but the fire was newly kindled, the house newly swept, and the bed newly made. Then who should come in but the hawk of Glencuaich and she said to him:

'Are you the young son of Cruachan?'

'I am,' said he.

'Do you know who were here last night?' said the hawk.

'I do not,' said he.

'There were the giant, King of Sorcha,' said the hawk, 'your wife, and the shaggy dun filly. The giant was threatening, saying that, if he got hold of you, he'd take the head off you.'

'I can well believe that,' said the herdsman.

Then the hawk gave him food and drink, and sent him to bed. She rose early in the morning, made breakfast for him, and baked a bannock for him to eat on the journey. Then he went away.

In the evening, he saw a house far away, but if it was far away, he did not take long to reach it. He went in, and sat down in the upper part of the house. The fire was newly kindled, the house newly swept, and the bed newly made. A green-headed duck came in and said:

'Are you the herdsman of Cruachan?'

'I am,' said he.

'Do you know who were here last night?'

'I do not,' said he.

'There were,' she said, 'the giant, King of Sorcha, your wife, and the shaggy dun filly. The giant was threatening to take off your head.'

'I believe you,' said the herdsman.

The green-headed duck prepared food and drink for him, and sent him to bed. She rose next morning, made breakfast for him, and baked a bannock for his journey. He set off, and he was walking on all day, till the soles of his shoes were blistered and his cheeks were sunken. The yellow-headed birds were going to rest at the roots of the bushes and the tops of the thickets, and the dark clouds of night were coming and the clouds of day were departing. In the evening he saw a little house far away, but though it was far away, he did not take long to reach it. He went in, and sat in the upper part of the house. The fire was newly kindled, the house was newly swept, and the bed newly made. The fox of the scrubwood came in, and said:

'Are you the herdsman of Cruachan?'

'I am,' said he.

'Do you know who were here last night?' said the fox.

'I do not,' said he.

'There were the giant, King of Sorcha, your wife, and the shaggy dun filly,' said the fox. 'The giant was threatening to cut your head off!'

'I can believe that,' said the herdsman of Cruachan.

The fox gave him food and drink, and sent him to bed. In the morning, the fox rose and baked a bannock for the journey. Then the herdsman set off. He went on and on, and in the evening he saw a house. He went in and sat down in the upper part of the house. The fire was newly kindled, the house newly swept, and the bed newly made. The brown otter of the burn came in and said to him:

'Are you the herdsman of Cruachan?'

'I am,' said he.

'Do you know who were here last night?' said the otter.

'I do not,' said he.

'There were the giant, the King of Sorcha, your wife, and the shaggy dun filly. The giant was threatening to take off your head!'

'I can believe that,' said the young herdsman of Cruachan.

The brown otter gave him food and drink, and sent him to bed. When he awakened in the morning, he saw the hawk of Glencuaich, the green-headed duck, the fox of the scrubwood, and the brown otter dancing together on the floor. They then prepared breakfast, which they had together, and they said to the herdsman:

'Should you be in trouble at any time, think of us, and we will help you.'

After that he bade them farewell, and went away.

On the evening of that day, he arrived at the cave of the giant, the King of Sorcha, and there was his own wife. The giant was away hunting. His wife gave him food and hid him at the upper end of the cave. She put clothes over him and told him to stay hidden. The giant came home, and said:

'Oh! Hohagaich! The smell of a stranger is in the cave.'

'No, my love,' said she, 'it's only the smell of the little birds of the air I am roasting.'

'Oh! If that's all it is, I'll not worry,' said the giant, and sat down.

Then the wife of the herdsman said to him:

'Pray tell me where your life is kept, that I may take good care of it.'

'It is in a grey stone over there,' said he.

When the giant went away next day, she took the grey stone, dressed it well and put it in the upper part of the cave. When the giant came home that evening, he said to her:

'What is that you have dressed over there?'

'Your own life,' said she. 'We must be careful of it.'

'I see that you are very fond of me, but it's not really there.'

'Where is it then?'

'It is in a grey sheep on yonder hillside.'

Next day, when the giant was away, she got hold of the grey sheep, took it in, dressed it well, and placed it in the upper part of the cave. When the giant came home that night, he said to her:

'What is that you've dressed over there?'

'Your own life, my love,' said she. But he said it was not there.

'Well, you're putting me to great trouble taking care of it, and twice you've not told me the truth.'

'I think I can tell it to you now,' said he. 'My life is below the feet of the big horse in the stable. There is a small lake down there. Over the lake, seven grey hides are spread, and over the hides are seven sods from the heath, and under all these are seven oak planks. There is trout in the lake, and a duck in the belly of the trout, an egg in the belly of the duck, and a thorn of blackthorn inside the egg. Till the thorn is chewed small I cannot be killed. Whenever the seven grey hides, the seven sods from the heath and the seven oak planks are touched, I shall feel it wherever I may be. Now, an axe is above the door, and unless all these things are cut through with one blow of the axe, the lake will not be reached; but when it is reached I shall feel it.'

When the giant went off next day to the hill of game and hunting, the wife said to the young herdsman:

'Should we not attempt to cut through the hides, sods and planks with the axe now?'

'We had better do that,' said he.

They went to the stable, and the herdsman took the axe in order to strike the spot with it, when the horse said:

'Hold the axe, and I will strike it.'

The herdsman of Cruachan held the axe over the top of the seven grey hides, seven sods and seven oak planks; and the horse rose on his forelegs, and drove the axe through them till they reached the lake. The trout sprang out of the lake into a nearby river, and they could not catch it.

'If I had the brown otter of the burn,' said the herdsman, 'it wouldn't take long to catch the trout.'

The brown otter came, and said:

'What do you wish, young son?'

'I wish you would go and fetch the trout for me, that sprang into the river,' said the herdsman.

Into the river sprang the brown otter. He found the trout and brought it to the herdsman of Cruachan. The herdsman opened the trout; and a duck sprang out of its belly, and flew into the air before he could catch it.

'If I had the hawk of Glencuaich, it would not take long to catch the duck,' said he.

The hawk came and said:

'What do you wish, herdsman of Cruachan?'

'I wish you would catch the duck that is flying away up there.'

The hawk flew after the duck, and caught it. The herdsman opened the belly of the duck, and an egg sprang out of it into the air.

'If I had the green-headed duck it would not take long to find the egg,' said he. And the duck came and said:

'What do you wish, herdsman of Cruachan?'

'Fly as fast as you can, and fetch the egg that has just sprung into the air, for I hear the giant coming!'

The green-headed duck went, and got the egg; the young herdsman broke it, and the thorn sprang out of it, and into the thorn-bush nearby. He could not distinguish it from any other thorn when he searched for it. He heard the giant coming nearer and nearer, and he said:

'Ah! If I had the fox of the greenwood, he'd not be long finding the thorn for me.' The fox came and asked what he wanted.

'Please, as fast as you can, find the thorn that sprang out of the egg and into the thorn-bush.'

The fox went, found the thorn, gave it to the herdsman of Cruachan; and he chewed it. Immediately, the giant, who was by now within twenty yards of him, fell down dead.

The herdsman and his wife spent that night in the cave. In the morning, they took away all the gold and silver that the giant had hidden there, his Sword of Light, the big dappled horse, and the shaggy dun filly. The wife rode the filly, and he rode the horse home to Cruachan.

They were to go round Cruachan next day. He took with him the White Sword of Light, and when he was setting off, his wife said:

'The young wizard-champion will come to meet you. Hand him the sword, and he will say: "Where is there the like of my sword in the red divisions of the world?" and you'll say to him: "Nowhere, were it not for one small flaw that it has," and he will say: "Show me the flaw." Now, as he intends to take off your head, you must catch hold of the sword to show him the flaw, draw it, and strike off his head, and say: "That is the flaw!"'

The herdsman set off, and went round Cruachan, and went round it twice. He sat on a pleasant green-sided hill on which the sun rises early and sets late, and he saw the brown-haired wizard-champion coming.

'You have come, herdsman of Cruachan?'

'I have, once more,' said he.

'Have you got the White Sword of Light for me?'

'I have,' said he, and handed the sword to the wizard-champion.

'Where is there now the like of my sword in the four quarters of the world?'

'Nowhere,' said the herdsman, 'were it not for the one small flaw that it has.'

'Show me the flaw,' said the wizard-champion.

'Give me the sword in my hand,' said the herdsman, 'and I will show you the flaw.'

The wizard-champion handed him the sword. The herdsman drew it, and struck off his head, saying:

'That is the flaw!'

The herdsman left the wizard-champion dead on the ground, and returned home, and he enjoyed the herding of Cruachan as long as he lived.

The Fian

THE FIAN were hunting and caught nothing. They did not know what to do. They went about strands and shores, gathering limpets, trying to find a pigeon or plover. They held counsel to decide how they should get game. They reached a hill and sleep came on them.

Finn saw in a dream how he would be on a rocky crag, on the longest night of the year, and in the dream he was driven backwards till he was able to set his back to a rock.

He sprang out of this dream, struck his foot on Diarmid's mouth, and drove out three of his teeth. Diarmid caught hold of Finn's foot and sent a drop of blood from every nail.

'What are you doing to me?' said Finn.

'What did you do to me?' said Diarmid.

'Do not be angry, son of my sister! When I tell you the reason, you'll understand.'

'What is the reason?' said Diarmid.

'I saw in a dream, that I would pass the night at yon rock, and that I was driven backwards till my back was set against the rock, and there was no escape from that place.'

'What is there to be afraid of? Who can frighten us? Who will come?' said the Fian.

'We are in trouble, for the chase has failed and we have no food. If this situation lasts we may become weak and useless. Some of us must go and search for food,' said Finn.

They cast lots to decide who should go and who should stay. All the Fian wished to go except Finn. He was not willing to go for fear their place would be taken by others before they returned.

'I'll not go,' said he.

'Whether you go or stay, we will go,' said the Fian.

And they stopped that night at the root of a tree where they made camp, and began to play cards.

Finn said to those who had stayed: 'Any man who will follow me out, I put him among heroes and warriors!' They followed Finn.

It was a fine frosty night, and they saw a light ahead of them. They went towards it and who did they find but the others; some were gambling and some were sleeping. Finn hailed them bravely, and when they heard his voice, they greeted him for they were pleased to see their leader.

On the road home, they passed a house where they used to stay. It was the house of a hunter. They went into the house, but inside there was only a woman, wearing a green kirtle.

'Finn, son of Cumhal, you and your men are welcome here,' said she.

They went in. There were seven doors to the house. Finn asked his gillies to sit in the seven doors, which they did. Finn and his company sat on one side of the house where they could get more air to breathe.

'Finn MacCoul,' said the woman of the green kirtle, 'I have long wished you well, but there is little I can do to help you tonight. The eldest son of the people of the Danan is coming here, with his eight hundred full heroes.'

'The other side of the house can be theirs and this side will be ours, unless the men of Ireland come,' said Finn.

When the people of the Danan came in, they sat down.

'No man may join us on our side of the house, unless he belongs to our company,' said Finn.

The woman came in again, and said:

'The middle son of the people's King of the Danan is coming, with five hundred brave heroes.'

They came, and some of them stayed outside the house, and rested on a knoll. Then the woman came in again and said:

'The youngest son of the King of the Danan is coming, and five hundred swift heroes with him!'

They came and sat down at the far end of the house.

Again the woman of the fine green kirtle came in, and said:

'The Gallaidh is coming, and five hundred full heroes!'

'This side of the house is ours,' said Finn, 'and that side can be theirs, unless there come the men of Ireland!'

The people of the Danan made seven ranks of themselves, but a quarter of them could not cram in. They still did not utter a word.

There came a gillie with a boar that had died of starvation; and he threw it in front of Finn with an insult. One of Finn's gillies caught hold of the man, tied him by his four smalls, that is his wrists and ankles, and threw him under the table, and the Fian spat on him.

'Loose me and let me stand up,' said he. 'Although I meant no harm I did it. I will bring you a boar as good as any you ever ate.'

'I will do that,' said Finn, 'but though you travel five-fifths of Ireland, unless you come before day-break, I will catch you.'

They loosed him and away he went, the gillies with him. They were not long before they returned with a good boar. They cooked it, and they ate it.

'You are not a good provider of meat,' said the Gallaidh to Finn.

'You shall not say that again,' said Finn, with the jawbone in his hand.

He raised the bone, and with it struck down seven men from every row of the people of the Danan, and this put a stop to them.

Then a gillie came back with the Black Dog of the people of the Danan, seeking a battle of dogs. Every one of the men had a pack of dogs, and there was a dozen in every pack. The Black Dog killed the dogs by the dozen until only Bran was left alive. Finn said to Conan:

'Let Bran slip. Unless Bran wins out, we are finished!'

Conan loosed him, and the two dogs attacked each other. It was not long before Bran began to take a beating. The Fian were afraid when they saw that, but Bran had a venomous claw. There was a shoe shielding the claw of venom, and they had not removed it. Bran looked at Conan, and Conan removed the shoe; and Bran went to meet the Black Dog again.

At the third bout, Bran struck the Black Dog with his venomous claw, and took his throat out. Then he took out his heart and liver.

Bran went to the knoll, where he knew he would find Finn's enemies, and attacked them. A message came to Finn that Bran was doing great damage to the people there.

'Come,' said Finn to one of his gillies, 'go and check the dog!'

But the gillie went and joined in the fight, and a message came that the gillie was now doing more damage than the dog. Man after man went out to join the dog, till only Finn was left inside and alone. The Fian had gone out and killed all the people of the Danan, and they did not remember that they had left Finn on his own.

When the children of the king saw that everyone had been slain by the Fian, they said they would get the head of Finn, and his heart. They attacked him, and drove him backwards till he reached the crag of the rock. He set his back to it and he was keeping them off.

Now Finn remembered his dream. He was sorely tried, but he had the Ord Fianna, the hammer of the warrior bands of Finn, which, when he was in extreme danger of his life, would sound of its own accord, and be heard in five-fifths of Ireland.

His gillies heard it. They gathered and returned to Finn. He was still alive, but only just. They raised him carefully on the points of their spears; and soon he recovered. They killed the sons of the king, and all that were still alive of the people of Danan.

Finn's Journey to Lochlann

ONE day Finn and his men were on the Hunting-hill. They had killed a great number of deer, and they were ready to go home, when they saw a Big Lad coming towards them. He came to meet Finn, and saluted him frankly, and Finn saluted him the same way. Finn asked him where he came from, and what he wanted. He answered:

'I am a Lad who has come from the east and from the west, seeking a master.'

'I want a Lad,' said Finn, 'and if we agree I will engage you. What reward do you want at the end of a year and a day?'

'Not much,' said the Lad. 'I only ask that, at the end of a year and a day, you will go with me, by invitation, to a feast and a night's entertainment at the Palace of the King of Lochlann; and that you will not take a dog, a calf, a child, a weapon, nor an ally – no one but yourself.'

So it was agreed and Finn engaged the Lad, who was a faithful servant to the end of his time.

On the morning of the last day of his engagement, the Lad asked Finn whether he was satisfied with his service. Finn said he was perfectly satisfied.

'Well, I hope I shall now receive my reward,' said the Lad, 'and that you will go with me as you promised.'

'You shall have your reward,' said Finn, 'and I will go with you.'

Finn went to his men and told them that he must fulfill his promise and go with the Lad, and that he did not know when he would return.

'But,' said Finn, 'if I am not back within a year and a day, let any man among you who is not whetting his sword, be bending his bow, to avenge my death on the Great Strand of Lochlann.'

Then Finn bade them farewell, and went into his house.

Finn's Fool was sitting beside the fire, and Finn said to him:

'Poor man, are you sorry I'm going away?'

The Fool, weeping, answered he was sorry because Finn was going in the way that he was going, but he would give him some advice if he would take it.

'I will,' said Finn, 'for often has the wisdom of a king been in the head of a fool. What is your advice?'

'It is that you should take Bran's chain of gold in your pocket. It is not an ally nor a weapon. But you should take the chain at any rate.'

'Yes, poor man, I will take it,' said Finn, bidding his Fool farewell.

He found the Big Lad waiting for him at the door. The Lad told him if he was ready, they would depart. Finn said he was ready, and told the Lad to lead, because he knew the way.

The Big Lad went off, and Finn followed him. Though Finn was swift and speedy, he could not touch the Big Lad with a stick. When the Lad was going out of sight at one mountain-gap, Finn was only coming into sight on the next mountain-ridge. And they kept that position in relation to each other till they reached the end of the journey.

They went to the palace of the King of Lochlann, and Finn sat down wearily, heavily, sadly. There was no feast awaiting him. Instead, the chiefs and nobles of the King of Lochlann were sitting within, putting their heads together to see what disgraceful death they could decree for him.

'We'll hang him!' said one.

'We'll burn him!' said another.

'We'll drown him!' said a third.

At last a man, who was in the company, stood up, and said that they should not put him to death in any of the ways the rest suggested. The men who spoke first asked what way Finn could die that would be more disgraceful than any they had mentioned. And he said:

'We'll take him to Glen More, and he'll not go far when he'll be put to death by the Grey Dog. You know, and I know, there is no death in the world more disgraceful in the estimation of the Fian, than that their earthly king should be killed by a cur.'

When they heard this man's sentence, they clapped their hands and agreed with him. Without delay they took Finn up Glen More, where the Grey Dog was. They had not gone far into the glen when they heard the dog howling. When they saw the dog, they knew it was time for them to flee. They turned and left Finn to the mercy of the dog.

Now, staying or running away was all one to Finn. If he ran away, he would be put to death; if he stayed he would die, and he would as soon fall by the dog as fall by his enemies. So he stayed.

The Grey Dog was coming with his mouth open, and his tongue hanging out on one side of his mouth. Each snort from his nostrils scorched everything three miles before him, and each side of him. Finn was tormented by the heat of the dog's breath, and he knew that he could not survive it much longer. He put his hand in his pocket, and as the dog approached him, he took out Bran's chain, and shook it at the Grey Dog.

The dog instantly stood still and wagged his tail. He came up to Finn and licked his sores, from the top of his head to the soles of his feet, till he had healed with its tongue what he had burned with his breath.

Then Finn clapped Bran's chain about the Grey Dog's neck, and descended down through the glen, with the dog on a leash.

An old man and an old woman, who used to feed the Grey Dog, lived at the lower end of the glen. The old woman was at her door, and when she saw Finn coming with the dog, she ran into the house, crying and clapping her hands.

'What have you seen?' asked the old man.

She said she had seen something extraordinary:

'A tall, fair, handsome man is coming down the glen,' she cried, 'with the Grey Dog on a gold chain.'

'Though all the people of Lochlann and Ireland were assembled,' said the old man, 'there would not be one man among them who could do that except Finn, King of the Fian, and Bran's chain of gold with him.'

'Whether it is the same,' replied the old woman, 'he is coming.'

'We shall soon know,' said the old man, and ran out of the house.

He went forward to meet Finn, and with a few words they saluted each other. Finn told him, from beginning to end, the reason why he was there. Then the old man invited him into the house till he had thrown off his weariness, and had had something to eat and drink.

Finn went in. The old man repeated Finn's story to the old woman. It pleased her so well, she told Finn he was perfectly welcome to stay in their house to the end of a year and a day. Finn gladly accepted their invitation, and stayed.

At the end of a year and a day, the old woman went out, and stood on a hillock nearby. She looked at everything she could see and listened to everything she could hear. At last, in the direction of the shore, she saw a great army of men on the Strand of Lochlann.

She ran back into the house, clapping her hands and crying: 'Alas!' and her eyes were as large as corn-fans with fear. The old man sprang to his feet, and asked her what she had seen.

'There is a great army on the Strand of Lochlann,' she said. 'Among them is a squint-eyed man with red hair, and I do not think there is his match in combat this night under the stars!'

'Oh,' said Finn, as he sprang to his feet, 'there you have the companions I love best! Let me go to meet them!'

Finn and the Grey Dog went down to the strand, and when the Fian saw Finn coming towards them, alive and well, they raised a great shout of joy, which was heard in the four quarters of Lochlann.

The Fian, and their king, Finn MacCoul, gave each other a hearty welcome. If the welcome between them was hearty, so was the welcome between Bran and the Grey Dog, for they were brothers.

Then the Fian took their vengeance on the men of Lochlann, because of the way they had planned to kill Finn. The Fian began at one end of Lochlann, and they did not stop till they went out at the other.

After they had subdued Lochlann, they returned home. When they reached the Hall of Finn, they made a great feast to celebrate his safe return.

How Finn Went to the Country of the Big Men

INN and his men were on a hillock behind the wind and in front of the sun, in the shelter of the Hill of Howth, where they could see everyone and no one could see them. They saw a dark speck in the sea coming from the west. At first they thought it was the dark of a shower, but when it came nearer they saw it was a boat, and it did not lower sail till it entered the harbour below.

There were three men in the boat, one in the bow, one in the stern, and one for the tackle in the centre. They came ashore, and drew the boat up seven times its own length on the dry grey grass, where the schoolchildren of the town could not make fun of it. Then they went to a green spot. The first man lifted a handful of round pebbles and commanded them to become a house, the best to be found in Ireland; and this was done. The second man lifted a slab of slate and commanded it to become the roof of the house, better than any other in Ireland; and this was done. The third man caught hold of some wood shavings, and commanded them to become the timber of the house, better than any in the whole of Ireland, and this was done.

Finn and his men were amazed when they saw this. They went down and spoke to the men. Finn asked them who they were and what they intended to do.

'We are three Heroes whom the King of the Big Men has asked to fight the Fian.'

'What is the reason for that?' said Finn.

'We don't know, except the Fian are strong, and we must challenge them,' they said.

Finn put the men under crosses and enchantments so that they could not move from the place. Then he went and made his coracle ready, turned the stern to land and the prow to the sea. Against the long mast he hoisted the spotted sails, cleaving the billows of a wind from the sea that would take the green leaves from the trees and heather from its roots. Finn was navigator in her prow, helmsman in her stern and crew in her centre. He did not pause till he reached the kingdom of the Big Men.

He went ashore, with Bran his dog, and drew his coracle up on to the grey grass. A Big Wayfarer met him, and Finn asked who he was.

'I am the Red-haired Coward of the King of the Big Men, and,' said he to Finn, 'you are the one I am in search of. You will make a dwarf for the king, and your dog will make a lapdog for him.'

The Big Wayfarer took Finn and Bran up in his hand, but just then another Big Man came along and tried to snatch them from him. The two Big Men fought and tore each other's clothes, but neither won.

'You must judge which of us will carry you to the king,' they said to Finn. Finn chose the first man, who took him and Bran to the king's palace, where everyone had assembled to see the tiny man and his dog.

The king lifted Finn on to the palm of his hand and went three times round the town, with Finn on one palm and Bran on the other. Then he made a sleeping place for Finn at the end of his own bed.

Finn was watching, waiting and observing everything that went on in the palace. He noticed that, as soon as night came, the king rose and went out, and did not return until morning. He wondered about this, and asked the king why he went away every night and left the queen alone.

'Why do you ask?' said the king.

'Because I am curious,' said Finn.

Now the king had taken a great liking to Finn. He had never seen anyone who had given him more pleasure, so at last he told him what was worrying him.

'There is a fierce monster who wants to marry my daughter and take half my kingdom from me for himself,' he said. 'There is no other man in the kingdom who can fight him except myself, so I must go every night to meet him in combat.'

'There is no one to fight him but yourself?'

'There is not.'

'That is strange when this is the kingdom of the Big Men!' said Finn. 'Is the monster bigger than yourself?'

'Never you mind!' said the king.

'I do mind,' said Finn, 'and tonight you must take your rest and I will go to meet the monster.'

'YOU?' said the king. 'Why, you would not be able to make half a stroke of your sword against him.'

When night came, everyone went to rest and the king was to go off as usual; but Finn prevailed on him to let him go instead.

'Sleep soundly tonight,' said Finn, 'and let me go. If the monster fights too violently, I will hasten back.'

Finn went to the place where the combat was to be. He saw no one there and he began to pace backwards and forwards. At last he saw the sea on fire, like a darting serpent, till the flames reached him. And out of the fire came the monster and looked at him.

'What dark speck do I see there?' he said.

'I am Finn MacCoul!'

'What are you doing here?'

'I am a messenger from the King of the Big Men. He is under great sorrow and distress. The queen has died and I have come to ask if you will be so good as to go home tonight without giving any trouble to that kingdom.'

'I will do that,' said the monster, and went away with the rough humming of a song in his mouth.

When the time came, Finn went back to the palace and lay down on his bed at the foot of the king's own bed. When the king awoke, he cried out in great anxiety:

'My kingdom is lost! My dwarf and lapdog are killed!'

'They are not,' said Finn. 'We're here, and you've had your sleep, a thing you said was rare for you to get.'

'How did you escape,' said the king,' when you're so small?'

'Though you are big, I am small and active,' said Finn.

Next night the king prepared to go, but Finn told him to take his sleep again.

'I will go in your place,' said he.

'He will kill you,' said the king.

'I will take my chance,' said Finn.

He went and, as happened before, he saw no one till he began to pace backwards and forwards. Then he saw the sea coming on fire like a darting serpent, and out of the fire came the monster.

'Are you here again tonight?' he said.

'I am, for when the queen was being put into her coffin, the king heard the coffin being nailed down, and he broke his heart with pain and grief. You are asked to go home until the queen is buried.'

So the monster went home that night, roughly humming a song, and Finn went back to the palace.

Next morning, the king awoke and called out:

'My kingdom is lost! My dwarf is dead!'

But he rejoiced when he found that Finn was alive and that he had had rest after being so long without sleep.

Finn went the third night. Things happened as before. There was no one before him and he began pacing backwards and forwards, until the fiery sea came up with the great monster.

'I have come to fight you,' said Finn.

Then Finn and Bran began the combat. Finn was going backwards, and the monster was pressing him. Finn called to Bran:

'Are you going to allow me to be killed?'

Now Bran had a venomous claw. He leapt and struck the monster on the breast with it, and took the heart and lungs out of him. Finn drew his sword, Mac an Luin, and cut off the monster's head. This he tied at the end of a hemp rope, and pulled it to the palace. He took it into the kitchen, and dragged it behind the door.

In the morning the servant could not turn the door handle of the kitchen. The king went down to the kitchen and saw the head of the monster. He knew

it was the head of the giant who had for so long tormented him, and kept him from sleep.

'How did this get here?' he said. 'Surely my dwarf has not done this?'

'Why not?' said Finn.

Next night the king wanted to go to the place of combat himself.

'Because,' said he, 'a yet bigger monster than before will come tonight, the kingdom will be destroyed, and you yourself killed, and that will not give me pleasure.'

But Finn went, and everything happened as it had done before, till the Big Monster came asking vengeance for his son, the kingdom for himself, or equal combat. He and Finn began to fight. Finn was driven back, and he said to Bran:

'Are you going to allow him to kill me?'

Bran whined, and went to sit down on the beach. Finn was still being driven back, and he called again to Bran. Bran jumped up, struck the Big Monster Man with his venomous claw, and took the heart and the lungs out of him. Finn struck

his head off, and took it with him, and left it in front of the house, and then went
off to bed. That morning the king woke in great terror, and cried out:

'My kingdom is lost! My dwarf and lapdog are killed!'

Finn raised himself up and said:

'They are not!'

And the king's joy was not small when he went out and saw the head that
was in front of the house.

The next night, a Big Hag came ashore, and the tooth in front of her mouth
was long enough to make a distaff. She sounded a challenge on her shield:

'You killed my husband and my son!' she cried.

'Yes, I did kill them,' said Finn.

They began to fight and it was difficult for Finn to defend himself from the
tooth, and she had nearly killed him, but then Bran struck her with his venomous claw, and killed her. Finn cut her head off, and took it with him and put it in
front of the house.

The king awoke in great anxiety, and called out:

'My kingdom is lost! My dwarf and my lapdog are dead!'

'They are not,' said Finn.

And when they all went out and saw the head, the king said:

'My kingdom will have peace after this! The mother of the brood is herself
dead now! But tell me who you are. It was foretold that it would be Finn Mac-
Coul who would relieve me of all threats, but he is now only eighteen years of
age. Who are you then, and what is your name?'

'There was never anyone to whom I would deny my name,' said Finn. 'I am
Finn, the son of Cumhal, son of Looach, son of Trein, son of Arthur, son of the
High King of Ireland. It is now time for me to go home. I have been wandering
far out of my way, coming to your kingdom. The reason why I came in the first
place was to discover what injury the Fian have done you, or why you sent three
of your Heroes to ask for combat, and bring destruction on my men.'

'You did me no injury,' said the king, 'and I ask a thousand pardons. I did not
send those three Heroes to you. They did not tell you the truth. They were three

men who were courting three fairy women, who presented them with a shirt each. When they wear the shirts, the combat of a hundred men is in the hands of each one of them. But they must take the shirts off every night, and put them on the backs of chairs. If these shirts were taken from them during the night, while they slept, they would be as weak as anyone else the next day.'

Finn was given every honour the king could bestow on him; and when he went away, the king and the people went down to the shore to wish him a good voyage with their blessing.

Finn sailed away in his coracle, keeping close to the shore, when he saw a young man running and calling to him. Finn came in close to land with his coracle, and asked the young man what he wanted.

'I am,' said he, 'a good servant wanting a master.'

'What work can you do?' said Finn.

'I am the best Soothsayer there is.'

'Jump into the boat then,' said Finn.

And the lad did so. They had not gone far when another youth came running.

'I am a good servant wanting a master,' said he.

'What work can you do?' said Finn.

'I am a good Thief, if ever there was one,' said he.

And Finn took him as well.

They then saw a third youth running towards them, and calling out.

'What man are you?' said Finn.

'I am the best Climber there is. I will take a hundred pounds on my back in a place where a fly could not stand on a calm summer day.'

'Jump into the coracle,' said Finn. 'I now have my pick of servants, and these must suffice.'

They went; and they did not stop till they reached the harbour of the Hill of Howth. He asked the Soothsayer what the three Big Men were now doing.

'They are preparing for bed, after their supper,' said he.

Finn asked a second time.

'They are going to bed; and their shirts are spread on the back of chairs.'

After a while Finn asked him the same question again:

'What are the Big Men doing now?'

'They are sound asleep,' said the Soothsayer.

'It would be a good thing if there was now a Thief to go and steal the shirts,' said Finn.

'I would do that but the doors are locked and I cannot get in.'

'Come on to my back,' said the Climber, 'and I'll let you in.'

The Climber took the Thief on his back, and climbed to the top of the chimney with him, let him down, and he stole the shirts.

Finn then went to his band of men, the Fian, and told them what he wanted them to do. Next morning, the Fian came to the house of the three Big Men. They sounded a challenge on their shields, and called to them to come out to combat. They came out, and said:

'Many's the day we have been better equipped for combat than we are today!'

They confessed to Finn how things were with them.

'You were impertinent!' said Finn; and he made them swear they would be faithful to him and to the Fian, ever after, and be ready for every enterprise he would put before them. And so they were from then on.

Finn and His Men

INN and nine of his men, among them Goll and Conan, each with a leash of dogs, were hunting on the Hill of Howth. At midday, they had found nothing, so they rested on a hill where game often passed, but they saw none. Finn drew apart from the others, and put his finger under his tooth of knowledge, to find out why there was no game. He returned to his men and told them that in a short time a hound with a white ear would pass. They were not to attack it. If they did, the game would stay away from them for seven years and a day.

The Dog with the White Ear passed. The Fian kept their dogs beside them, but Finn's own dog, Bran, broke loose and gave chase to the strange hound. Bran chased it down the hill, but it threw up mud, which struck Bran on his muzzle. The mud that Bran threw up from his forepaws struck the Dog with the White Ear.

'Bran will hurt himself, and not catch White Ear,' said Finn. 'Let us go after him!'

They went, and found Bran lying on the ground, his tongue lolling out. He had not caught the strange dog.

'Well, my fine dog,' said Finn. 'I am glad to find you; though you have now driven the chase away from us for seven years and a day. Now let us go home!'

They went on their way. Towards dusk they lost their direction, wandering over the hill. They saw a light. They made for the light and when they reached it, they found a bothy. The gillie of the bothy was standing at the door. He greeted Finn, and Finn saluted him.

'We've lost our way,' said Finn, 'and we have come to ask for room and shelter for the night, if we are welcome.'

'You would get room and shelter in my house even if there were a hundred men with you,' said the gillie of the bothy.

The Fian went in and sat close to each other. Finn looked at them to see if all his men were safe, when he noticed that Goll was missing. He said he would go to find him; but that no mother's son, born in Ireland, was to follow him.

'If I find Goll, I'll bring him back. If I don't find him I will return alone.'

Finn had not gone far when he heard the sound of someone following him. He turned and saw it was Fergus.

'Fergus,' said he, 'why are you following me, when I ordered anyone born in Ireland not to do so?'

'But I was born in Jura!' said Fergus. So Finn allowed him to go with him.

At last, they found Goll and the Red Man of Tara, playing chess. The man from Tara said to Finn:

'Do not be anxious about the Fian, although the chase has stayed away from you. Divide yourselves into two parties. My brother will lead one and I will lead the other. We will feed you all, and none of you will be allowed to suffer want.'

Finn thanked him, but said he could not accept his offer. He must go back to the Fian and provide meat for them himself.

'Goll, were you afraid we would not find enough food for you?' said Finn. 'Is that why you stayed away?'

'No,' said Goll, 'I wanted to come here and play chess with this man.'

They returned to the bothy, and the Fian, who sat close to each other. Then there was a great commotion outside, and the gillie, owner of the bothy, went out to see what was happening. He returned to say that the son of the King of Sheanaidh, with one hundred men, was outside seeking shelter, and would Finn allow them in to share the bothy.

'I am not strong enough to keep them out,' Finn replied.

Soon one hundred and one men were in the bothy. Then there was another commotion outside; and the gillie went out to investigate. He returned to say that the second son of the King of Sheanaidh with his hundred men were outside, seeking shelter. Again, Finn said they could come in, as he was not strong enough to keep them out; and so the second son came in with his hundred attendants. Before long the third son of the King of Sheanaidh and his one hundred men were also allowed into the bothy. Finn MacCoul and his nine men, with a leash of dogs apiece, the King of Sheanaidh's three sons, with their three hundred attendants and six hundred dogs were now all in the bothy.

Each company kept together to themselves and apart. Finn and his men sat close to each other. Then the King of Sheanaidh's daughter and her one hundred handmaidens were admitted, as her brothers had been. After sitting down and looking about her, she told Finn that she would like to try a bout of wrestling with him. He said it was not usual for him to try feats of strength before his men had been defeated.

So Conan agreed to wrestle with her. At once, she threw him, and tied together his four smalls – that is, his wrists and ankles – and threw him into a corner of the room, behind all the others.

As he lay there, he heard Goll laughing and having fun with the handmaidens. At last he cried out:

'Goll, son of Morna, if I were a maiden, you would not allow me to lie here, tied up like this!'

'That is true,' said Goll; and went to untie him.

Conan had not been worth considering in any feat of strength or daring after disgracing himself thus, but once he was untied he asked for fair play, and this was given, and he wrestled again with the king's daughter, and this time threw her down.

Later, the King of Sheanaidh's daughter asked Finn to go outside and bring in the wild boar that was lying at the door, and which would provide food for the entire company. Finn replied that he had never been without a servant, and it was only when his servants could not perform a task, that he himself undertook such a menial duty. So she told one of his men to bring in the boar. He went, but enchantments had been laid on the boar, and he could not move it. Another was sent but he also failed, and so did the rest of the nine members of the Fian.

Finn said he would go and fetch it in himself, and though seven times its own weight in earth stuck to the boar, he brought it in easily.

Conan dressed the boar and prepared it for the pot. He took the jawbone as his share, and as he was picking at it, one of the king's sons asked for it.

'If you had asked for it earlier,' said Conan, 'you would have got more flesh on it!'

And he threw the bone at the King of Sheanaidh's eldest son, and knocked him down. The king's sons then demanded a fight between their six hundred dogs and the five hundred dogs of the Fian. And that was how the great dog-fight began.

The Fight between Bran and the Black Dog

ON a day that we were on the Hunting-hill,
Seldom were we without dogs,
Listening to the cries of the birds,
Roaring of the deer and elks.

We did slaughter, doubtless,
With our dogs and death-inflicting weapons;
And came to our dwelling at noon,
Joyful, musical, and with right good will.

That night in Finn's dwelling,
Dear me! delightful was our condition,
As we struck strings,
And ate birds, deer and elk.

Early rose Finn next day,
Before sunrise,
And he saw coming on the plain,
Between the hills and the sea,
A man with a red cloak and a Black Dog.

Like this was his appearance:
His two cheeks were ripe as fruit,
His breast like the mountain down,
Though his hair happened to be black.

He came to us for increase of enjoyment,
This fine lad, so desirable;
On his appearance no shadow would rest,
Asking from the rest a dog-fight.

We let towards him at the beginning of the fight,
The best hounds within our walls,
The Black Dog, rough was his onset;
Killed by him were fifty of our dogs.

Then Finn spoke:
'This is a contest that is not weak.'
He turned his back to the people,
And, with a frown, struck Bran.

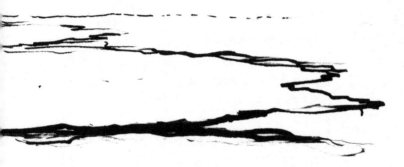

Victorious Bran looked at him,
Wondering that he should strike him,
'The hand with which I struck Bran,
Pity from the shoulder it was not separated.'

Then Bran shook the golden chain,
Among the people loud was his yelp,
His two eyes burned in the head,
And his bristles rose for the fight.

'Take the thong from my dog without delay;
Good was his prowess till today;
And let us see sharp strife,
Between Bran and the Black Dog.'

'Goodly shaped was my dog,
Its neck-joint far from its head;
The middle broad, its side burly,
Its elbow sloping, and its claw crooked.'

'Yellow paws Bran had,
Two black sides, and underneath white,
The back green (on which hunting would rest),
Erect ears, strongly red.'

They placed the dogs, nose to nose;
Among the people they shed blood,
There was a strong, rough struggle,
Before the Black Dog was left dead by Bran.

'I thought there was not in the Fian host,'
(Said Eibhinn Oision from the place of tying dogs),
'One dog, for all its prowess,
That could give such a deadly wound.'

'Were it not for every twist and trick,
That Bran had, and its very strength,
No dog that could be bound with such a thong,
Would be left by him west in our fort.'

'Many a fair brown maiden,
Of bluest eye and golden yellow hair,
In the kingdom of the king, Tork's son,
That would give my dog food tonight.'

The true, generous hero buried,
In a narrow clay bed, his dog;
And the Fians buried,
In that west fort fifty dogs.

We went with MacCoul of the golden cups,
to pay, and to the fort,
King! joyful and full was our dwelling,
Though none are here today within its walls.

The Lad of the Skin Coverings

ON A certain day of old, Finn thought he would go hunting in the White Glen. He took with him as many of his men as were at hand at the time, and they went together to the glen.

The hunt began, and when it was over, no man who was present had ever seen such a pile of dead deer.

It was a custom with the Fian, after they had gathered together the deer they had killed, to sit down and take a rest. They would divide the deer among themselves, each man taking as small or large a burden as he was able to carry. But on this day, they killed many more than they could carry with them.

While Finn was considering what he should do with the remainder, he saw a Big Lad coming over the side of the mountain at very great speed, making straight for the place where they were gathered.

'Someone is coming towards us,' said Finn, 'intent on the business before him, unless I am mistaken.'

They all stood looking at the Big Lad, dressed in the skins of various animals, and it was not long before he was in their midst.

He saluted Finn frankly, energetically, fluently; and Finn saluted him in a similar manner. Then Finn asked him where he had come from, where he was going, and what he wanted. The Lad said he was the son of the Lady of the Green Isle, and he had come from there to here, seeking a master.

'I am in need of a servant,' said Finn, 'and I don't mind engaging you if we agree about the reward.'

'That would not be my advice,' said Conan.

'Conan, you had better keep quiet, and mind your own business, and I will do my own business,' said the Lad.

Everyone present was wondering about the Big Lad's dress of animal skins. Not less did they wonder about his great strength of body. And they were somewhat afraid he would put them to shame, before he parted from them.

Finn then asked what reward he would be asking at the end of a year and a day. He said he would ask nothing but that he should eat and drink with the Fian at table, in the house or outside on the moor, or wherever they took their meals, to the end of a year and a day.

'You shall get that,' said Finn, and so they agreed.

Then the Fian began to lift the deer. One would take with him one deer, and another would take two, until all had their burdens except the Big Lad. Finn told him to take his burden, and the Lad pulled the finest and longest pieces of heather, till he had a great heap beside him. He began to make a rope of the heather branches, and placed a deer on every deer's length of the rope. He tied them twined together, till he had all the deer left to him tied into one great burden.

When it was ready, he told the Fian to lift it on to his back. They came, as many of the Fian as were present that day, they tried but they could not put the wind between the burden and the earth. When the Big Lad saw this, he told them to stand out of his way. He took hold of the rope, twisted the end of it around his fist, bent his back, put firm pressure on his foot, and threw the burden over his shoulder. Everyone of the Fian looked at his neighbour, but spoke not a word. When the Big Lad had the burden steady on his back, he said:

'I am but a stranger in this place, therefore let one of you go in front and show me the way.'

Everyone looked at his neighbour to see who would volunteer to go. At last, Conan said he would go if the rest would carry his deer. Finn agreed that his deer would be carried for him if he led the way. So Conan threw off his deer, sprang in front of the Big Lad, and went off as fast as he could.

The Big Lad followed him barefoot. They had gone but a short distance, when the Lad drew close behind, and the two very long nails which were on the Lad's toes were so close to Conan's back that they scratched the skin from between his shoulders to the back of his heels, and tore it off.

At last Conan began to slow down, for he was growing weak with the loss of blood from the deep scratches on his back. In a short time he had to stop and sit down.

When the Big Lad saw that Conan had weakened, he ran past him, and did not stop till he laid down his burden at the house of Finn. He sprang inside, and lit a fire. He cooked food for every man who was at the hunt, and set each man's food apart, except Finn's food and his own.

The Fian came home, and when they went into the house, they were greatly surprised to see the food ready before them; but they made no remark about it.

After the supper was over, the Fian went to Finn, and Conan said:

'Did I not tell you that we should be disgraced by the Lad you engaged? His strength cannot be matched by the Fian. You must send him away until his time with us is up.'

'Well,' said Finn, 'I do not know what I can do with him unless I send him away to Lochlann to seek the four-sided Cup of the Fian. He would have a year and a day's journey there and back, however well he may walk.'

The Fian were all quite pleased with this, and they told Finn to send him off as soon as he could. Finn answered and said:

'Before one sun shall rise on a dwelling, he will get his order to travel on the journey.'

Without delay he sent for the Lad of the Skin Coverings, and said to him that he was sorry to ask him to go on such a long journey, but he hoped he would not refuse. The Lad asked him on what business he was being sent, and where he had to go. Finn said he had got word from Lochlann that he would get the four-sided Cup of the Fian if he sent a man for it.

'I sent word to them to come and meet us with the cup, and that someone would meet them and bring it back here. Will you go and fetch it?'

'Well, Finn,' said the Big Lad, 'you know and are quite sure, that the men of Lochlann will not meet me with the cup, for numerous are the heroes who have shed their blood on the field beneath the spears of Lochlann, for the sake of the four-sided Cup of the Fian, which has been held in Lochlann for years. How do you think, Finn, that I can take it out of their hands unassisted? But since I promised to do whatever you would ask me, I will go and fetch the cup for you.'

Next morning, before sunrise, the Big Lad was ready for the journey. He dressed himself in his animal-skin coverings, and strode away. The swift March wind that was before him, he would overtake, and the swift March wind that was behind him, could not keep pace with him. Travelling thus, he did not slacken his speed till, that night, he struck his palm against a door of the palace of the King of Lochlann.

The King of Lochlann's palace was kept by seven guards. The Big Lad knocked on the first gate, and the first guard asked him where he had come from and where he was going. He said he was the servant who had come from Finn, the King of the Fianna, with a message for the King of Lochlann. Word went to the king that such a man was at the door. The king asked if anyone was with him. When the king was told there was no one with him, he gave orders to let him in.

The first gate was opened for him and he went in. In like manner, every gate with a guard, until he passed through seven gates and past seven guards. He was taken to the king, who told him to sit down. The Big Lad sat down, for he was tired after his journey. He looked about the room, and there, standing on a table, was the most beautiful four-sided cup he had ever seen.

'That is a very beautiful vessel you have there,' he said to the King of Lochlann.

The king agreed that it was, and said it was a Cup of Virtues.

The Big Lad asked what virtues the cup possessed. The King said there was nothing one could think of to be in the cup, that would not be in it immediately.

The Big Lad, being thirsty after the journey, thought that if the cup was filled with drinking water, it would be a very good thing. Then he rose up, took hold of the cup, and drank all the water that was in it, and he turned his face to the door.

Although he had asked for an entrance, he did not ask for an exit, but leapt over the seven guards, taking the cup with him. He lifted his skin coverings over him, and strode down the path by which he had come. The swift March wind before him, he would overtake, and the swift March wind behind him, could not keep pace with him. At this rate of travelling, he did not slacken his speed till, that night, he struck the palm of his hand against a door of Finn's house. He went in and handed the cup to Finn.

'You were not long away,' said Finn. 'Did I not tell you that someone would meet you with the cup?'

'You know full well they did not meet me with it! But I reached Lochlann, and I got the cup from the king's palace. I made the journey forward and back again,' said the Big Lad.

'Silence, babbler!' said Conan. 'There are some in the Fian, who can run on the hillside on the glen-strath as well as you can, and they could not do the journey to Lochlann in double the time you said you did it. But come as far as the Little Green Loch at the foot of the Hill of Howth and try a leap with me.'

'Oh, Conan, I am more in need of food and a wink of sleep than trying leaps with you.'

'If you do not go, we will not believe that you made the journey,' said Conan.

The Big Lad rose and went with him; and they reached the Little Green Loch. Conan asked the Big Lad to try a leap across the lochan.

'You brought me here,' said the Big Lad, 'therefore make the first leap yourself.'

Conan took a run and made a leap, but sank to his two hip-bones in the leafy marsh on the other side of the lochan. The Big Lad, without a take-off run, took his leap, went over Conan's head and on to the hard ground on the other side of the lochan.

He leapt the lochan backwards then forwards, before Conan had got his haunches out of the bog. When Conan at last got his footing on hard ground, he told the Big Lad that the roots had given way under his feet, and that was why he had slipped.

'But come and race with me to the top of the Hill of Howth, then I will know that you made the journey.'

'Conan, I am more needful of a wink of sleep than racing you to the top of the Hill of Howth!'

However he went. At a stride, the Big Lad passed Conan, and did not give another look at him till he was on top of the hill. He then stretched himself on a green hillock and slept. He did not know how long he had slept, but it was the panting of Conan climbing the hill that wakened him. He sprang quickly to his feet, and said:

'Now, did I make the journey?'

'Come, wrestle with me, and I'll know if you made it.'

They embraced each other ready to wrestle, and Conan told the Big Lad to take the first turn.

'No, you take it, it was your idea, you wanted to begin.'

Conan tried to wrestle, but he could not move the Big Lad, who then bent over, and with his great strength, threw Conan and bound his wrists and ankles with his leather thong.

The Big Lad had taken it as an insult that the most contemptible man of the Fian had despised and bullied him. He made a vow that he would return to Finn no more. So he went away and left Conan bound, on the top of the Hill of Howth.

Night was coming, and Finn was wondering why the two men had not returned. At last, fear struck him that the Big Lad had killed Conan, and he told his men to go and look for them. Before the sun rose next morning, he divided his men into two companies. He sent a company to each side of the hill, and told them to travel till they all met at the top. About evening of that day, they met, and found Conan bound, wrists and ankles, with one thong.

Finn told one of his men to unbind Conan. Oscar went, and took a long time trying to undo the knots. For every knot he untied, seven appeared. At last he said to Finn:

'I cannot loosen this thong.'

Then Goll sprang over, thinking he could do better, but, as had happened to Oscar, the knots defeated him. If it was not tighter when he stopped, it was not a bit looser. Mad with aggravation, he raised his head in wrath, and cried:

'There is not a man in the Fian who can unbind Conan!'

Finn was afraid that Conan would be dead before they could release him. But he remembered his tooth of knowledge; and putting his finger under it, learned that there was not a man in the world who could unbind Conan except the Smith of the White Glen; or else the man who had bound him in the first place.

He sent Oscar and Goll to tell the Smith what had happened to Conan. The Smith told them they must gather together every four-footed beast they could find between the back of the Hill of Howth and the head of the White Glen; and drive them past the door of the smithy.

'And,' said he, 'if I then come out in peace, my peace is good, but if I come out in wrath, evil is my wrath!'

Oscar and Goll returned to Finn and told him what the Smith had said. Finn said the hunt must commence. The hunt that started was the Great Hunt of the White Glen. Since the first hunt, there never had been such a great number of four-footed beasts assembled as were together on that day. They were driven past the door of the smithy. And the Smith came out, and asked what was there.

'All the four-legged beasts between the top of the Hill of Howth and the head of the White Glen,' said the Fian.

'You have done well enough,' said the Smith, 'but return every one of those creatures to the place from which you have taken them, and I will go and unbind Conan.'

They did that, and the Smith went to the top of the Hill of Howth, and released Conan.

Conan was so ashamed of what had happened that he walked down the hill as fast as he could, and did not look behind him till he reached the sea. He would not come away from it for Finn or for any man in the Fian. But the tide was rising at the time, and when the water began to enter his mouth, he thought it was better for him to go ashore and return home after the rest.

One evening after, when Finn and his men were on their way from the Hunting-hill, they saw a Lad coming to meet them. He made his way to Finn, and told him that he had been sent from the Queen of Ruaidh, to Finn, King of the Fianna, and that he was laying on him, as spells, as crosses, and seven fairy fetters of travelling and straying, that he would neither stop nor take rest until he reached the Queen of Ruaidh's palace. Having said this, he turned his back on them and departed, and they had not a second look at him.

The Fian looked at each other. They were afraid some evil was to happen to Finn, because no one else had been asked to go with him. They told him they were sorry he was going alone, because they knew not when he would return, nor where they would find him. But Finn told them not to be anxious about his return at the end of a year and a day.

After that he departed, with his arms and weapons. He travelled far long and full long over hills, glens, and heights; and he did not stop till he came within sight of the Green Isle. There he saw a man about to lift a bundle of rushes on to his back. When he saw the man throwing the burden over his shoulder, he thought he looked like the Lad with the Skin Coverings.

He approached the man under cover till he was close to him. Then he showed himself, and when the man looked him in the face, he knew it was indeed the Lad with the Skin Coverings. Finn sprang quickly towards him, seized hold of his arms, and said:

'Dearest man in all the world! Is it you?'

'If I were the dearest man in the world,' said the Lad, 'would you have allowed the most insignificant man in the Fian to bully me and make me the subject of mocking wit?'

'Well,' said Finn, 'I was sorry, but I could not help it. I was afraid the Fian would rise against me, and become unruly; therefore I allowed Conan to have his own way, but I knew you had made the journey. Now we will be good friends as we ever were. Will you go with me once more on this journey?'

'Well,' said the Lad, 'I do not know. Look down there in that hollow below us, and you will see my mother on her knees cutting rushes. If you can catch hold of her, do not let go till you get your first request from her.'

Finn crawled for a while on his hands and feet, and then for a while dragged himself along on his belly, till he got near enough to take a spring. He sprang, and got hold of the Lady of the Green Isle, who cried out:

'Who is there?'

'Finn, King of the Fian, is here, making his first request. Let your son go with me once more on this journey.'

'Had I known what you would ask of me,' said the Lady of the Green Isle, 'you would not have caught me. But I will have one promise from you before you go, and that is that you shall bring him back to me and all that shall fall with him.'

'I hope things will not end that way, and that he will return home well and whole.'

'If he does, good luck will not fail you, Finn. However, be off on your journey,' said the Lady of the Green Isle.

Then Finn and the Big Lad went on their journey, ascending hills, descending hollows, travelling over bens and glens and knolls, till the gloaming of the night was coming. They were growing weary, and wished to reach some place where they could get permission to rest. Soon after that, they saw an exceedingly fine place before them, with fine large houses built in green fields. Said Finn to the Big Lad:

'Take courage, we are not far from houses which will give us shelter.'

Finn saw a man coming to meet them and knew he was the very Lad who had come to him with the message from the Queen of Ruaidh. He asked him what need he had of him now. The Lad said there were two great houses opposite, one with doorposts of gold and doors of silver, and the other with doorposts of silver and doors of gold, and that he was to take his choice of which one to stay in. He would see when he entered what he had to do there. Having said this, the Lad turned away and left them where they were standing. Finn looked into the face of the Big Lad, and said:

'Which of these houses shall we stay in?'

'We will have the more honourable one,' said the Big Lad. 'We'll take the one with the doors of gold.'

They went over to the door. The Big Lad took hold of the bar, and opened the door. Then they went in. They saw a great sight before them, but the Big Lad thought nothing of it. There were eighteen score and eight Avasks standing on the floor. When they got Finn and the Big Lad inside the door, they sprang towards it, and shut it, and put on it eighteen score and eight bars. The Big Lad went over and put one great bar on the door, and so firmly did he put it on, that all the other bars fell off. Then the Avasks gave eighteen score and eight laughs, but the Big Lad made one great guffaw and deafened all other sound. Then the Avasks said:

'What is the cause of your laugh, little man?'

The Big Lad said:

'What is the cause of your own laughter, big men all?'

'The cause of our laughter,' said they, 'is that it is a pretty, clustering, yellow head of hair you have on you to be used as a football out there on the strand tomorrow!'

'Well,' said the Big Lad, 'the cause of my laugh is that I will seize the man of you with the biggest head and the smallest legs, and I will brain the rest of you with him.'

He then saw a man with a big head; and having laid hold of him by his two feet, began braining the Avasks from one end of the band to the other. When he had done this, he had only as much of the man as he held in his fists.

The Big Lad and Finn put out the dead bodies, and made three heaps of them at the door. Then they shut the door and made some food ready, for there was an abundance of it in the house.

After they had taken the food, the Big Lad asked Finn:

'Will you sleep or keep watch at the door?'

'You sleep, and I will watch the door,' said Finn.

They did so. But before the Big Lad slept, Finn asked him:

'How shall I waken you if I am in trouble at the door?'

'Strike me on the breastbone with the block of stone from behind the hearth, or take the breadth of your thumb of skin from the top of my head with your dirk.'

'All right,' said Finn, 'now sleep on.'

Finn was watching the door, but for a long time heard nothing coming. At the break of dawn, he heard the conversation of ten hundred coming to the door. He lifted the block of stone, and struck the Big Lad on the chest with it. The Big Lad sprang quickly to his feet, and asked Finn what he had heard.

'The conversation of ten hundred at the door,' said Finn.

'That is right,' said the Big Lad, 'but let me out.'

The Big Lad went to meet the bands of men, and beginning at one end of them, attacked them below and above, and left none of them alive to tell the tale, but one man with one eye, one ear, one hand, and one foot, and he let him go. Then he and Finn collected the dead bodies, and put them in three heaps at the door with the rest. They went in and waited till the next night came. After supper, the Big Lad asked Finn:

'Will you sleep or keep watch tonight?'

'You sleep and I will watch,' said Finn.

The Big Lad went to sleep, and Finn was watching the door. A short time before sunrise, Finn heard the conversation of two thousand coming, or the son of the King of Light alone. He sprang up, and with his dirk took the breadth of his thumb of skin from the top of the Big Lad's head. Instantly the Big Lad sprang to his feet, and asked Finn what he had heard.

'The conversation of two thousand, or the son of the King of Light alone, is at the door.'

'Oh, then, I dare say you must be as good as your promise to my mother,' said the Big Lad, 'but let me out.'

Finn opened the door, the Big Lad went out, and it was the son of the King of Light who was before him.

Then the two Champions embraced each other, and wrestled from sunrise to sunset, but one did not throw the other, and the one did not speak to the other

during the whole time. They let each other go, and each one of them went his own way.

Early next morning, before sunrise, the Big Lad went out, and his companion met him. They wrestled from sunrise to sunset, but the one did not throw the other, and the one did not speak to the other. They let each other go, and each went his own way.

The third day the Heroes met, and embraced each other. They fought all day long till twilight, and the two fell side by side cold and dead on the ground.

Finn was very sorry for the Big Lad. He remembered his promise to the Lad's mother, and said to himself that it must be fulfilled. He took out the silk covering which had been over them where they slept, wrapped it about the two bodies, and took them with him on his back. He returned with a hard step over bens and glens and hillocks, ascending hills and descending hollows, and made no stop nor rest till he reached the house of the Green Island.

The mother of the Big Lad met him at the door, and said to him:

'Have you come?'

Finn answered that he had come, but not as he would wish.

'Did you do as I told you?'

'Yes,' said Finn, 'but I am sorry indeed I had to do it.'

'Everything is all right,' she said. 'Come in.'

Finn went in, and laid the burden on the floor. He removed the covering, and there were the two Lads, locked in each other's arms, just as they fell.

When the Lady of the Green Isle saw them, she smiled and said:

'Finn, my Darling, well is it for me that you went on this journey!'

She went into a closet, and having lifted a flagstone from the floor, she took out a little vessel of balsam which she had there. She then placed the two Lads face to face, knee to knee, thumb to thumb; and rubbed the balsam on the soles of their feet, on the crowns of their heads, and on all parts of their skin that touched one another. The two Lads immediately stood up on the floor and kissed each other.

'Now, Finn,' said she, 'there you have my two sons! This one was stolen from me in his infancy, and I was without him until now. But since you have done all that I told you, you are welcome to stay here as long as you wish.'

They were so merry in the house of the Green Isle, that time went past unknown to them. One night, the Lady of the Green Isle, said to Finn:

'Tomorrow it will be a year and a day since you left the Fian, and they have given up hope of you. The man of them who is not whetting his sword, is pointing his spear for the purpose of going to look for you. Make ready to depart tomorrow, and I will let my son go with you. If you go alone, they will give you such a tumultuous welcome they will smother and kill you. But when you arrive, my son will enter before you, and tell them that if they will promise to rise up one by one, and give you a quiet, sensible welcome, he will bring their earthly king home whole and sound to them.'

Finn agreed to this with all his heart. He and the Big Lad went on the journey homeward on the morning of the next day. They had a long way to go, but they did not take long accomplishing it.

When they reached Tall, Finn's Hall, the Big Lad went in first, and what his mother had said proved true. Every man of the Fian was getting ready his sword and spear. The Big Lad asked them what they were doing, and they told him they were preparing to go and look for Finn. Then the Big Lad told them that if they promised to rise, one after another, to give Finn a quiet and sensible welcome when he came, he, the Big Lad, would bring Finn to them. They willingly consented to do this. Then the Big Lad called on Finn to come in. He came, and one by one, the Fian rose and welcomed him quietly, as they had promised. The Fian now had their earthly king back once more.

(The Big Lad returned home, and if he is not dead, he is still alive.)

The Day of the Battle of Sheaves in the
Hollow of Tiree

THE FIANS were at harvest work in Kilmoluag, in the true hollow of Tiree. It was oats they were harvesting. The day they went to reap, they left their weapons of war in the armoury of the Fairy Hill of Caolis.

When they were at the reaping they saw the Norsemen coming ashore at Besta. The Fians had neither spears nor any weapons of war. They sent away the swift Caoilte and back-of-the-wind Mac Rae, son of Ronan, to fetch the weapons.

The Norsemen attacked them, but a sheaf of oats was driven by the wind up to the waist of the body of Norsemen that day. Then Finn said to the man near to him:

'Look, can you see any man coming with the armour?'

'I see one man.'

'What is he like?'

'He is as if he had bare, stripped wood on his shoulders.'

'Are you seeing anyone else?'

'I do not see anyone but him.'

'What does he look like now?' said Finn after a while.

'He appears to have three heads on.'

'In that case he must be running at full speed, with his two feet lifting as high as his head as he runs. Do you see anyone else?'

'Yes, I see another.'

'Is he making good speed?'

'Yes, well enough!'

Then Caoilte came and every man took his weapons, and they and the Norsemen attacked each other, and they drove the Norsemen to the shore.

Finn's Ransom

ONCE upon a time Finn and his three foster-brothers, the Red Knight, the Knight of the Cairn and the Knight of the Sword, went to the Hunting-hill. They sat down to look around them, on a sunny, rocky hillock, sheltered from the wind and in the sun's warmth, where they could see everyone, and no one could see them. When they had sat for some time, the Knight of the Sword said:

'Is it possible that anyone who has walked on the earth, could despise Finn MacCoul, when his three foster-brothers are near him?'

These words were hardly uttered, when they saw the darkening of the sky of a passing of a shower from the north-east, and heard the sound of a rider on a black horse.

The rider came straight to Finn, struck him on the mouth, knocking out three upper and three lower teeth. Then the Knight of the Sword said:

'The earth will make a hollow in the sole of my foot, and the sky will make a nest in the crown of my head, before I fail to restore Finn's loss.'

The other foster-brothers said the same. Then they went down to the shore, and began to fit out a ship to sail away. They were not long working on it, when they saw a little twisted, thickset man approaching them. They addressed him, and he asked the Knight of the Sword if he could accompany them on the ship.

'No,' said the Knight of the Sword. 'What use could a little man like you be to us on a ship?'

He made the same request of the Knight of the Cairn, who made the same reply, and so did the Red Knight, when he was asked.

'Who would have the audacity to take such a small insignificant creature like you to sea in a ship?' said he.

The little man then went to Finn, and told him that the others had refused him, and asked if Finn would allow him to accompany them.

'I'll give you permission,' said Finn, 'for you are of more value than a stone.'

They launched the ship, turned the prow seaward, the stern landward and raised the speckled towering sails against the tall strong mast, with wind that would strip the green leaves from the trees and the young heather from its roots, lashing the sea wildly into waves, while the little crooked whelk that was seven years at the bottom of the sea, gave a creaking sound on the gunwale and a thump at the bottom of the boat. The ship could have cut a grain of oats with the edge of her prow, from the excellence of her steering. Finn MacCoul was the guide at the prow and they directed her course for the kingdom of the Big Men.

When they had been sailing for two days, Finn asked the Knight of the Sword to look from the mast, to report if he could see land. He went a short way up the mast and said there was no sign of land. Then Finn asked the Knight of the Cairn to try and see if there was any sign of land, but he also returned and said there was no trace of land in sight. Finn asked the Red Knight to look carefully for a sign of land. The Red Knight only climbed a short way up the mast when he returned to report that there was neither land nor earth to be seen. Then the little insignificant man stood up and said:

'If you could not do better than that you might as well have remained behind!' And he gave a bound and reached the top of the mast. When he came down he said to Finn: 'I saw something too large for a hooded crow, and too small to be land; but keep the course and you will reach your destination.'

Next day they were in the harbour of the kingdom of the Big Men. When they reached the anchorage, they found they could not land. There were three fiery darts gleaming all round the harbour. Then the little man put a hollow shield on his right hand, gave a leap of three bounds, and reached the shore. After that he took Finn and his three foster-brothers safely on shore with him.

The four of them walked with the little man through the island. They met

a tall woman with a little brown lapdog at her heels, and every time the lapdog looked at Finn, Finn's lost teeth were restored to his mouth, but when the lapdog turned away from him, Finn's teeth vanished.

The foster-brothers now thought that Finn's ransom of lost teeth had been found, and they carried off the tall woman and her dog to their ship, leaving the little man alone on the island.

He travelled across the island, and in the dusk of the evening, saw a small house at the roadside, with a light shining in it.

He went into the house and found a fire burning in the hearth, but nobody there. He was not long waiting and listening, when a tall man came in and said:

'What news has the little Swaddler?'

The little man had no news, and asked the tall man if he had any.

'My news is sorrowful,' said he, 'for my beautiful sister who used to bathe me after battle and made me fresh and strong again has been taken away and is lost to us.'

'If that is all she did,' said the little man, 'perhaps I can do it for you.' And he washed the tall man in a tub, so that he had never felt more refreshed and happy.

Another brother came in, and said:

'What news has the little Swaddler?'

'I've no news unless I get some from you!'

'My news is sad,' said the second tall brother, 'for my dear sister who bathed me after battle so that I was as well as ever, has been taken away with her little brown dog that always followed at her heels.'

'If that's all she did, I may be able to do that myself.'

And he put the tall second brother in a tub and washed him so that he too was as fresh as ever to go to fight next day. Then a third tall brother came in and said:

'What news has this little Swaddler?'

'I've no tale to tell better than that of the last tall man who came in!'

'My story is poor,' said the third brother, 'for my handsome sister who always bathed me when I returned from battle, has been taken away, and now I shall be without strength or counsel.'

'If that is all she did,' said the little man, 'I may try to do it myself.'

He took the third brother off to the far end of the house, washed and bathed him so that he was refreshed and ready to engage in battle.

'Will you allow me to go into battle tonight in your place?' said the little Swaddler.

One of the brothers said:

'What can a little creature like you do, when they keep the three of us at bay?'

'Tell me how many are coming to trouble you,' said the little man.

'A regiment of soldiers, and though I beheaded every one of them,' said one brother, 'they were followed by a tall old woman, who came after them with a life-restoring stoup in one hand. When she dipped the finger of the other into the stoup and put it into the mouths of the dead soldiers, they then sprang up alive.'

'Will there be others to fight?' said the little man.

'There will then come another regiment of soldiers,' said the second brother, 'and they'll be led by musical harpers, who will send you to sleep.'

'Will any others come?' said the little man.

'There will come a tall old man of terrifying appearance,' said the third brother, 'who will take your life unless you can keep fighting him all through the night. After him, a tall old woman will come, and if you allow her to come near you, her breath will kill you.'

The little man asked if any others would follow, and the brothers told him that no one else would come.

That night the little man got permission to go to the battle. When he saw the first regiment approaching, he hid himself until they had passed, then he went up behind them and killed every one of them. Then he saw the enormous old woman coming with the life-saving stoup in her hand. As she drew near, he lay down among the dead men.

The old woman dipped her finger into the stoup of life-giving liquid, and put her finger into the mouth of the dead soldier nearest to him. The man sprang up alive. She then put her finger into the mouth of the little Swaddler, but he bit it off at the knuckle, and she cried out:

'Of all the men lying here, may you be the last of your mother's race to rise!'

'No, I shall be the last of all men here to rise,' said the little man, and he struck off her head and that of the soldier.

Soon after that he heard the musical harpers drawing near, and the next regiment hurrying towards him. He was almost overcome with fatigue and falling asleep. To keep himself awake, he placed the hilt of his sword on the upper part of his foot and the point of the blade to his eyebrows, and whenever he began to nod, the point of the sword kept him awake. When the last band of soldiers passed near him, he leapt after them and killed them all.

He now thought that the tall old man would not be long appearing, and he began to dig a deep wide hole in the earth, and cover it over with branches, grass and moss. When the pitfall was nearly complete in the gathering dusk, the terrific and dreadful old grey man came. He and the little Swaddler began to fight. They attacked each other roughly and fiercely. In the heat of the conflict, they drew near the pitfall, and the terrible old grey man fell in. Then the little Swaddler took advantage of him, and struck off his head.

Shortly after that fight was over, the old woman appeared. As she came close to him, her breath was weakening him. He tried to keep her away from him and they fought all through the night.

At the break of day, when the brothers woke, the first rose and said to the others:

'I am certain that little man who went to fight in my place must be dead.'

'That's not the worst of it,' said another. 'Your kingdom will be destroyed!'

'We had better go together to the place where the battle was fought,' said the third.

So they set off.

When they arrived at the battlefield they found the little Swaddler and the enormous old woman fighting together, quite exhausted.

'Oh! Give me the sword that I may cut off the wretched old one's head!' said one brother.

'Since I finished the foot measure,' said the little man, 'I'll undertake the inch measure! But first, put your finger into the stoup of life-saving liquid, and then put that finger into my mouth.'

When one of the brothers had done this, the little Swaddler rose, swept off the old woman's head and she fell back dead. The tall brothers carried the little man home on their shoulders, and they continued to live in peace together.

One day, when the little Swaddler went to the hill to look out over the country, he saw a darkening shower coming from the north-west, out of which came a rider on a black horse. The little Swaddler fiercely attacked him. He drew his sword, and cut off the head of the rider of the black horse. Then, finding the rider was quite dead, he searched the body for any valuables. He found only two combs and a slim silken purse, in which were the six teeth of Finn MacCoul. He took them and returned home.

One of the tall brothers asked him what he had seen that day on his travels.

'I saw nothing that gave me pleasure,' said he, 'but I did see the gloom of a shower from the north-west, out of which came a rider on a black horse. He tried to cut off my head, but I drew my sword, and separated his head from his body.'

'What treasure did you find on his body?'

'I found only two combs and a slim silken purse, in which there were six teeth.'

'Alas,' said the tallest brother, 'you never did us any good equal to the evil you have brought us today! You have killed our father's only brother. He went abroad once a year, through every kingdom of the universe to its remotest bounds, and returned to give us a history of everything that was taking place.'

'It has long been foretold that it would be the restorer of Finn MacCoul's loss, who would deliver us from our conflicts and warfare,' said another of the tall brothers. 'We will agree to make peace with the little Swaddler, for he has helped us more than he has harmed us.'

The little man thanked them and said that as he had found Finn's ransom, he would rather leave them and return to the Fian.

'We will give you a black horse to ride the green ocean as if it is the green grassy land, and you will bring news of us to our sister. And when you find her, make her your lawful wife,' said the three tall brothers.

The little man mounted the black horse, and set out for the land of the Fianna. In the dusk and twilight of the evening, he was with Finn MacCoul, and asked him and his foster-brothers whether they had found the ransom. They all answered that they had not found it. He then drew out the slim, silken purse, with the six teeth contained in it, and handed it to Finn.

'Your ransom is there,' said the little man, 'but your foster-brothers did not get it for you. I did.'

Finn thanked him; and he was always to remember,

'The little, low-set Swaddler,
His russet coat and sinewy muscles,
The hair of his chest pointing upwards,
The hair of his head reaching down to his chest,
His bag of arrows death-inflicting,
Without wax or feathering.'

The Daughter of the King under the Waves

HE FIAN were together, on the side of the Hill of Howth, on a wild night, and there was pouring rain and snow falling from the north. About midnight, a creature of uncouth appearance knocked on the door of Finn. Her hair was down to her heels, and she cried to him to let her in, and give her shelter under his covering.

'You strange creature,' said he, 'your hair is down to your heels, how can you ask me to let you in?'

She went away, and gave a scream. She reached Ossian and asked him to let her in and give her shelter. Ossian lifted the corner of his covering, and saw her.

'You strange, hideous creature, how can you ask me to let you in?' he said. 'Your hair is down to your heels. You shall not come in.'

She went away and gave a shriek. She reached Diarmid, and cried aloud to him to let her in under his covering. Diarmid lifted a fold of his covering and saw her.

'You are a strange, hideous creature. Your hair is down to your heels, but come in,' said he, and she came in under the border of his covering.

'Oh, Diarmid,' said she, 'I have spent seven years travelling over ocean and sea, and in all that time I have not passed a night under cover till this night, till you let me in. Let me in to the warmth of the fire.'

'Come up to the fire,' said Diarmid.

When she drew up to the fireside, the Fian began to move away, so hideous was she.

'Go to the far side,' said Diarmid to them, 'and let the creature feel the warmth of the fire.'

They went to the far side, and let her be at the fire, but she had not been long there, when she sought to be under the warmth of the blanket, together with Diarmid.

'You are growing too bold,' said Diarmid. 'First you ask to come under the border of the covering, then you seek to come to the fire, and now you seek leave to come under the blanket with me; but come all the same.'

She went under the blanket, and he turned a fold of it between them. She was not long thus, when he gave a start, and gazed at her. He saw at his side, the finest woman that ever was, from the beginning of the universe till the end of the world. He shouted to the others to come over, and said to them:

'It is not often that men are unkind. Is this not the most beautiful woman man ever saw?'

'She is,' said they, 'the most beautiful woman man ever saw.'

She was asleep, and did not know that they were looking at her. Diarmid let her sleep, and did not waken her, but after a short while she awoke, and said to him:

'Are you awake, Diarmid?'

'I am,' said he.

'Where would you like the finest castle you've ever seen to be built?'

'If I had my choice, up above Benn Eudainn,' said Diarmid and then slept, and she said no more to him.

One of the Fian was out before day, riding, and he saw a castle built on a hill. He cleared his sight to see if it was surely there; then he saw it, and went home, and did not say a word.

Another of the Fian went out, and he saw it, and he did not say a word. Then the day brightened, and the two came in saying that a castle was surely there.

'Arise, Diarmid,' said she, as she sat up. 'Go to your castle, and do not lie stretched there any longer.'

'If there is a castle, which way should I go?' said he.

'Look out, and see if there is a castle there.'

He looked out, and saw a castle, and came in saying: 'I'll go up to the castle if you will go with me.'

'I'll do that, Diarmid, but don't say to me three times how you found me.'

'I'll never say to you how I found you,' said Diarmid.

The two of them went to the castle, together with Diarmid's greyhound bitch and three pups. It was beautiful. In the castle there was nothing lacking that would be required, even to a herd for the geese. There was meat on the table, and there were maid-servants and men-servants about it.

They spent three days in the castle together, and at the end of the three days, she said to him:

'You are turning sorrowful because you are not with the others.'

'I am not feeling sorrowful, surely, because I'm not with the Fian,' said he.

'You had best go with the Fian. Your meat and drink will be no worse than they are now,' said she.

'Who will take care of my greyhound bitch, and her three pups?' said Diarmid.

'Oh,' said she, 'what is there to fear for the greyhound bitch and the three pups?'

He went away when he heard that. He left a blessing with her, and reached the people of the Fian, and Finn, the brother of his mother, and there was a chief's honour and welcome for Diarmid when he arrived. But they had ill will for him, because the woman had come first to them, and they had turned their backs to her, and he had given in to her wishes, and the matter had turned out so well.

She went out after he had gone away, and what should she see but a man coming in great haste. She stayed outside till he came, and who was there but Finn. He hailed her and caught her by the hand.

'You are angry with me, damsel,' said Finn.

'I am not,' said she. 'Come in and take a drink with me.'

'I will, if you grant my request,' said Finn.

'What request could there be that you should not get?'

'One of the pups of the greyhound bitch.'

'Oh, the request is not great,' said she. 'Take the one you choose.' And he took the pup and went away.

At the opening of the night came Diarmid. The greyhound bitch met him outside, and gave a yelp.

'It is true, my lass, one of your pups has gone. But if she had remembered how I found her, how her hair was down to her heels, she would not have let your pup go.'

'What did you say, Diarmid?' said she.

'Oh,' said Diarmid, 'I am asking pardon!'

'Oh, you shall get that,' said she, and he slept in the castle that night, and his meat and drink were as before.

Next morning, he went to where he had been, and while he was gone she went out to take a stroll. While she was strolling about, what should she see but a rider coming. She stayed outside till he reached her. And who should it be but Ossian, son of Finn.

They gave welcome and honour to each other. She told him to go in with her, and take a drink with her, and he said he would if he might get his request.

'What request do you have?' said she.

'One of the pups of the greyhound bitch.'

'You shall get that,' said she. 'Take your choice of them.' He took the pup with him, and went away. At the opening of night, Diarmid came home. The greyhound met him and she gave two yelps.

'That is true, my lass,' said Diarmid, 'another pup has been taken from you. But if she had remembered how I found her, when her hair was down to her heels, she would not have let one of your pups go.'

'What did you say, Diarmid?' said she.

'I am asking pardon,' said Diarmid.

'You shall get that,' she said, and they seized each other's hands, and they went in together, and there was meat and drink that night, as there had ever been.

In the morning, Diarmid went away. A while after he had gone, she went outside to take a stroll. She saw another rider coming, and he was in great haste. She thought she would wait and not go home before he'd arrived. Who was this but another of the Fian. He went to the damsel with civil words, and they gave welcome and honour to each other. She told him to come and have a drink with her. He said he would if she granted his request. She asked him what that might be.

'One of the pups of the greyhound bitch,' said he.

'Though it is a hard matter for me,' said she, 'I will give it to you.'

He went with her to the castle, took a drink from her, and he got the pup, then went away.

At the opening of night came Diarmid. The greyhound bitch met him, and she gave three yelps, the most hideous ever heard.

'Yes, it is true my lass, you are without any pups today,' said Diarmid, 'but if she had remembered how I met her, when her hair was down to her heels, she would not have let the pup go.'

'What did you say, Diarmid?' said she.

'Oh, I am asking pardon,' said Diarmid.

He went inside, but there was no wife nor bed for him that night.

Next morning, he awoke in a moss-hole. There was no castle, and no stone left of it. He began to weep, and said to himself that he would not stay, head or foot, till he should find her. Away he went across the glens. There was neither house nor fire on the way. He glanced over his shoulder, and what should he see but the greyhound bitch, who had just died. He seized her by the tail, and slung her over his shoulder. He would not part with her for the love he bore her. He went on and who should he see but a shepherd.

'Did you see, today or yesterday, a woman passing this way?' said Diarmid.

'I saw a woman early yesterday morning, and she was walking hard,' said the herd.

'Which way did she go?'

'She went down to yonder point, to the strand, and then I saw her no more.'

Diarmid took the road she had taken, till there was no going further. He saw a ship, put the slender end of his spear under his breastbone, sprang on to the ship, and sailed to the other side of the water. He lay down on the side of the hill, and slept. When he woke there was no ship to be seen.

'A man to be pitied am I,' said he. 'I shall never get away from here. There is no help for it!'

He sat on a knoll, and had not sat there long when he saw a boat coming, and a man in her. He went down to the boat. He grasped the greyhound by the tail, put her into the boat, and went in after her.

Then the boat went out over the sea, and then went down under the sea. He had just gone under, when he saw ground, and a plain on which he could walk. In this land he walked on and on.

He was but a short time walking, when he came across a clot of blood. He gathered up the blood, put it in a napkin, and into his pouch.

He was a while walking, when he came across the next clot of blood, and he did the same with it.

A short time after that, what should he see but a woman gathering rushes as though she was crazed. He went up to her and asked her what news she had.

'I cannot tell till I gather the rushes,' said she.

'Be telling it while you are gathering rushes,' said he.

'I am in a great haste,' said she.

'What place is this?' said he.

'Here,' said she, 'is the Realm Under the Waves.'

'Realm Under the Waves?'

'Yes,' said she.

'What use have you for rushes?' said Diarmid.

'The daughter of the King Under the Waves has come home. She was seven years under spells, and now she is ill. The doctors of Christendom are gathered here, but none are doing her good, and a bed of rushes is what she finds most comforting.'

'I would be in your debt if you would take me where that woman is,' said Diarmid.

'Well then, I'll see to that. I'll put you into a sheaf of rushes. I'll put rushes under you and over you, and I'll take you with me on my back.'

'That is a thing you cannot do,' said Diarmid.

'Be that on me,' said she.

She put Diarmid into the bundle, and took him on her back. When she reached the chamber, she let down the bundle.

'Oh hurry with that to me,' said the daughter of the King Under the Waves.

Diarmid sprang out of the bundle. He ran to meet her, and they seized each other's hands joyfully.

'Three parts of the illness are gone, but I am not well,' said she, 'and I shall not be. Every time I thought of you as I came here, I lost a clot of my heart's blood.'

'I have those three clots of your heart's blood. Take them in a drink, and all will be well.'

'I will not take them,' said she. 'They will not do me any good, since I cannot get the one thing to cure me, and I shall never get it.'

'What thing is that?' said Diarmid.

'It is no good telling you, you will not get it, nor will any man in the world.'

'If it's on the surface of the world, I'll get it, so tell me,' said Diarmid.

'It is three draughts from the cup of the King of Wonderplain. No man ever got that, so I shall not get it.'

'Oh!' said Diarmid, 'there are not on the surface of the world as many as will keep it from me. Tell me if King Wonderplain is far from here.'

'He is not. He is within a stone's throw of my father, but there is a river between, and in it there is the sailing of a ship, with the wind behind her, for a day and a year before you reach your destination.'

He went away. He reached the river, and spent a good while walking along it.

'I cannot cross it, that is true,' said Diarmid. Before he had let the words out of his mouth, there stood a little russet man in the middle of the river.

'Diarmid, son of Duibhne, you are in trouble,' said he.

'Yes, I am in trouble just now,' said Diarmid.

'What would you give to a man to bring you out of this trouble? Come here and put your foot on my palm.'

'Oh, my foot cannot go into the palm of your hand!'

'It can.'

Diarmid put his foot on the russet man's palm.

'Now, Diarmid, it is to the King of Wonderplain that you are going.'

'It is indeed.'

'It is to seek his cup you are going.'

'It is.'

'I will go with you myself.'

'You shall go,' said Diarmid.

Diarmid reached the house of King Wonderplain. He shouted for the cup to be sent out, or battle or combat; but it was to be combat, not the cup. There were sent out four hundred strong heroes, four hundred brave heroes, and in two hours he had left not a man of them alive. He shouted again for battle or combat, or the cup to be sent out.

That was the thing he would get, battle or combat, but not the cup.

There were sent out eight hundred strong heroes, and eight hundred brave heroes. In three hours he left not a man of them alive. He shouted again for battle or combat, or else the cup to be sent out to him. There were sent out nine hundred strong heroes, and nine hundred brave heroes, and in four hours he left no man of them alive.

'Whence came the man that has just brought my realm to ruin?' said the king, as he stood in his own great door. 'If it be the pleasure of the Hero, let him tell from whence he came.'

'It is the pleasure of a Hero; a Hero of the people of the Fian. I am Diarmid.'

'Why did you not send a message to say who you were? I would not have wasted my realm on you, for it was written in the books, seven years before you were born, that you would kill every man of them. What do you want from me?'

'The cup. It comes from your own healing hand.'

'No man ever got my cup but you. It is easy for me to give you a cup, but for the healing, it is all I have.' Then Diarmid got the cup from King Wonderplain.

'I will now send a ship with you, Diarmid,' said the king.

'Great thanks to you, oh king. I am much in your debt; but I have a ferry of my own.'

Here the king and Diarmid parted from each other. He remembered when he had parted from the king, that he had not said a word about the little russet man, and that he had not taken him into the castle. It was only when he was coming near to the river, and he did not know how he should get across, that he thought of him.

'There's no help for it. Now I shall not get over the ferry,' said he, 'and pride will not let me return to the king.'

While the words were in his mouth, who should rise out of the river but the little russet man.

'You are in trouble, Diarmid,' said he.

'I am.'

'This day you are in extreme trouble.'

'I am. I got the thing I desired, but I am not getting across.'

'Though you did to me all you have done; though you did not say a word about me yesterday; put your foot on my palm, and I will take you over the river.'

Diarmid put his foot on his palm, and the little russet man took him over the river.

'You'll talk to me now, Diarmid,' said he.

'I will.'

'You are going to heal the daughter of the King Under the Waves; she is the lass you like best in the world?'

'Yes, it is she.'

'You shall go to a well. You will find a bottle at the side of the well, and you will take it with you, full of water. When you reach the lass, put the water in the cup, and a clot of blood in it, and she will drink it. Fill the cup again, and she will drink. You shall fill the cup a third time, and you'll put the third clot of blood into it, and she will drink it, and there will not be a whit wrong with her. When you have given her the last drink, and she is well, she will be the one you care for least.'

'Oh! Not she!' said Diarmid.

'She it is. The king will know that you have taken a dislike to his daughter. She will say: "Diarmid, you have taken a dislike to me." Say you that you have,' said the little russet man. 'Do you know what man is speaking to you?'

'I do not,' said Diarmid.

'In me, there is the messenger of the Other World, who helped you because your heart is warm and willing to do good to another. The King Under the Waves will come, and offer you silver and gold for healing his daughter. Take not a jot, but ask that the king should send a ship to take you to Ireland, to the place from whence you came.'

Diarmid went. He reached the well. He got the bottle and filled it with water. He took it with him and he reached the castle of the King Under the Waves. When he went in he was honoured and saluted.

'No man ever got that cup before,' said the daughter of the king.

'I would have got it from anywhere on the surface of the world,' said Diarmid. 'No man could have turned me back.'

'Although you went, I did not think you would get it, but I see that you have it,' said she.

He put a clot of blood into the water in the cup. She drank it. She drank the second cup of blood in water, and she drank the third. And when she had drunk the third cupful, there was nothing wrong with her. She was whole and hearty. But, as it had been foretold, when she was well he took a dislike to her. Scarcely could he bear to see her.

'Oh Diarmid!' she said, 'You are taking a dislike to me!'

'Yes, I am,' said he.

Then the king sent word throughout the town that his daughter was healed. Music was raised, and lament ceased, and the king went to Diarmid and said to him:

'Now you can take as much as you can count for healing my daughter. And you shall have her in marriage.'

'I will not take the damsel. I will not take anything except a ship to take me to Ireland, where Finn and the Fian are gathered.'

A ship went with him, and he reached the Fian and Finn, the brother of his mother. There was joy for him there and pleasure that he had returned.

Leoän Creeäch, Son of the King of Ireland, and Kaytav, Son of the King of Colla

HERE were three men called Leoän Creeäch, son of the King of Ireland, his companion, Kaytav, son of the King of Colla, and Boinne Geal Jeerach, son of the King of the Universe. These three scholars went to Greece to improve their education. When they were out walking one day, they saw the daughter of the King of Greece and her maids-in-waiting; and Leoän Creeäch said to Kaytav:

'You must go to speak to the daughter of the King of Greece. I shall not be happy unless I win her in marriage.'

Kaytav went to the daughter of the King of Greece with the message that the son of the King of Ireland wished to marry her. But she replied that she could not live unless he, Kaytav, would marry her himself. Kaytav said that he could not marry her, for if he did he was afraid Leoän Creeäch would kill him. But she insisted that he did marry her and that they would go away and leave the place together.

They set off, and resolved to go to the court of Finn MacCoul. After their arrival, Finn MacCoul asked Kaytav what work he could do. Kaytav said that he was a good cook.

'You are well bred,' said Finn MacCoul, 'but if you are willing to be a cook, I will engage you, for this very day our cook left us. What reward do you ask for your labour?'

'I only ask,' said Kaytav, 'that my wife be allowed to go to rest and to rise before the women of the Fian.'

'Your request shall be granted,' said Finn.

Kaytav began his work as cook; and there never was such a fine cook in the court of Finn MacCoul.

A message came from the King of Lochlann, inviting Finn to go to a feast and a night's entertainment that night with him, the king, at Lochlann. The cook had to go with Finn and his men to Lochlann.

'If you take him with you,' said the cook's wife, 'I'm afraid that he will not return, but whether he be alive or dead, bring him home to me.' Finn promised that he would do this.

Finn and his men set off, and reached Lochlann. The cook began to prepare the feast in the house of the King of Lochlann. Who should then come to the house but Leoän Creeäch, after travelling over seven red divisions of the universe in search of Kaytav.

When Kaytav became heated with cooking, he raised the cook's hat he had on. Leoän Creeäch did not know him till he pushed the cook's hat up off his forehead, but when he recognised Kaytav, he attacked him and the two of them

fought on the floor. At last Leoän Creeäch, son of the King of Ireland, overcame and killed Kaytav.

When Finn MacCoul returned home, he took with him Kaytav's body in order to give it to his wife, as he had promised. The Fian left Kaytav's body on the shore and sent word to his wife to come to it. Lamenting and sorrowing, she went and sat beside him. Now, what did she see but a boat passing, quite near the shore where she was sitting. Two men were in it, one in the stern and one in the bow. The man in the stern had a gold apple and a silver apple. He was throwing the apples at the man in the bow. When he threw one of the apples at the man, he knocked his head off, and when he threw the other apple at him, his head went on again, and he became alive and well.

Kaytav's wife saw what the man was doing; and she called to him, and asked for a loan of the apples for a short while. He gave her the apples and she did with them what she had seen him do. She threw a silver apple at Kaytav's head and knocked it off. Then she threw a gold apple at him, and this put his head on again; and he got up, alive and well as he ever was.

A King of Scotland

THIS king had one son and one daughter. An enormous giant, who lived in a cave, came and took the daughter away by force.

The king was seized with a mortal illness, and died. He was buried, and his son was mourning him and lamenting him. He was in the habit of going to the grave to weep, and at times to sleep. One day, as he slept at the gravestone, a big, ugly lad came to him, and said:

'I must be a servant with you for a year and a day.'

'I cannot have such an ugly man to serve me,' said the young king, 'for when my servants see you, they will be afraid of you.'

'Be that as it may,' said the Big Lad, 'I must be your servant and you must stop lamenting your father, or worse will befall you. I will join you tomorrow.'

The young king went home, grieved that he had fallen in with such a servant. Next morning there was a knock on the door, and a handsome lad entered and said:

'Are you in want of a servant today, King of Scotland?'

'I am not,' said the king. 'I got an ugly servant yesterday. Were it not for that, I would gladly take you.'

The Lad gave himself a turn, and who should the king see but the ugly lad he had engaged yesterday. And he said to the king:

'Is this the Lad?'

'Yes, yes,' said the king, 'but do become the handsome lad again, and I will gladly engage you.'

The Lad gave himself another turn, and became as handsome as he had been when he came in. He then said to the king:

'I requested you to stop lamenting your father!'

The king again went to his father's grave, and slept, till he heard a voice saying:

'Are you asleep, young King of Scotland?'

The king wakened, and said:'I am not asleep now!' And the voice said:

'You must tell me what has kept the King of Ireland cheerless and from laughing for the last seven years.'

'I cannot find that out,' said the king, 'it is impossible!'

'If you do not, you will lose your head.'

The king returned home very grieved indeed. His servant asked him what was troubling him, for he looked so sad.

'That is not to be wondered at,' said the king.

'Tell me what the matter is,' said the Lad.

'It is because I must go and find out what has kept the King of Ireland cheerless and without laughter for the last seven years.'

'Well,' said the Lad, 'did I not tell you to stop lamenting your father? Now you've got a difficult problem indeed, for many a hero has gone to seek that information, but none have returned. You must go, at all events, and I will go with you.'

They set off the next day. When evening came, the king said:

'Where shall we stay tonight?'

'With your sister and the giant,' said the Lad.

'Not so,' said the king. 'He will kill us both.'

'Two thirds of fear be on him and a third on us!' said the Lad.

They arrived at the giant's cave, but the giant was not there. When the king's sister saw her brother, she put her arms round him, kissed him, and began to weep. In one way she was so happy to see him, but in another, she was sorry, for she was afraid the giant would kill him. She begged them to go away before the giant returned. The Lad asked her where the giant was. She told him the giant was on the Hunting-hill, hunting for game.

'You remain with your sister, and I'll go and meet the giant,' said the Lad to the king. And he went off, and met the giant who said:

'Come here, and play some music to me.'

The Lad went over to the giant, drew his sword and struck off the giant's head. He took the head back with him, and threw it in a corner of the cave, and said to the king's sister:

'There is the giant's head for you!'

She glanced at it and began to weep, and said to him:

'I knew you were a hero! Tell me where you and my brother are going.'

'We're going to find out what has kept the King of Ireland cheerless and without laughter for the last seven years.'

'Well,' said she, 'I have seen many go to try and discover that, but I have not seen any of them return.'

She then prepared food for them, showed them to their beds, rose early the next morning, and made breakfast for them. The giant had a beautiful white bird that could warble the notes of any other bird as well as its own. The Lad said to the king's sister:

'We will take the bird with us, for if anything will persuade the King of Ireland to speak to us, it is that bird.'

'You shall get the bird on condition you take care of it.'

'If we return safely so will the bird,' said the Lad.

'When may I expect you back?'

'If we are alive you can expect us at the end of a year,' said the Lad.

They bade the sister goodbye and set off. It was night when they arrived at the King of Ireland's palace. It was surrounded by a very high wall, allowing no one in until the gates were opened in the morning. They remained beside the wall till morning, walking about, trying to keep themselves warm. This wall was surmounted by a row of iron spikes. On each of them, except two, was a man's head. These were the heads of those who had gone to inquire about the king's condition.

'Do you see that?' said the Lad to the young King of Scotland.

'It cannot be helped,' said the king. 'I believe it will end like that for us.'

'Take it easy,' said the Lad, 'you are not sure.' And he went and put the bird on one of the spikes, and said to it:

'If you have ever sung, sing now!'

The bird began to sing; and the King of Ireland heard it, and thought he had never heard such charming music. He lifted the window, and saw two men standing on the outside of the wall, and the beautiful bird on one of the spikes. He said to his manservant:

'Go and ask yon men to come in here with their bird, that I may hear it sing a while. Tell them they'll be well paid for it, and order them to let no one see them enter the palace.'

The servant went and told them that the king wished them to go in, but that no one was to see them entering the palace, and he added:

'Bring the bird with you.'

'Certainly,' said the Big Lad.

In they went, and the Big Lad caught the doorkeeper by the legs, and brained him against the doorpost.

The King of Ireland's servant went and told the king what had happened.

'Go, tell them to come in,' said the king, 'that I may hear the bird warbling for a while.'

'He shall hear it,' said the Lad, 'if he pays well.'

They went in, and the king said to them:

'What impudent men you are to brain my doorkeeper!'

'Are you not yourself to blame?' said the Lad.

'How am I to blame?' said the king.

'I'll tell you,' said the Big Lad. 'Did you not order your servant to let no one see us enter? But for that I'd not have touched your doorkeeper.'

'We'll let that pass for the present. Now I want to hear your bird sing, and will pay you for it. Put the bird up on the press.'

The Big Lad put the bird up on the press; and it began to warble. The king was very pleased with it, and asked what payment they wanted.

'The payment I ask, is that you tell us what has kept you so cheerless and without laughter for the last seven years.'

'Ah!' said the king, 'Do you think I'd tell you that? Many a man has come to find that out and has never returned home to tell the tale; and it will be the same for you and your master. On each one of those spikes on yonder wall there's a man's head, except for two. Your head and that of your master will be placed on spikes at twelve o'clock today.'

'You're not quite sure,' said the Lad to the king. 'You had better tell me; for if you don't willingly, you'll be forced to tell it.'

'You impertinent fellow! Is that the way you answer the King of Ireland?'

'That is just the way,' said the Big Lad, 'and if you don't tell it you'll be forced to tell it!'

The Big Lad then caught the king by the legs and threw him over seven crossbeams and backward over seven crossbeams. At this the king called:

'Oh! Spare my life, and you shall be told all that you wish to know.'

'That is wise of you,' said the Big Lad.

'Be seated now,' said the king. 'I had a gentleman dining with me seven years ago. After dinner we went out to hunt, and saw a hare. We chased it with our dogs in order to kill it, and followed it until we reached a very steep promontory where there were many caves. The hare doubled upon us, and went into a cave. We followed it and when we entered the cave we found a big giant sitting inside, with his twelve sons. The giant said:

"Hail to you, King of Ireland. Be seated on the other side of the cave."

We sat down, and the giant continued:

"Which do you prefer to play at, the venomous apple or the hot grid iron?"

I said we would try the venomous apple. Every time the giant threw the apple he killed one of my companions; and when I threw it back, he intercepted it with the point of a penknife. He killed my twelve companions with the venomous apple. I was then caught and kept at a large fire of oak wood till I was almost burnt. Then I was thrown out of the cave, and was barely able to crawl home. My good lad! Many a man has come to find out these things without success but you have found them out. That is what has kept me cheerless and unable to laugh for the last seven years.'

'I wish that day was today,' said the Big Lad, 'then you would get sport. Had we not better go and hunt today for the hare?'

'No,' said the king, 'I'll not go. I've had enough of the hare.'

'I'll make you go,' said the Lad, 'and if you do not, I'll toss your head downstairs like a shinty ball.'

'Oh! My good lad, spare my life,' said the king, 'and I'll go with you wherever you wish.'

Then the King of Ireland, the King of Scotland and the Big Lad went hunting. They saw a hare, and the Big Lad said to the King of Ireland:

'Is that the hare you saw previously?'

'I am not sure, but it is similar,' said the king.

The hare made off, and they followed it. It made for the steep promontory as before, then they lost sight of it among the holes and caves in the rocks. They went into the cave where the giant and his twelve sons were seated. When they arrived, the giant said:

'Oh! King of Ireland, have you come to see me again?'

'Two thirds of fear on yourself!' said the Big Lad, 'and a third of it on us. Would you prefer to play at the venomous apple or the hot grid irons today?'

'We will play the venomous apple,' said the giant.

The giant caught the venomous apple and threw it across at the Big Lad, who intercepted it on the point of a penknife. When the Big Lad threw the apple back, he killed one of the giant's sons with it. The King of Ireland gave a gleeful laugh that came from the bottom of his heart. If many a year had elapsed since he laughed, he had a good laugh that day. The Big Lad killed the giant's twelve sons with the venomous apple. Then they caught the giant, stripped his clothes off him, kindled a fire of peeled oak, and roasted him. Then they threw him more dead than alive out of the cave. They took away all the gold and silver the giant had, and returned to the palace of the King of Ireland. The King of Scotland and the Big Lad spent the night with the King of Ireland, who was exceedingly kind to them, and wished the Big Lad would stay with him permanently.

Next day, the King of Scotland and the Big Lad set off to return to Scotland. They did not halt till they reached the dwelling of the king's sister – she who had married the giant, whose head had been struck off by the Big Lad before the journey to Ireland. She had been sad when they had left for Ireland, fearing her brother would not return, but when she saw him, she put her arms round him with delight. The king and the Big Lad passed that night in the cave with her. Next morning, she, her brother and the Big Lad set out for Scotland.

There was great rejoicing when they arrived at the palace of the King of Scotland. Then the Big Lad said:

'Now I must leave you. If you have ever heard of Murdoch Mac Brian, that is my name! I was under some obligation to serve you and that I have done. Now I must leave. Stop lamenting your dead father, King of Scotland, and there will be nothing for you to fear. I now bid you goodbye, and will go on my way.'

And so he went.

How Finn Was in the House of the Yellow Field

ONE day Finn and his men were on the Hunting-hill. They had travelled a long way before they fell in with the deer, but before the close of day, they killed a great number. They then sat down to rest and consult each other about the direction they should take next day. While they were conversing, Finn gave a look into the glen below them, and saw a strong Hero making straight towards them.

'A stranger is coming this way,' said Finn.

'If he is coming on business,' said Conan, 'he'll not leave before settling it.'

But before they had much more conversation about him, the Young Hero was there standing before them. He gave Finn the salutation of the day, and Finn saluted him courteously. Finn then asked whence he came, and what business he had.

'I am a servant who has travelled long and far, seeking a master,' said he, 'and I will go no further unless you refuse me.'

'Well,' said Finn, 'I want a servant. If we agree about the reward, I may engage you.'

'That would not be my advice to you,' said Conan. 'I thought you had had enough of those Wandering Lads!'

'Silence, rascal!' said the Young Hero. 'Often has your tongue put your head into trouble, and I am deceived if you do not experience some trouble after this day's talk.'

'Never mind,' said Finn, 'your appearance will answer for you at any rate. What is the reward you want till the end of a year and a day?'

'That you and your men will accept an invitation from me to a feast and a night's entertainment when my time is up.'

When Finn heard that his men were to go with him, he took courage that, being together, no evil would befall them, and so he said that the Lad should get the reward he asked for.

After a year and a day, Finn and his men considered which of them should follow after the Lad, for he was very swift.

'We will let Caoilte go after him,' said Finn. 'I believe he will be able to keep him in sight. Cuchulin will follow Caoilte, and we will follow them both.' And so they did.

The Big Lad set off bareheaded, bare-footed, without any preparation, leaping from gap to height, from height to glen, and through glen to strath. Caoilte went after him, and when the Big Lad would be going out of sight on the first gap, Caoilte would be coming into sight on the next ridge. Cuchulin was the same distance to Caoilte as the Fianna were to Cuchulin. They kept that order till they reached the House of the Yellow Field.

The Big Lad stood and waited till the last man of the Fianna had arrived. Then he walked over to a fine yellow house, opened the door and invited them to go in and be seated.

Finn went in first, and his men followed him. All of them got seats against the walls, except Conan. He was behind, and because all the seats were filled before he arrived, he had no choice but to drop down and stretch himself on the hearthstone. They were all tired after the journey they had made, and were at first content to stay where they were. But, after they had rested, they began to grow impatient because there was no sign of a feast.

At last Finn told one of his men to go and see if anyone was coming with food for them. One or two of the men tried to rise from their seats but they could not. Their haunches stuck to the seats, the soles of their feet to the floor, and their backs to the walls. They looked at each other, and Conan cried from the hearthstone, to which his back and hair was stuck:

'Did I not tell you in good time what would happen to you with these Wandering Lads!'

Finn did not speak a word. He was very anxious about the straits they were in. Then he remembered his tooth of knowledge, so he put his finger under it, discovered that the only thing that could release them from their predicament was the blood of the three sons of the King of Insh Tilly, and that the blood must be filtered through silver rings into cups of gold.

Finn did not know who would get the blood for him, but he remembered that Lohary, son of the King of Hunts, and Oscar were, that day, absent from the company. He had with him his Wooden Crier, his magical whistle, which he only blew when he was in some dire strait or other. Whenever he blew it, the sound would pass through the seven borders of the world, to the extremity of the Uttermost Earth. He knew that when Lohary and Oscar heard the sound, they would come from any quarter of the world they were in.

Finn blew the Wooden Crier three times, and before the sun rose next day, Oscar was outside the walls of the house crying:

'Are you there, Finn?'

'Who is that?' asked Finn from inside the house.

'You are changed indeed if you do not know my voice when there is only the thickness of a house between us. I, Oscar, am here, and Lohary with me. What must we do?'

Finn told them their situation and peril, and that nothing could release them except the blood of the three sons of the King of Insh Tilly, filtered through rings of silver into cups of gold.

'Where shall we find them?' said Oscar.

'You must watch the ford at the mouth of yon river, at the going-down of the sun,' said Finn. 'But it is still early in the day. See if you can find some food for us for we are very hungry. And Oscar, remember to take your lance with you.'

Oscar and Lohary set out in the direction of the Big House. When they got there, the people living in the house were preparing their meal.

'You take the lead,' said Lohary to Oscar.

Oscar took the lead, keeping his eye in every corner to see what he could see. When he reached the kitchen, he looked in, and saw a fierce Hero lifting a quarter of a deer out of a pot.

'Follow me,' said he to Lohary. 'I will take care of the man and you take the food with you.'

Oscar went into the kitchen, but the man was nowhere to be seen. Instead there was a large buzzard with outspread wings ready to pounce down on his head. He aimed his lance at the buzzard and broke its wing. The buzzard fell to the ground and vanished. He and Lohary took every bit of food they could find.

They returned to the House of the Yellow Field, and to Finn and his men. They made a hole in the wall of the house, and threw in piece after piece of food for each man, till all there had got something except Conan, who lay on his back on the hearthstone. Having his hands, feet, and back stuck to the hearthstone, they could not give him any food except what they could let down through the roof of the house, which he then seized with his mouth. This way he got a morsel or two.

Oscar asked Finn what they had to watch for at the ford at the mouth of the river, besides the three sons of the King of Insh Tilly.

'An army of men will accompany them,' said Finn.

'And how shall we know the three sons of the King of Insh Tilly from all the other men?'

'They will wear green apparel and walk apart from the others on the right hand side.'

'Now we will know them,' said Oscar.

Then Oscar and Lohary went to find the silver rings and the cups of gold for filtering and holding the blood. After they had been found, they went to watch at the ford. At the setting of the sun, they heard a loud sound of many men approaching. Oscar looked in the direction of the sound, and saw a great army come into view. He called on Lohary to be ready.

'We will go ashore and meet them on hard land,' said Lohary.

When the great army of men came near, they cried:

'Who are the two tall, ugly lubbers, standing there at the ford? Whoever they are, it is time for them to be afraid!'

'A third of the fear be on yourselves,' said Oscar, 'and a small third of it be on us!'

Then they went to meet each other, but Oscar and Lohary fought them violently, and not a man of them was left alive to tell the tale.

Oscar and Lohary turned back. Next morning they told Finn what had befallen them, adding that they had not seen the king's sons.

'Where shall we watch tonight?' said Oscar.

'Watch well again the ford of the river,' said Finn, 'but in the meantime get us some food, for we are very hungry. And Oscar, remember to take with you your three-edged blade and your shield.'

They reached the Big House, and Oscar was more guarded this time. He did not know what might meet him. When he looked into the kitchen, he saw a dreadful giant with four hands, lifting meat out of a cauldron. He went inside, but the man had vanished, and in his place was a large eagle about to throw an egg at him that she held in her talons. He lifted his shield, but the blow sent him onto one knee beside the cauldron. He saw he could not be ready with his blade before the eagle reached him, so he lifted the cauldron of boiling broth, and poured it on the eagle's head. She gave a terrible shriek, went through the wall, and he did not get a second look at her.

Then he and Lohary took the food and, as on the day before, succeeded in giving every man of the Fianna a share, except Conan, still stuck to the hearth. Again, his share was smaller.

When evening came, they went to the ford, and advanced further on the other side of the river than on the previous night. Soon they saw an army of men, who cried:

'Who are the two tall ugly lubbers, standing over there above the ford? Whoever they are, it is time for them to be afraid!'

'Two thirds of the fear be on yourselves, and a little third of it on us!' said Oscar.

Then they assailed the army until they fought through their ranks, and not a man was left of them to tell the tale. They turned back, and told Finn that the king's sons had not come yet. Finn told them again to bring food.

'And Oscar, remember your spear and shield. If your spear tastes the blood of the Winged Dragon of Shiel, the King of Insh Tilly shall be without a son tonight.'

They went and turned their faces towards the Big House. Oscar took the lead, as was his custom. He looked to see what was in the kitchen, and there he saw a handsome, strong man with two heads and four hands, lifting meat out of the cauldron. It was time to be ready. When Oscar entered the kitchen, no man was to be seen, instead a Great Winged Dragon, with two heads, was standing on the floor. Oscar whispered to Lohary:

'You make for the food, and I'll fight the dragon.'

He lifted his shield, drew his spear, thrust it through one head, and halfway through the other head of the dragon. The Winged Dragon of Shiel fought hard, but at last he grew weak with the loss of blood. Then Oscar drew back the spear to thrust it again into the monster, but as the spear came out of the flesh, he disappeared.

The two heroes got the food and took it to the Fianna. When they arrived, Finn asked Oscar:

'Did your spear taste the dragon's blood?'

'A cubit length and a hand's breadth of it drank greedily,' Oscar said.

Then they managed to give a share of the food to every man as on previous days. But Conan's share was still smaller.

As soon as the greying of the evening came, Finn said to Oscar:

'Let the silver rings and the cups of gold be with you tonight.'

They went to the ford at the mouth of the river, and they advanced farther on the other side of the river than before. They were but a short time waiting, when they saw that a great army was coming towards them, and on the right, wearing green garments, were the three sons of the King of Insh Tilly. Oscar said to Lohary:

'Will you face the three sons of the King of Insh Tilly, or the great army of men?'

'I will face the three sons of the King of Insh Tilly,' said Lohary, 'and you shall face the great army of men.'

As they approached, the army of men cried:

'Who are the two ugly lubbers, standing above the ford of the river in the greying of the evening? Whoever they are, it is time for them to flee.'

'Three thirds of the fear be on yourselves, and none of it on us!' said Oscar.

Then he advanced to meet the army, and Lohary faced the three sons of the King of Insh Tilly. There was a hard fight between Oscar and the army of men, but he prevailed over them, and not a man of them was left alive. Then, in great haste, he went over to Lohary, who had the three sons of the king on their knees, but they had Lohary on one knee. When Oscar saw that Lohary had the upper hand, he did not help him, but directed his attention to the blood of the three sons of the King of Insh Tilly; pouring rapidly out on to the meadow. He began

to filter it through the silver rings into the cups of gold, but before all the cups were full, the bodies grew so stiff that out of them no more blood flowed.

The two Heroes went with what they had got, to the house where Finn and his men waited. Oscar cried that they had come, and that they had the blood with them.

'Well,' said Finn, 'you must rub it onto every part of you that may touch this house, from the top of your heads to the soles of your feet.'

Oscar and Lohary did as Finn instructed them, then they went into the house, and rubbed the blood onto every bit of the Fianna's bodies that had stuck to the seats, or the walls, or the floor. In that way they released every man of the Fianna in the House of the Yellow Field. All except Conan. Only the dregs remaining in the cups were left for him, but these released all but the back of his head. And so his hair and the skin round it, still stuck to the hearthstone, and there was no alternative but to leave him as he was.

Finn and his men had not gone far from the house, when they looked back and saw Conan coming. At once they stood and waited till he overtook them. There he was, without a single hair on his head, or a strip of skin between the top of his head and the back of his neck; for, when he perceived that the rest of the Fian had gone and left him behind, he gave his head a mighty pull, and left his skin and hair bound to the hearthstone. From that day on, people called him 'Bald Conan'.

Finn and his men reached home, and Finn gave his word that he would never again engage a Wandering Lad, a promise he was to break when he met the Lad with the Skin Coverings many years later.

KYLE RHEA

T a certain time, when the Fian had come home from the chase to the House of Farabhuil, at the foot of Farabhein, in Ardnamurchan, they were astonished to find their wives so lusty, fair and comely; for the deer was very scarce at that time with the Fian.

The Fian determined that they would know what their wives were getting to make them so lusty; and when they went away again to the chase, they left Conan, one of themselves, at the house to find this out.

Conan kept watch. The meal that the wives had was the hazel tops boiled, and they were drinking the bree. It is said that they also used to wash themselves with this.

The women understood that Conan had been left in the house to watch them, and they were in a great fury.

One night, when Conan lay down to sleep, they tied his hair to two stakes, which they drove into the earth on either side of his head. Then the women went out to the front of the house, and struck their palms, one against the other, with great lament, till they woke Conan.

Conan sprang to his feet with great haste, but he left part of his hair, and the skin of his head, stuck fast to the stakes.

When Conan got the women back into the house, he shut the door against them, and set fire to the faggots and heather in front of the house, so that he might suffocate them with the smoke.

The Fian were, at the time, opposite the House of Farabhuil, on the other side of the strait. They saw the smoke rising, and they cried out loudly, striking their left hands on their face, with their eyes towards the sky.

They ran to save their set of wives, but the strait was between them. Then with their blades, they leapt the strait. All of them got across except Mac an Reaidhinn. He fell into the strait and was drowned. Since then, the name of Kyle Rhea has stuck to those narrows.

By good fortune, the women survived, all bùt one or two of them, for the Fian ran swiftly to save them.

The Fian were furious with Conan for what he had done. They seized him and condemned him to death. Conan asked as a favour that his head should be cut off with Finn's own sword, Mac an Luin, which would not leave a shred of flesh behind. And that it should be his son, Garbh, who should smite him, and cut off his head as it rested against Finn's thigh.

This request was allowed him, but first, the Fian laid seven grey hides and seven faggots of wood against and around Finn's thigh. Then Conan's head was rested against it, and Garbh, his only son, struck off his father's head with the Mac an Luin. And the folds in the palm of a hand were not deeper or more injurious than the severed hides on the thigh of Finn.

But Garbh went mad, for he had killed his father, and now he knew no one, although they spoke to him; and he ran down the hill to the sea, slashed at it with his sword, and drowned himself.

FINN'S QUESTIONS

FINN maintained that he would only marry the woman who could answer his questions. One day, Gráinne, daughter of the fifth King of Ullin, answered all his questions and proved herself the wisest as well as the most beautiful of women. Finn married Gráinne in Ireland. It is said that they followed the track which has been assigned to the Celtic race, and while *Gradh* means 'love', *Finn* means 'wisdom'.

Finn: What is more plentiful than grass?

Gráinne: The dew; for there will be many drops of it on one blade of grass.

Finn: What is better than fire?

Gráinne: A woman's reasoning between two men.

Finn: What is swifter than the wind?

Gráinne: A woman's thought between two men.

Finn: What is blacker than the raven?

Gráinne: There is death.

Finn: What is whiter than the snow?

Gráinne: There is truth.

Finn: What is a ship for every cargo?

Gráinne: A smith's tongs; they will hold hot and cold.

Finn: What is it that will not abide lock or chain?

Gráinne: The eye of a man about his friend; it will not brook shutting or holding, but looking at him.

Finn: What is redder than blood?

Gráinne: The face of a good man when strangers come his way, and he
has no meat by him to give to them.

Finn: What is sharper than a sword?

Gráinne: The reproach of a foe.

Finn: What is the best of food?

Gráinne: Milk. Many a change comes out of it; butter and cheese are
made from it, and it will feed a very young child and a very old man.

Finn: What is the worst of meat?

Gráinne: Lean flesh.

Finn: What is the best jewel?

Gráinne: A knife.

Finn: What is more brittle than the new thistle?

Gráinne: The words of a boar pig.

Finn: What is softer than down?

Gráinne: The palm on the cheek.

Finn: What is the best deed?

Gráinne: A high deed and low conceit.

From her answers it appeared that Gráinne had a quick wit and beauty. But when mature wisdom marries young love, young love runs away with young valour, as we will hear in the next story of Diarmid and Gráinne.

DIARMID AND GRÁINNE

FINN was going to marry Gráinne, daughter of the King of Carmag, in Ireland. The nobles and the gentles of the Fian were gathered to the wedding. A great feast was made, and lasted seven days and seven nights. When it was past, a feast of the leavings was made for the hounds.

Diarmid was a truly fine man. There was a mole, a love spot, on his face, and he always kept his cap down over this beauty spot, for any woman who chanced to see the mole, fell in love with him.

Now the hounds fell out over the food, and the heroes of the Fian went to drive them apart. When Diarmid was driving the dogs apart, he pushed back his cap and Gráinne saw the mole and fell in love with him. She told Diarmid, and said:

'You shall run away with me.'

'I will not,' said he.

'I am putting a spell on you so that you go with me.'

'I will not go with you. I will not take you in softness, and I will not take you in hardness. I will not take you within, and I will not take you without. I will not take you on horseback, and I will not take you on foot,' said Diarmid, and went away in anger. He went to a place apart, made a house and lived in it.

One morning, who cried out to him but Gráinne.

'Are you there, Diarmid?'

'I am.'

'Come out and go with me now.'

'Did I not say to you already that I would not take you on your feet and I will not take you on a horse. I'll have nothing to do with you.'

But Gráinne was between the two sides of the door, on a billy goat.

'I am not without, and I'm not within,' said she. 'I am not on foot and I'm not on a horse, so you must come with me.'

'There is no place we can go, where Finn will not find us when he puts his finger under his tooth of knowledge, and he will kill me for going with you.'

'We will go to Carraig. There are so many Carraigs, he'll not know which one we are in.'

They went to Carraig an Daimh, which is the Stag's Crag.

Finn was furious when he found that his wife had gone away, and went to search for her. He and the Fian went over to Kintyre, and no stop was on their foot and no stay on their step, till they reached Carraig an Daimh in Kintyre, near to Cille Charmaig.

Now Diarmid was a good carpenter, making wooden dishes, and he was good at fishing. Gráinne would go about selling his dishes, and they had their beds apart.

One day, a great sprawling old man came that way, who was called Ciofach Mac a Ghoill. He sat, playing at wedges. Gráinne took a liking for the old carl, and they laid a scheme together to kill Diarmid.

Diarmid was working at his dishes, when the old man laid hands on him. Diarmid turned against the old man, and they got to grips and wrestled. The old man was strong, but at last Diarmid put him under. Gráinne caught hold of the dagger and thrust it into Diarmid's thigh.

Diarmid left them, going from hole to hole, barely alive. His hair and beard grew so thick and long he was not recognisable. One day, he came by way of Carraig. He had fish with him, and asked leave to roast it. He got a cogie of water in which to dip his fingers while he was roasting the fish.

Now there was a taste of honey in anything that Diarmid touched with his finger, and he was dipping his finger into the cogie. Gráinne took a morsel of the fish and tasted the honey in it. So she recognised Diarmid, and Ciofach attacked

Diarmid. They got to grips for a while but at last Diarmid killed Ciofach, and fled. He went over Loch Chaistei.

When Gráinne saw that Ciofach was dead, she followed Diarmid. About the break of day, she came to a strand, and there was a heron screaming. Diarmid was up the face of the mountain, and Gráinne called:

> 'It is early the heron cries,
>
> On the heap above Sliagh Gaoil,
>
> Oh Diarmid! O Duibhne! To whom I gave love,
>
> What is the cause of the heron's cry?'

And Diarmid replied:

> 'Oh Gráinne, daughter of Carmaif of Steeds,
>
> That never took a step right,
>
> It seems that before she gave the cry,
>
> Her foot had stuck to a frozen slab.'

Gráinne replied:

'Would you eat bread and flesh, Diarmid?'

'I would if I had it.'

'Here, I will give it to you. Where is the dagger that will cut it?'

'Search the sheath in which you last put it,' said Diarmid.

The knife had remained in Diarmid's thigh ever since Gráinne had put it there. She drew out the knife, and that was the greatest shame she had ever felt, drawing the knife out of Diarmid.

Fear was on Diarmid that the Fian would find them out, and so they went forward to Glen Elg. They went to the side of a burn and still their beds were apart. Diarmid was making wooden dishes, and the shavings he was making floated down with the burn to the beach.

The Fian were hunting along the beach. They were on the track of a venomous boar that was bothering them. Finn noticed the wood shavings at the mouth of the burn.

'These are the shavings of Diarmid's work,' said he.

'They are not,' said the Fian, 'for he is dead.'

'Indeed,' said Finn, 'they are. We will sound the Forhaid, our hunting horn. He is sworn to answer it wherever he may be.'

Diarmid heard the Forhaid.

'That is the Forhaid of the Fianna, and I must answer it.'

'Do not answer it, Diarmid, it is a lying cry,' said Gráinne.

But Diarmid answered the call, and went down to the beach.

It was set before Diarmid by the Fian that he should hunt the boar. And he roused the boar from Benn Eidin to Benn Tuirc. While withdrawing down the mountain, the boar cornered Diarmid, and his tempered blades were twisted like withered rushes. Diarmid drew the sword that Lon Mac Liobhain had made for him, and he put it under his armpit, and killed the boar.

This was no revenge for Finn on Diarmid. There was a mole on the sole of Diarmid's foot. Should one of the boar's bristles pierce the mole, Diarmid would surely die. And Finn said to him:

'Oh Diarmid, measure the boar. How many feet from his snout to his heel?'

Diarmid measured the boar, and said:

'Sixteen feet of measure true!'

'Measure the boar against the hair.'

Diarmid measured the boar against the hair, but one of the bristles pierced his mole, and he fell. Finn was full of sorrow for him as he fell, and asked:

'What will make you better, Diarmid?'

'If I could drink a draught of water from the palms of Finn's hands, I would be better.'

Finn went to fetch the water, but when he thought of Gráinne, he spilt the water. When he thought of Diarmid, he was full of sorrow, and hurried to take the water carefully. But he delayed too long, and Diarmid was dead by the time Finn returned to his side.

The Fian walked up the side of the burn till they came to where Gráinne was. They went in, saw the two beds; and they understood that Diarmid was without guilt. Finn and the Fian were exceedingly sorrowful about all that had happened.

In a faggot of grey oak they burned
Gráinne, daughter of Carmaig of the Steeds,
Who never took a step right.

The Fair Gruagach, Son of the King of Ireland

HE FAIR Gruagach, son of the King of Ireland, went with his company of men to hold court. He met a woman whom they called the Lady of the Fine Green Kirtle, and she asked him to sit a while and play at the cards. They sat down to play, and the Fair Chief won the game against the Lady of the Fine Green Kirtle.

'Ask for the forfeit,' said she.

'I do not think you have the forfeit I want,' said the Fair Chief, son of the King of Ireland.

'Be here tomorrow, and I will meet you,' said she.

'I will be here,' said the Fair Chief.

Next morning, he met her. They played at the cards, and she won.

'Ask for the forfeit,' said the Fair Chief.

'I am laying you under spells,' said the Lady of the Fine Green Kirtle, 'under crosses, under holy herdsmen of quiet travelling, wandering women, and the little calf, feeble and powerless, to take your head and your ear and your life from you, if you take rest by night or day. And where you take your breakfast, you'll not take your dinner, where you take your dinner you'll not take your supper; until you find the place where I am, under the four brown quarters of the world.'

She took a napkin from her pocket and shook it. Then there was no knowing where she had gone. She had vanished.

He went home heavy and black sorrowful, and put his elbow on the table and his hand under his cheek, and let out a sigh.

'What ails you, my son,' said the King of Ireland. 'Are you under spells? If so I will lift the spells off you. I have a smithy on the shore, and ships on the sea. So long as my gold and silver last, I will use them to lift the spells off you.'

'You are good, father,' said the Fair Chief, 'but you cannot lift the spells. You will lose many of your men. Keep your men by you. If I go alone, I shall only lose myself.'

In the morning of the next day, he went without man or dog. He went on and on, journeying, till there were blisters on his soles, and holes in his shoes. The bright, quiet clouds of day were going away, the black clouds of night were coming, and still he found no place to stay or rest. He spent a week from beginning to end, without seeing a house or castle. He grew sick, sleepless, restless, hungry and thirsty, walking all week. Then he looked about him and saw a castle. He walked towards it, then round it, and there was not so much as a small hole into the house. Heavy minded and sorrowful, he turned back, for he heard a shout behind him.

'Fair Chief, son of the King of Ireland, come back! There is a feast of a year and a day awaiting you, with unimaginable delicious meat and drink!'

So he returned, but there was no sign of the person who had shouted after him.

Now, there was a door for every day in the year, and a window for every day in the year in the house he found. This was a great marvel to him, for he had gone round the house, with not so much as a small hole in it; and now, when he returned, there was a door and a window for every day of the year in it.

He entered. There was meat and drink and music, and the company was feasting along with him, and the fine damsel who called to him from the palace.

A bed was made for him in the castle, with pillows, a hollow in the middle, and a bottle of warm water for his feet; so he lay down and slept.

Next morning he rose, and the table was laid with the best of food. Thus, for a time, he did not feel time pass. Then, one day, the damsel stood in the door, and said:

'Fair Chief, son of the King of Ireland, how are you?'

'I am well,' said he.

'Do you know when you came here?'

'I think I shall have completed a week tomorrow.'

'It is a quarter of a year today,' said she. 'Your meat and your drink will not grow less, nor your bed less comfortable, till you decide to return home.'

There he stayed, by himself, till he imagined he had been there a month, and again she stood in the door.

'Fair Chief, how do you find yourself today?' said she.

'Very well,' said he.

'Do you know when you came here?'

'I am thinking I have stayed one month here,' said he.

'Today is the end of two years,' she said. 'In what frame of mind are you?'

'I will tell you,' said he. 'If my two hands could reach yonder peak, I would set it on that other steep hill. I do not believe that any man on the surface of the world could gain victory over me in strength,' said he.

'You are silly,' said she. 'There is a band of men here they call the Fian, and they will win victory over you. There never was a man they could not defeat.'

'Morsel I will not eat, draught I will not drink, sleep will not come on my eye, till I reach the place where they are, and find out who they are,' said he. 'I will not rest by night or day, till I reach the Fian.'

'The day is soft and misty, and you've made up your mind that you will go. But I know you will return,' said she. 'The Fian are in a place, with a net, fishing for trout. You shall go over to where they are. You will see the Fian on one side of the river and Finn MacCoul alone on the other side. You shall go to where he is and you will bless him. Finn will bless you in the same way. You will ask to serve him. He will say that he has no service for you now, that the Fian is strong enough, and he'll not dismiss a man. He'll ask your name, and you will answer the name you never did hide, the Fair Gruagach, son of the King of Ireland. Finn will then say: "Though I do not need a man, why should I not give service to the son of your father, but be not high-minded among the Fian." Now, Fair

Gruagach, take this napkin,' said the lady of the Green Kirtle, 'and tell Finn that, whether you are alive or dead, you should be wrapped in it when the time comes and there is need for it.'

The Fair Gruagach went to the place where the Fian were.

He saw the Fian fishing for trout. Finn was on one side of the river, and the rest were on the other side. He went to Finn and blessed him, and Finn blessed him in the same manner.

'I hear there are such men as the Fian, and I have come to offer my service to you,' said the Fair Chief.

'I have no need of a man at this time,' said Finn. 'What is your name?'

'The name I've never hid, the Fair Gruagach, son of the King of Ireland.'

'Of all the bad luck to befall me! To turn away the son of your father, for who should get service with me, unless it is your father's son,' said Finn. However, do not be high-minded with the Fian. Come here and I will help you cross to the other side of the river. Then catch the end of the net, and drag it along with them.'

He began dragging the net with the Fian. He glanced above the bank, and there he saw a deer.

'Would it not be better for swift, strong, young men, like yourselves, to be hunting that deer, rather than fishing for trout in the river. A morsel of fish or a mouthful of juice, will not satisfy you as well as that deer – a morsel of whose flesh or a mouthful of whose broth, would satisfy you.'

'If yonder beast is good, we're seven times tired of his flesh,' said the Fian. 'We know him well enough!'

'Well, I've heard there is one man of you, so fleet of foot, he could catch the swift March wind, and whom the swift March wind could not catch,' said the Fair Gruagach.

'Since it is your first request, we'll send someone to seek him,' said Finn.

He was sent for, and Caoilte came. The Fair Gruagach shouted to him:

'I have a challenge for you, to overtake that deer yonder.'

'The Fair Chief came amongst us today, and his advice may be taken on the first day,' said Finn.'He saw the deer standing above us, and said it would be better for strong, young men like us to be hunting the deer, than fishing for trout here; so you, Caoilte, go and chase the deer.'

'Many is the day I've given to chasing him, but it's little I've had from it, and my grief that I never caught him,' said Caoilte,'but I will try again.'

Then Caoilte began running at speed.

'How will Caoilte look when he is at full speed?' said the Fair Gruagach.

'There will be three heads on Caoilte when he is at full speed,' said Finn.

'And how many heads will there be on the deer?'

'There will be seven heads on him when he is at full swiftness.'

'What distance before he reaches the end of his journey?'

'Seven glens and seven hills,' said Finn,'that is what he has to do before he reaches a place of rest.'

'Let us take a hand at dragging the net,' said the Fair Chief. Then he looked and said to Finn:'Finn, son of Cumhal, put your finger under your tooth of knowledge, to see what distance Caoilte is from the deer.'

Finn put his finger under his tooth of knowledge.

'There are two heads on Caoilte, and there are but two heads yet on the deer,' said Finn.

'How far have they gone?' said the Fair Gruagach.

'Two glens and two hills. They still have five to pass.'

'Let us take a hand at fishing for trout,' said the Fair Chief. When they had been working a while, he looked about him and said:

'Finn, son of Cumhal, put your finger under your tooth of knowledge to see how far Caoilte is from the deer.'

'There are three heads on Caoilte, and four on the deer, and Caoilte is at full speed.'

'How many glens and hills are before them?'

'There are four behind them and three before them.'

'Let us take a hand at fishing for trout,' said the Fair Chief. And, for a while, they fished.

'Finn, son of Cumhal, what distance is the deer from the end of his journey?' said the Fair Chief.

'One glen and one hill,' said Finn.

The Fair Gruagach threw the net from him, and he took off at speed. He would catch the swift March wind, and the swift March wind would not catch him, till he caught Caoilte, passed him, and left his blessing with him. Going over the ford of Struth Ruadh, the deer sprang – the Fair Gruagach gave the next spring, and caught the deer by the hind leg. The deer gave a roar, and the Carlin of the Ford cried:

'Who seized the beast I love?'

'I, the son of the King of Ireland,' said the Fair Gruagach.

'Let him go, son of the King of Ireland, let him go!' said the carlin.

'I'll not let him go; he's my beast now!'

'Give me my fist full of his bristles, a mouthful of his broth, or a morsel of his flesh,' said the carlin.

'Not one share are you getting.'

'The Fian are coming,' said she, 'and Finn at their head, and there will not be one of them that I will not bind back to back.'

'Do that,' said he, 'but I'm going away.'

He went away, taking the deer with him, till he met Finn.

'Finn, son of Cumhal, keep that,' said he, leaving the deer.

Finn sat by the deer, while the Fair Gruagach went away. He reached the smithy of the twenty-seven Smiths. He took three iron hoops, for every man of the Fian. He took a hand-hammer and he put three hoops over the head of every man that was in the Fian, and he tightened the hoops with the hammer. The carlin came out, and uttered a great screech.

'Finn, son of Cumhal, give me the creature I love!'

The highest hoops that were on the Fian, burst with her screech. She came out a second time, let out a yell, and each of the second hoops burst. Then she went indoors. It was not long before she came out a third time, and let out a third scream, and then each third hoop burst. She took herself off to the wood, twisted a withy from the wood, and took it with her. She went over and bound every man of the Fian, back to back, except Finn.

The Fair Gruagach laid his hand on the deer, and flayed it. He took out the blood and every bit of the inside, and buried them under the earth. He prepared a cauldron, cut the flesh of the deer into the cauldron, and lit a fire to cook it.

'Finn, son of Cumhal,' said the Fair Gruagach, 'would you rather go and fight the carlin, or stay and boil the cauldron of venison?'

'Well, venison is hard enough to boil,' said Finn. 'If there was a morsel of flesh uncooked, the deer will rise as he was before. If a drop of broth goes into the fire, he will arise as he was before. I would rather stay and boil the cauldron of venison.'

The carlin came, and said:

'Finn, son of Cumhal, give me my fist full of bristles, or a squeeze of the blood, or a morsel of flesh, or a mouthful of the broth.'

'I know nothing about it,' said Finn, 'I have no authority to give any of it away.'

Then the Fair Gruagach and the carlin began to fight each other. They made a bog of the rock and a rock of the bog. In the place where they would sink the least, they sank up to the knees; in the place where they would sink the most, they sank up to their eyes.

'Are you satisfied with your sport, Finn, son of Cumhal?' said the Fair Gruagach.

'It is long since I was satisfied with that,' said Finn.

'You'll have a chance now,' said the Fair Chief.

He seized the carlin, struck her a blow with his foot in the crook of the hough, and felled her.

'Finn, son of Cumhal, shall I take her head off?'

'Please yourself, I do not know,' said Finn.

'Finn, son of Cumhal,' said the carlin, 'I am laying you under spells and under crosses, to be husband, three hours before day breaks, to the wife of the Tree Lion.'

'I am laying you under spells and crosses to lie with a foot on either side of the ford of Struth Ruadh, and every drop of water be flowing through you,' said the Fair Young Gruagach.

'Raise your spells from me, and I will raise them from Finn,' said the carlin.

The Fair Gruagach took the cauldron off the fire. He seized a fork and knife, and put the fork into the flesh of the deer. He seized the knife, cut a morsel of the flesh and ate it. He took hold of a turf, and laid it on the mouth of the cauldron.

'Finn, son of Cumhal, it is time for us to be going,' said he. 'Are you a good horseman?'

'I can try.'

He caught hold of a rod, and gave it to Finn. 'Strike me with it,' said he. Finn struck him with the rod, and he turned into a brown mare.

'Now mount me,' said the Gruagach. Finn mounted him.

He gave a spring, and Finn stayed on his back. He galloped over nine ridges. He speeded up. He could catch the swift March wind, and the swift March wind could not catch him.

'There is a little town down here,' said the mare. 'Go down and fetch three stoups of wine and three wheaten loaves. You will give me a stoup of wine and a wheaten loaf, and you will comb me against the hair, and with the hair.'

Finn did as he was told, and they reached the wall of the Tree Lion's Castle.

'Get down, Finn, son of Cumhal, and give me a stoup of wine and a wheaten loaf.'

Finn dismounted and gave the mare a stoup of wine and a wheaten loaf.

'Now comb me against the hair, and comb me with the hair.'

He did that. Then the mare leapt and put a third of the wall below her. There were two-thirds above, so she returned to the earth.

'Give me another stoup of wine and wheaten loaf. Comb me against the hair and with the hair!'

He did that. Then she took a second spring, put two-thirds of the wall below her, and a third above her head, then she returned to earth.

'Give me another stoup of wine and wheaten loaf. Comb me against the hair, and with the hair.'

He did that. Then she took a spring and was on top of the wall.

'You're in luck, Finn,' said the mare, 'the Tree Lion is away from home.'

Finn entered the castle. 'My chief!' and 'All hail!' greeted him; and meat and drink were set before him. He rested that night, and was with the Tree Lion's wife three hours before the break of day.

As early as his eye saw the day or earlier than that, he rose and reached the mare, the Fair Gruagach, and they went off.

'The Tree Lion is away from home; anything that passed between you, his wife will not hide from him,' said the Fair Gruagach. 'He is coming after us. He'll not remember his book of witchcraft; and since he does not remember his book of witchcraft, it will go well with me but against him; but if he should remember the book, the people of the world could not withstand him. He has every magical spell.

He will spring as a bull when he comes, and I will spring as a bull before him. The first blow I give him, I will lay his head on his side, and I will make him roar. Then he will spring as an ass, and I will spring as an ass before him. The first thrust I give him, I will take a mouthful out of him, between flesh and hide. Then he will spring as a hawk in the heavens, I will spring as a hawk in the woods, and the first stroke I give him, I will take his heart and liver out. I will come down afterwards, and you shall seize that napkin yonder. You shall put me in the napkin, cut a turf, put the napkin under the earth, and you shall stand upon it.

Then the wife of the Tree Lion will come. You'll be standing on the top of the turf, and I under your feet. She, with the book of witchcraft on her back in a straw band, will say: "Finn, son of Cumhal, man that never told a lie, tell me who, in all the world, killed my comrade?" and you'll say: "I know no one on the earth who killed your comrade." And she will run away weeping.'

When they had gone forward a short distance, whom did they see coming but the Tree Lion. He became a bull, and the Fair Gruagach became a bull before him, and the first blow he struck, he laid the Tree Lion's head on his side, and he gave out a roar. Then the Tree Lion sprang as an ass, and the Gruagach sprang as an ass before him. At the first rush, he took a mouthful between flesh and hide. The Tree Lion then sprang as a hawk in the heavens, and the Gruagach sprang as a hawk in the woods, and he took the heart and liver out of the Tree Lion.

The Fair Gruagach as a hawk fell down after that, and Finn seized him, and put him in a napkin. He cut a turf, and put the napkin under the earth and the turf upon it. Then he stood on the turf.

The wife of the Tree Lion came, with the book of witchcraft on her back, tied with a straw band.

'Finn, son of Cumhal, the man who never told a lie,' she said, 'tell me who killed my comrade.'

'I know no one on the earth who killed your comrade,' said Finn.

The wife of the Tree Lion went away weeping; and when she was out of sight, Finn lifted the turf, removed the napkin that held the hawk, that was the Fair Chief who had changed his shape, and took it to the castle of the Lady of the Fine Green Kirtle. He gave her the napkin, and she took it away with her into her room. It was not long before she came back to Finn.

'Finn, son of Cumhal,' said she, 'the Fair Gruagach, son of the King of Ireland, is asking for you.'

'That is the best news I have ever heard,' said Finn, 'that the Fair Chief is asking for me.' And Finn went with her to him.

She set meat and drink before them, but they would not eat a morsel, nor drink a drop, till they could eat their share of the deer with the Fian in Struth Ruaidh.

They reached the place where the Fian was bound. They loosed every one of them, and they were all very hungry. The Fair Gruagach set the deer before them, and they left three times as much as they ate.

'Now, I must go and tell my tale,' said the Fair Chief.

He reached the carlin at the ford of Struth Ruaidh, and he began to tell her all that had happened to him. With every tale he told her, she began to rise; and every time she rose, he would seize her, crush her bones, and would break them until he had told her all his tales. When he had told them all, he returned to the Fian.

Then Finn went with the Fair Chief to the castle of the Lady with the Green Kirtle.

'Blessing be with you, Finn son of Cumhal,' said the Fair Gruagach. 'I have found all I sought – a sight of every matter and every thing, and now I will be returning to the palace of my own father.'

'Is it thus that you are about to leave me?' said the Lady of the Fine Green Kirtle. 'After all that I have done for you, you will take another and I shall be left alone.'

'Is that what you say?' said he. 'As though I could think of such a thing. I have never seen a maiden that I would take rather than you; but I will not marry you here. You must come first to my father's palace with me.'

So the Fair Gruagach, the Lady with the Fine Green Kirtle and Finn, went to the palace of the King of Ireland. A churchman was found, and the Fair Gruagach and the Lady of the Fine Green Kirtle were married. A hearty, jolly, joyful wedding was made for them. Music was played and lament was laid down; meat was set in the place for eating and wine was set in the place for drinking; and music in the place for listening; and the feast and merriment lasted for a year and a day.

CONAL

HERE was once a King of Ireland who had no children. His sister, whose name was Maobh, had three sons: Fergus, the eldest, then Lagh an Laidh, and Conal, the youngest.

The king decided to make Fergus, the eldest, his heir. He gave him the schooling of a king's son, and when he was finished with school and learning, brought him home to live with him. One day they were in the palace, and the king said to Fergus:

'This year has passed well, but the year is coming to an end, and trouble and care is coming with it.'

'What trouble and care, uncle?' asked the young man.

'The vassals of the country are coming to reckon with me today.'

'You've no need to be in trouble,' said the young man. 'It has been proclaimed that I am the heir. It has been set down in papers and in letters, at each end of the kingdom. I will build a fine castle for you in front of the palace. I will engage the best carpenters, stonemasons and smiths to build this castle.'

'Is that what you have in mind, son of my sister?' said the king. 'You have neither claim nor right to my realm unless I have given it to you of my own free will. You shall not rule Ireland until I am buried under the earth.'

'There will be a day of battle and combat before I allow that to happen,' said Fergus.

He went away, and sailed to Scotland. A message was sent to the king of Scotland, saying that the Young King of Ireland had come to see him. Fergus was carried on the points of spears in honour to the king. He found meat laid out in the place of eating, wine in the place of drinking, music in the place for listening, and the whole company feasting.

'Young King of Ireland,' said the King of Scotland, 'you have not come here without reason.'

'I cannot tell you why I have come, until you promise to help me.'

'Anything I have, you can share. If I were seeking help, perhaps I would go to you for it, so tell me your story.'

'Trouble began between my uncle and me. He had proclaimed that I was King of Ireland, then he told me that I had no right to the realm until a clod of earth had been placed over him. I wish to stand by my rights, and to get help from you.'

'I will give you that help,' said the king. 'Three hundred swift heroes, three hundred brave heroes, three hundred fully armed heroes; and that is not a bad helping!'

'I have no chief to lead them, so I have yet another request to make,' said Fergus.

'Anything I have that I can part with, you shall have,' said the king, 'but what I have not, I cannot give you.'

'I want your son, Boinne Breat, to head the men you send me,' said Fergus.

'My curses on you! Had I not promised whatever I had, you would not have got my son. But there is no one in Scotland, or Ireland or England, who can gain victory over my son, if they keep to fair play. If my son does not return as well as he went, then the word of an Irishman will never again be taken, for it is only by treachery that Boinne Breat can be overcome.'

Fergus, Boinne Breat and the company of nine hundred heroes set sail next day for England. A message was sent to the King of England saying that the young King of Ireland had come to see him. The King of England went to meet him, and Fergus was carried in honour on the deadly points of spears to the palace of the King of England. There meat was set out in the place of eating, wine in the place of drinking, music in the place for listening, and the whole company was feasting.

'Young King of Ireland,' said the King of England, 'you have not come here without reason!'

'I have not. I tell you I had the schooling of a king's son, then my mother's brother took me home. He spoke of the vassals of the country, the people of the realm; and that care and trouble were on him and that he wished the end of the year had not come at all. I told him I would build a palace for him, so that he would only have to wash his face and stretch his feet in his shoes; but he said that I had no right to the realm until a clod of earth was over him. I said there would be a day of fight and combat between us before the matter was settled. Then I took my ship and sailed to Scotland. There I got three hundred swift heroes, three hundred brave heroes and three hundred fully armed heroes. Now I come to you for help.'

'I will give you as many more, and a hero at their head,' said the King of England. And he did this, and kept his promise in every way.

So Fergus, Boinne Breat, the England chief and the six companies of three hundred men in each, sailed back to Ireland. They landed on a crag in Ireland, called Carrick Fergus. Fergus went to the old king, and said:

'Uncle, are you ready to fight?'

'Fergus, I did not think you would really take my words in anger, and so I have not gathered my people together to fight in my defence.'

'That is no answer,' said Fergus. 'You still have Ireland under your rule. I am here with my men, and I have neither place nor meat nor drink to give them.'

'The storehouses of Ireland are open to you,' said the king, 'and I will go and gather my people together.'

The old king went round Ireland, till he came to a place called Iubhar, which is now Newry. There was only one man in Iubhar, who was called Goivlan Smith. The old king decided to go into the Smith's house, for he was thirsty and wanted to quench his thirst, and rest a while. He found only the Smith's daughter inside the house. She brought him a chair to sit on; and he asked for a drink. The Smith's daughter did not know what to do, for the Smith only had one cow, called Grey Goivlan. Three times a day, a vessel was placed under the cow to catch the milk she gave. Always the Smith was thirsty. He would drink a vessel full of milk, and if the vessel was not full, his daughter would be punished. When the old king asked for a drink of milk, she was afraid lest the vessel would not be refilled in time for the Smith. In spite of this, the daughter decided that the vessel of milk should be offered to the king, so she brought the vessel, and set it before him. The king drank a draught; he took a quarter of the milk and left three-quarters of it.

'I would rather you drank it all,' said the daughter, 'for my father has vowed that unless I have the vessel full, I shall die.'

'Well, then,' said the old king, 'it is the spell of my spells to leave the vessel full.'

And he set the vessel on the table, struck his palm on it, and at once it was full; and before he left the girl was his own.

'Now you are going, oh King of Ireland, and I am shamed; what will you leave for me?'

'I will give you a thousand creatures of every colour, and a thousand of every kind.'

'But how shall I care for them? I will not find enough salt in Ireland to give them.'

'I will give you glens and high moors to feed them from year to year.'

'What shall I do with that? If Fergus kills you, he will take it all from me, unless I have it all down in writing, with a drop of blood to bind it.'

'I am in a hurry tonight, but tomorrow go to the camp at Croc Maol nam Mue,' said the king, and left her with a blessing.

Her father came, and said to her:

'My daughter, I think a stranger has been here with you today.'

'How do you know that?'

'You had the slow eyelash of a maiden when I went out, and the brisk eyelash of a wife when I returned.'

'Who would you like to have been here?'

'There is no man I would like to have been here more than the King of Ireland!'

'Well, it was he,' said the daughter, 'and he left me a thousand creatures of every colour, a thousand of each kind, and high moors to feed them, and said that I should have all this in writing and a drop of blood to bind it.'

The Smith and his daughter slept in their clothes that night, and if it was early that day broke, it was even earlier that the Smith rose.

'Come, daughter, let us be going.'

She went, herself, and the Smith, and they reached the king in his camp.

'Were you not in Newry yesterday?' said the Smith to the king.

'I was,' said he.

'Do you remember your promise to her?'

'I do; but the battle will not be until tomorrow. I will give you all that I promised to the girl, if you leave her here tonight.'

The Smith agreed to this, and went home.

That night, after the girl had slept for a while, she awoke for she had had a dream. She turned to the king and touched him, saying:

'Are you awake?'

'I am,' said he. 'What do you want?'

'I had a dream, and in it a young fir shoot was growing from the heart of the king, and also from my own heart. The two shoots were twining about each other.'

'That was our baby son.'

They slept and it was not long before she saw the next dream, and said:

'Are you awake, King of Ireland?'

'I am; what do you want now?'

'I had another dream, and this time Fergus was coming and taking the head from me.'

'That is Fergus killing me, and taking off my head,' said the king.

She slept again, and had another dream, and she said:

'Are you sleeping, King of Ireland?'

'I am not. What do you want now?'

'In my dream I saw Ireland, covered from side to side, and from end to end with sheaves of barley and oats. And there came a wind from the east, the west and from the north, and swept every tree and stalk off the land, till there were none to be seen.'

'Your dream means that Fergus will kill me, and take my head. As fast as you ever did anything, you must remove my weapons and keep them. If a baby son is born to us, you must suckle and nurse him, and train him well. Keep the weapons and when you see that he can look after himself, send him off into the wide world to wander until he finds out who he really is. He will be king over Ireland and his son will be king over Ireland, until it reaches the ninth knee. Then a child will be born to the ninth king, who will eat a fish that will be cooked for him, and a bone will stick in the child's throat and he will choke, and that will be the end of my line, and another race will rule over Ireland.'

Now, Maobh, the old King of Ireland's sister and mother of Fergus, had two other sons, Lagh an Laidh and Conal, and when they heard that the battle was to be on the morrow, they wondered whose side they should fight on, their uncle's or that of their brother, Fergus.

'If our mother's brother wins, and we are on the side of Fergus, it is a stone in our shoe for ever; but if Fergus wins, he will turn his back on us, because we were on the other side.'

'Well, then, you can be with Fergus, and I will be with our mother's brother.'

'That is not a good idea; let us leave it to our mother to decide.'

'If I were a man,' said Maobh, 'I would fight on the field with my own brother.'

So Lagh an Laidh and Conal both decided to side with their brother, Fergus.

Fergus went to Finn and blessed him with calm, soft words. Finn blessed him with better words; and if they were no better, they were no worse.

'I hear there is to be battle and combat between you and your mother's brother,' said Finn.

'That is so, and I have come to you for help.'

'It would be unwise for me to go against your uncle, since it is on his land that I get my keep. If he should win, the Fian will get neither furrow nor clod of the land of Ireland as long as we live. I will do this: I will not strike a blow for you, but I will not strike a blow against you.'

Fergus went home the next day and prepared for the battle. The king's company was on one side, and that of Fergus was on the other. Fergus had no dashing Champion Heroes but Boinne Breat and his company. There was the great Saxon Hero and his company, and Lagh an Laidh. Boinne Breat put on his armour of battle and hard combat. He set his silken-netted coat above his shirt of armour, with a great shield at his left side. And how many deaths were in the sheath of his sword!

He strode out with stern steps, like a sudden blaze. Each pace he put from him was less than a hill and greater than a knoll on the side of the mountain. He turned on the enemy and drove three ranks of them, dashing them from their shields and sending their flesh and blood to the skies. He would not leave one to tell the tale, report the bad news, put holes in the earth or a shelf in the rock. But there was one little russet man, one-eyed, one-handed and on one knee.

'You shall not live to tell this tale of me,' said Boinne Breat, and took off the little man's head. Then he took off his armour and left the fight, saying:

'Go down, Fergus, and strike the head off your mother's brother, or I will do it.'

Fergus went, and struck off the head of the old King of Ireland; and the Smith's daughter went and removed the king's weapons and armour, and took them away with her.

Lagh an Laidh kept on his armour, and when he saw Fergus take off his uncle's head, he took fright. He went to the hill to seek for Boinne Breat who was unarmed. Boinne Breat saw him coming and thought he was drunk with battle. He turned round to the other side of the hill, hoping to find his own company. Lagh an Laidh turned again to see if the battle had abated, and the third time he turned, he met Boinne Breat.

'I'll not turn again for all those who come from Scotland, Ireland or England,' said he.

'It is strange that you were with me throughout the battle, and now are against me? I believe that you are drunk with battle,' said Boinne Breat.

'I am quite beside myself,' said Lagh an Laidh.

'Well, then,' said Boinne Breat, 'though I am unarmed, and you are armed, remember that you are no more to me than I can hold between these two fingers!'

'I will not be a traitor to you, there are behind you three of the best Heroes in Scotland, Ireland and England.'

Boinne Breat turned to see the three Heroes, and as he turned, Lagh an Laidh struck off his head.

'My torture!' cried Fergus. 'I had rather that was my head. An Irishman's word will not be taken now as long as man shall live. It is a stone in your shoe every day for ever, and not a pinch of the land of Ireland shall you have.'

Lagh an Laidh went away, and he went to the mountain. He made a hollow for himself there and stayed in it.

The Smith's daughter came on well till she bore a son. She named him Conal Mac Righ Erin, or Conal, son of the King of Ireland. She nourished him well and when he could walk and speak, she took him with her to the mountain among the high moors and forests. She left him there to make his own way, and then she went home.

The boy did not know what he should do, nor where he should go, till he found a finger of a road. He followed the road. And what should he see in the evening of the day but a little hut. He went inside, but there was no one there, so he sat down at the fireside. There he stayed till, at the end of the night, a woman came in with six sheep. She saw, beside the fire, the slip of a lad, who seemed to be a fool. She told him he had better go down to the king's house, where he would get something with the servants in the kitchen. But he would not go, and said that if she gave him something to eat, he would herd her sheep for her.

'If I really believed that, I would give you meat and drink,' said the woman, whose name was Caomhag Gentle, and she gave him food and drink all the same.

The next day, the lad went away with the sheep.

'There is no grass for them,' said she, 'only the road; and you must keep to the edge of the road, and not let them off it.'

At night, the lad came home with the sheep, and the next day took them away again. Nearby, there were three fields of wheat, belonging to three farmers. As the sheep were wearing him out in their search for food, the lad levelled the dyke into the fields and let the sheep in, from one to the other until they had eaten the wheat in all three fields. One day the three farmers came, and when they came the three fields had all been eaten by the sheep.

'Who are you?' they said. 'You have eaten the fields!'

'It was not I who ate them, it was the sheep,' said the lad.

'It's no good talking to him, he is but a fool. We will go to Caomhag, and see if the sheep are hers.'

They went to Caomhag, and they took her with them to court. This was the first court that Fergus had made, since he became King of Ireland. Kings had a tradition at that time. When they did not know how to administer justice properly, the judgement-seat would begin to kick, and the king's neck would twist until judgement was indeed just.

The king listened to this case, but could make no sense if it.

'It was the teeth that did the damage,' said he. 'The teeth are guilty.'

The judgement-seat began to kick and the king's neck twisted, and the king begged someone to pronounce a fairer verdict and free him. Although there were thousands there, no one would go and give judgement in the king's place, for fear of showing him disrespect.

'Is there no man here who will free me?' cried the king.

'There is not, unless it is Caomhag's young herdsman,' they said.

So the lad was taken before the king, who said:

'Free me little Hero, and do justice as it should be done, and let me out of this predicament.'

'I can do nothing until I have had something to eat,' said the lad.

He was given a meal and then he asked what the verdict had been.

'I did but condemn the teeth that did the damage to the fields.'

'It was Caomhag who had the sheep, but even if her six sheep were taken from her, this would not compensate the three farmers. Caomhag will still have six lambs. Better to let the three men have the lambs and Caomhag herself keep the sheep.'

The twist went out of the king's neck and the seat of justice stopped kicking. And the lad left the court without hurt, and no one asked who he was.

Now, there was another man, who had a horse which he sent to the smithy to be shod. The Smith had a young child in the care of a nurse. It was a fine day, and because the nurse had not seen a horse shod before she took the child with her to watch. She sat nearby with the child, as the Smith took a nail to the shoe. But instead of hammering the nail into the hoof, the Smith drove it into the flesh. The horse kicked with pain and struck the child on the head. This matter was taken to the king for his judgement, and the king's verdict was that the horse's leg should be removed. The judgement-seat began to kick and the king's neck began to twist. Caomhag's lad was there, and he was asked to release the king by giving a fairer judgement. He said he would only do so after he had had something to eat. He was given this and then taken to the king.

'What verdict did you give?' he asked the king, who was Fergus.

'That the leg that did the damage, should be taken off the horse.'

'That will not compensate the Smith for his son. Send for the groom who broke in the horse and the man to whom the horse belongs. Also send for the Smith and his child's nurse.'

The man and his groom came.

'Well, my man, did you instruct your groom how to break in your horse?'

The man said that he had, and the groom said that he had done the job as well as he knew how to do it.

'No more could be asked of you,' said the lad. 'Well, Smith, did you order the nurse to stay indoors with the child?'

'I did not,' said the Smith, 'she could decide that for herself. She could do as she wished.'

'Gentleman,' said the lad to the owner of the horse, 'since you are the richest, I will levy a third of the reparation for the injury to the Smith's son on you, another third on the Smith himself, because he did not measure the nail before he used it, and another third between the nurse and the groom, because she did not stay indoors and because the groom left some instruction untaught to the horse.'

The judgement-seat stopped kicking, and the twist went from the king's neck. Caomhag's young herd went away, and they let him go as usual.

'There must be a drop of royal blood in that lad,' said Fergus the king, 'for he could not judge so well if that was not so. Let the three Heroes I have go, and let them take off his head and bring it to me.'

They went after the lad, who glanced round and saw them coming. They caught up with him, and he asked them where they were going.

'We are going to kill you. The king has sent us to do so.'

'Well, that was just an order that came into his mouth! It is not worth your while to kill me.'

'The lad is but a fool,' they said to each other.

'Since the king sent you to kill me, why don't you kill me?'

'Will you kill yourself, little Hero?'

'How shall I kill myself?'

'Here's a sword. Strike it on your neck and cast your head off.'

The lad seized the sword and gave it a twirl in his fist.

'Fall to killing yourself, little Hero!' they said.

'Go,' said he, 'and return home, and do not hide from the king that you did not kill me.'

'Well then, give me back the sword,' said one of them.

'I will not give it up. There are none in Ireland who will take it from my fist,' said the lad.

The three Heroes of the king returned home, and the lad said to himself as he went on his way:

'I was not born without a mother, and I was not begotten without a father. I do not remember ever coming to Ireland, and I know that it was in Ireland that I was born, so I will not leave a house where there is smoke un-entered in Ireland, till I know who I am.'

He went on to Newry. It was a fine warm day, and who did he see but his mother washing. He understood that this was indeed his mother, and he went behind her and put his hand on her.

'I am your foster-son,' said he.

'I never had a son or a foster-son who looked a contemptible servant, like you,' she said.

'My left hand is behind your back, and a sword is in my right hand. I will strike off your head if you do not tell me who I am.'

'Still your hand, Conal mac Righ, Conal son of the King of Ireland.'

'I knew myself that was who I was,' said he, 'and that there is a drop of the blood of a king's son in me. Now, tell me who killed my father?'

'Fergus killed him, and a loss as great as your father was slain on the same day – that was Boinne Breat, son of the King of Scotland.'

'Who slew Boinne Breat?'

'It was the brother of Fergus, whom they call Lagh an Laidh.'

'And where is that man now?'

'Once he had slain Boinne Breat, he could not get a bite of food, nor a bit of land in the whole of Ireland, so he went to the high mountain and found a cave, and lived there among the wild beasts, monsters and untamed creatures.'

'Who kept my father's weapons, and armour?'

'I did.'

'Go and fetch them and bring them here to me.'

She went and she brought them. He put them on and they fitted him as though they had been made for him.

'I will not eat a bite, and I will not drink a draught, nor stop to rest after this night, till I reach the man who killed my father, where so ever he may be.'

Conal, son of the King of Ireland, passed the night there, and next morning he went away. He went on and on till there were holes in his shoes and the soles of his feet were black. The white clouds of day were going and the black clouds of night were coming, and still he had found nowhere to rest. He saw a forest, and made a hollow in one of the trees where he stayed all night.

In the morning of the next day, he looked down about him and what should he see stretched out on the ground below, but a poor wretch of a man, naked but for the hair grown long from his head and his beard, matted and dirty, all over him. He thought he would climb down, but he was unsure of what the wretch would do. So he put an arrow in his crossbow and shot it at him. He struck the wild man on the right forearm, and he gave a start.

'Do not move a muscle, nor a hair of your head, till you promise to see me king over Ireland,' said Conal, 'or else I will send down a shower of oaken darts enough to sew you to the earth.'

The wild man took no notice of Conal, so he fired again, and this time struck him on the left forearm.

'Come down from the tree and let me see you. I promise to do as you ask.'

Conal climbed down, and the wild man looked at him and said:

'Had I known it was a mere drudge of a lad, dictating to me like that, I would have done nothing for you, but since I said I would do what you asked me, I will do it, for I am Lagh an Laidh, the second son of the sister of the old King of

Ireland, who is now dead, and Fergus, my brother, and his eldest nephew rules in his place.'

'I am the young son of that old king. I am his heir and I will avenge his death,' said Conal.

They went together to the palace. They shouted for battle or combat or the head of Fergus, or Fergus himself as captive.

Battle and combat they got. There were four hundred swift heroes, four hundred fully armed heroes, and four hundred strong heroes against them. They fought until Lagh an Laidh and Conal had killed them all. Then they shouted again for battle or combat, or the head of Fergus or himself as captive.

'It is battle and combat you shall have but not at all my head nor myself as captive,' said Fergus.

There were sent out twelve hundred swift heroes, twelve hundred fully trained heroes, and twelve hundred stout heroes. They fought till all were killed.

Again Conal and Lagh an Laidh shouted for battle or combat, or else the head of Fergus, or himself as captive. They were told they would get battle and combat, but not the head of Fergus, nor himself as captive. There was sent out to them four hundred score heroes and all were killed. So they shouted again for battle and combat.

'Those who are outside the walls are so hard to please, they will take my head, and unless they get it they will kill all there are in Ireland, and myself after them. Take the head of one of the slain, and when Lagh an Laidh comes and asks for my head, give it to him, and he will think it is my head.'

The head was given to Lagh an Laidh. He went to Conal with it.

'What have you there?' said he.

'The head of Fergus.'

'That is not the head of Fergus. I saw him for a shorter time than yourself, but I know that this is not his head.'

Lagh an Laidh returned the head. And Fergus told another to go and offer himself as captive. But when this one went to meet Lagh an Laidh, he was seized and his head struck off his neck, and the head taken to Conal, who said: 'What have you there?'

'The head of Fergus.'

'That is not the head of Fergus; turn back and bring me his head.'

Lagh an Laidh returned, and Fergus said to himself:

'The one outside the walls is so watchful and the one who comes is so blind, that there is no one in Ireland they will not kill till they get me!' Then he turned to Lagh an Laidh who stood before him, 'Where are you going, Lagh an Laidh?'

'I am seeking your head, or yourself as captive!'

'You shall get my head but not myself as captive,' said Fergus, 'but what kindness are you giving your brother?'

'The kindness you gave to me, I will give to you!'

And he drew his sword and struck off the head of Fergus, and took it to Conal, who said:

'What have you there?'

'The head of Fergus.'

'It is not.'

'Truly it is.'

'Let me see it,' said Conal.

Lagh an Laidh gave him the head. Conal took it, and struck Lagh with it, and made two heads from one. Then he and Lagh an Laidh began to fight. They made a bog on the rock and a rock on the bog. In the place where they would sink the least, they sank up to their knees, and in the place where they would sink most, they sank up to their eyes.

Conal thought it would be a pity if he fell now, after he had got so near to victory, so he drew his sword, and struck off the head of Lagh an Laidh, and cried:

'Now I am King over Ireland, as I have the right to be.'

Then Conal took his mother and her father from Iughar, and took them to the palace; and his race ruled in that place until the ninth knee. The last member of his race was choked as a baby, with a splinter of bone that went crosswise in his throat, and he died, and another tribe came to rule in Ireland.

The Tale of Young Manus, Son of the King of Lochlann

WHEN Manus was born, his mother put him on her knee to suckle him, but with the first sip he took the breast and heart out of her, and now she was dead.

The king, his father, got a nurse for him, but he did the same to her and fifty others, so he was given to the gardener that he might deal with him, but every nurse the gardener got for him, Manus killed the same way.

One day, the Slender Woman with the Green Kirtle came that way. She offered to be his nurse for a reward, which was half of all he had in the world. The gardener willingly agreed to this. Then the Woman with the Green Kirtle asked him to fetch her three wheaten loaves, three bottles of wine, and seven strong men, the strongest in the land. The gardener got all this for her, and she ate a loaf and drank a bottle of wine. She went on her knees and urged the seven strong men to take hold of her and keep her down while Manus was suckling her. They did so; but the first sip was so violent, the woman scattered the seven men through the house.

'Are these strong men,' said she, 'when they cannot keep down a slip of a woman?'

She ate another loaf, and drank another bottle of wine, and said:

'Keep me down this time if you can.'

They held on to her again, but the next sip that Manus took was so violent she scattered the men for a second time.

'Dear me,' said she, 'are these your stalwart, strong men?'

She ate another loaf and drank another bottle of wine, and said:

'Now men, keep me down this time, so that he may get another sip.'

She went on her knee; the men took hold of her, and Manus got a sip: but she threw the men about the house as if they were flies. Then she stood up.

'Now,' said she, 'he is done with suckling.'

The boy, Manus, began to walk, and the part of him that did not grow during the day, grew during the night.

The Slender Woman with the Green Kirtle said to the gardener:

'Pay me my wages.'

'I'll do that; you shall get my share of the world!'

'Thank you, poor man,' said she. 'I'll not take anything from you. My foster-son will pay for it himself.'

And she remained with him for a short time after this, and when the boy was playing and frisking about the place, she said it was time for her to go. She asked the gardener and Manus to go part of the way with her. They set off and, as they were walking towards the shore, they came to some high, rocky cliffs. Here she took hold of the boy and threw him over the precipice, and she was seen no more.

The gardener was sad and did not know what to do. At last he found a gap in the rocks by which he descended to the foot of the precipice. He looked to see if he could find the boy dead or alive. He was more than surprised to see Manus playing shinty on the shore below, with a gold shinty club and a silver ball which his nurse had given him. The gardener took him home and kept him for seven years.

The king then invited the high nobles of Lochlann to the feast of his son's home-coming. When the feast was set and Manus came home, his father and the guests were very proud of him. But when the feast was at its height, the alarm of a challenge on a shield sounded on the Castle lawn. It was given by the Slender Woman of the Green Kirtle and brown hair, who called for combat or the sending to her of the young Manus.

Three hundred strong heroes, three hundred fully trained heroes, and three hundred brave heroes were sent out to her, and she destroyed them all. She called again for combat or Manus, son of the King of Lochlann. She was told she would get combat but not Manus. The same number of heroes were sent out a second time, but she treated them as she had treated the others, and destroyed them all. She called again for combat or Manus. When Manus saw the great loss of men, he said to the king:

'Father, it is me she wants, and I will go.'

'What can you do, my son?' said the king.

'Whatever I may do, I'll go out.'

He went out to the Slender Woman of the Green Kirtle, and they met.

'Well Manus, you have come at last. Which do you choose, wrestling or combat?'

'I prefer wrestling.'

They then caught hold of each other. They made the boggy place more boggy and the rocky place harder. In the softest places they sank to their eyes, and in the hardest places they sank to their knees. In the twists they gave each other, she brought him to his knees.

'Aah!' he said, 'A king's son on his knees; allow me to rise.'

'Manus,' said she, 'no one has gone on his knees who has not gone on his elbow. We will give over wrestling for the present; but I shall put you under spells. I lay on you spells and crosses and nine fairy fetters, and a little fellow, more feeble than yourself, will deprive you of your head, your ears and your powers of life, unless you get information about your nurse. Here is a rod for you, and when you strike a rock with it, a three-masted ship will appear on the sea for you.'

She went away and was seen no more. Manus returned to the feast, and laid his elbow on the table and sighed. His father said to him:

'That is the sigh of a king's son under spells.'

'That is so,' said Manus.

'What spells has she laid on you?'

'That I get information about my nurse.'

'Tut! That is easy to get,' said the king. 'The gardener knows about it.'

The gardener was brought that he might raise the spells off Manus; but he did not know where the Woman of the Green Kirtle came from, who she was, nor where she had gone.

Next day Manus set off to get information about his nurse. He took a man-servant with him. They reached the shore. Manus struck a rock with the rod, and a three-masted, fully equipped ship appeared on the sea. They went aboard, hoisted masts and the spotted, towering sails. And there was not a mast unbent nor a sail unrent, as they were cleaving the slashing, light blue Scandinavian sea. The lulling music they heard was the squealing of pigs and the roaring of boars. The loud, surly wind blew from the top of the mountains to the bottom of the glens, tearing the young willows from their stocks and roots. Eels were twisting about, and gulls were screaming. Sea-tangle was making dents in the bottom of the boat. The spiral, dusky, periwinkle-blue weed, that for seven years was at the bottom of the sea, made a hissing noise on her gunwale and a creaking noise on her floor.

Manus played chess in the middle cabin. He told his servant to go on deck to see how the ship was sailing.

'She goes as fast as a deer on a mountain,' said the man.

'There is not enough speed, put more sail on her.'

They hoisted the towering, wind-tight sails to the masts, and there was not a mast unbent, nor a sail unrent, as they were cleaving the Scandinavian sea. Manus bade his servant again to look, and see how she was faring.

'She will overtake the swift March wind that is before, and the swift March wind that is behind will not overtake her.'

'There is still not enough way on her. Put more sail on her.'

Then they hoisted the sails to the long masts; and there was not a mast unbent nor a sail unrent, and they were cleaving the Scandinavian sea. But Manus sent his servant again to see how she fared.

'She moves as fast as the thoughts of a silly woman,' said he.

'That will do. There is enough sail on her,' said Manus.

Then he called to his man to see if there was any sign of land.

'I can see a little land.'

'We will steer towards it.'

When they reached the harbour, Manus caught the ship by the bow, and drew her up where the fops of the town would not mock her, and where the sun would not crack her, nor the water rot her.

He walked through the town, and night came. He saw a fine building lit by the blaze of brilliant wax candles. He went in, and found himself in a large room where there was a table covered with every kind of food. On it were twelve wheaten loaves and twelve dishes of rare foods. Manus took a bite out of each of the loaves, and a mouthful from each of the dishes. Then he hid himself in a corner, for there was no one to be seen.

Twelve Big Men came home. They sat round the table, and each of them said: 'There's a bite out of my loaf.'

The Red-haired Man, who was their leader, said:

'There is a bite out of mine too, so look for the one who took it. Find him, for he has not yet left this place.'

They found Manus hiding; and one of them took him up on the palm of his hand; and they passed him from one hand to another, till at last they stood him on the table. They had never seen so small and pretty a manikin. Then they took their food and went to sleep; but the Red-haired Man could not get to sleep. He said to Manus:

'Tell me a tale, to see if it will send me to sleep.'

Manus began, and repeated a tale to the Red-haired Man who soon fell asleep. When he awakened, he said:

'Well, my boy, I've not had so much sleep for seven years. Repeat another tale, and you'll have success and blessing from it.'

Manus repeated another tale, and the man slept, and when he awakened, he said:

'That is the best sleep I've had for seven years and a day. If I get more I will be all right. Repeat another tale.'

'Tell me first what has kept you sleepless for such a long time.'

'I will tell you that,' said the Red-haired Man. 'I have been for the last seven years fighting three great giants, their mother, and their hosts, together with their ten hundred strong heroes, their ten hundred fully trained heroes, and their ten hundred brave heroes; and those we kill during the day, come alive at night. They maintain the fight every day, and are devastating the kingdom. It is prophesied that this state of things will last till the son of a sister of mine, Manus, son of the King of Lochlann, comes to destroy them, but he is too young as yet.'

'I am he,' said Manus.

'What! You! You insignificant creature? Be quiet and do not boast, but repeat another story, to see if I can get a little sleep.'

Manus did this, and when the Red-haired Man was asleep, he took the sword that his mother's brother had at the side of the bed, and set off to the battlefield. He lay down among the dead men. He was not long there when he saw a big, ugly giant coming along with a reviving drink to bring to life the dead, and he was calling:

'Is there anyone alive among you? Anyone who will help me?'

'If you'll help me, I'll help you,' said Manus.

'Come here, that I may put my finger in your mouth.'

'Come you here, for you're more able than I am.'

'How is it, poor man, that you've been left alive?'

'I don't know, but I have been left.'

The giant dipped his finger in the reviving drink, and put it in the young man's mouth, and Manus bit it.

'Ah! Ah! You rascal, you'll pay for what you've done to my finger! It was prophesied that Manus, son of the King of Lochlann, would do this, but you shall not do it to me for nothing. Which do you choose, wrestling or combat?'

'I prefer wrestling,' said Manus.

Manus stretched his young white arms around the giant's swarthy old sides, and the giant stretched his withered old arms around the white young sides of Manus; and they made the boggy place more boggy, and the rocky place harder. In the softest place, they sank up to their eyes, and in the hardest place they sank up to their knees, but when Manus remembered that he was far from his friends, he gave the giant a lift, broke his arm under him and a rib above him. And he raised his sword.

'Death is over you, churl, what is your ransom?'

'I am of little account compared with my brother,' said the giant. 'Spare my life, for my brother who is coming, is much bigger than I am, and I'll help you against him.'

'Your help has not been asked,' said Manus, as he lopped off the giant's five heads.

Being tired, Manus lay in the battlefield. He saw a second giant coming. He was bigger and uglier than the first, and began to revile his brother for not having brought the slain men to life, saying:

'You're away courting the children of kings, and have left this work for me to do. Is there no one who will help me?'

'If you'll help me, I'll help you,' said Manus.

'Ah, poor man, how have you been left alive? Come here, that I may put my finger in your mouth.'

'I cannot. You come here, you're more able.'

When the giant put his finger in his mouth, Manus bit it. The giant understood who this was, and that this man had killed his brother, and said:

'This was prophesied. You'll have to pay for my brother's death. Although you have killed him, you'll not kill me. Which do you prefer, wresting or combat?'

Manus chose wrestling, and the same fate befell the second giant, as befell the first. Manus lopped off his five heads. Then he lay down in the battlefield to await the third giant. When he came, he was bigger, more horrible, and wilder than the other two. Because the slain men had not been brought to life, the giant reviled his two brothers, saying:

'Shame on you! Away after the children of kings, while the slain should have been brought to life, and the work is undone. Is there no one here to help me?'

'I am here,' said Manus.

'Come here, that I may put my finger in your mouth!'

'I cannot. You come, you're more able.'

The giant came, and put his finger into his mouth, and Manus bit him.

'Ah! You rascal, you are Manus, son of the King of Lochlann. It was long ago prophesied that you would come. You have killed my two brothers, but you'll not kill me. You shall pay for their deaths. Which do you prefer, wrestling or combat?'

'Wrestling, for I have practised it most.'

Manus stretched his strong white arms round the giant's swarthy sides, and the giant stretched his two hard, swarthy arms round Manus' soft white sides; and they made the boggy place more boggy, and the rocky place harder. At last Manus put the giant down.

'Death is over you,' said he. 'What is your ransom?'

'My brothers and I are of little account compared to my mother. If you allow me to rise, I'll help you and tell you how she can be killed,' said the giant.

'Tell me first,' said Manus.

'There is a mole under her right breast. Unless you hit it, she'll not die.'

'You shall not have the power to tell what will befall me,' said Manus, and took off the five heads of the third giant, then rested himself.

When day was approaching, he saw a giantess coming. She was calling to her sons:

'Where are you? Courting the children of kings, as usual, when you've not yet brought my men to life! Is there anyone alive that will help me?'

'I am here,' said Manus.

The hag at once understood who he was and offered him wrestling or combat. The wrestling began, and he had a hard struggle with her. At last he hit the mole and felled her. But she maintained the fight after she was down. When he lopped a head off her, another would appear; and he was hard-pressed. Then a voice from above him said:

'Keep your sword on the neck, till the blood becomes cold and the marrow freezes.'

He did this, and so destroyed all the giants.

He was very tired and sat down. Harpers came and played music to him to put him to sleep. He rose and killed the harpers, but as soon as he was seated, they were alive again and played to him. This went on and on until he was exhausted. Then a voice came from above which told him he would not succeed in killing the harpers unless he took the corners of their harps and attacked them. He did this, and destroyed them all. He then lay down on the battlefield.

When his mother's brother, the Red-haired Man, awoke, it was daylight. He missed his sword, and there was no sign of Manus. He set off for the battlefield to meet the giants, but as he drew near, he could not see a single creature moving there. So he rose into the air in the form of a griffin, and saw that the battlefield was full of bodies, just as he had left it.

When Manus saw the ugly griffin hovering above him, he stood up ready for battle, but when the griffin saw that it was Manus, he came down and resumed his own shape. They greeted each other, and Manus told his uncle the reason for his journey.

They set out to find the nurse that Manus had once had. They reached the castle where she was, and she was overjoyed at seeing him again, and he had to lie down beside her. They had not long lain down, when the most handsome beauty eye ever beheld, came to the side of the bed, and was walking backwards and forwards. Manus rose to take hold of her. She went out of the room and he followed her closely. She went into a great hall in a rock, and he went in after her. She struck him with a magic rod, and made him into a pillar of stone. When his nurse wakened and found that Manus was no longer with her, she began to cry and was very angry.

The Red-haired Man came down and was very puzzled. The nurse told him that there was a wicked woman in the cave near them who was in the habit of coming to the castle to wile away every king's son that came that way; she had tried to destroy her but she could not manage it.

'Perhaps you can manage it. You shall lie down beside me tonight, and should she come in in the form of a beautiful maiden, you must rise and follow her. Take this rod with you; and when she goes into the cave, strike her with the rod before she can do anything to you. You will then order her to become any creature you see fit. You will find in the hall a reviving cordial. Dip the rod into it, and strike the pillars with the rod. The pillars will then change back into the young men, and among them, I am sure, you will find my foster-son, your nephew.'

It was thus that it turned out. After the nurse and the Red-haired Man had lain down, the beautiful woman came. He rose and followed her. She took the road to the shore. She reached a high, rocky precipice. She struck it, and a door opened. Just at the entrance, the Red-haired Man approached and struck her with the rod, and turned her into a deer-hound bitch, which followed him wherever he went. Inside he found the reviving drink. He dipped the rod into it, and struck the stone pillars with it. Each one he struck with the rod, changed into a handsome youth. They rose and walked out of the cavern, but Manus was not among them. The Red-haired Man was afraid that the wonderful reviving cordial would be exhausted and that the rod would lose its virtue before he could reach Manus, so he went forward cautiously, till he struck a pillar in the innermost corner, and Manus rose up. They greeted each other warmly and set out for the nurse's castle. When she saw them both she rejoiced greatly.

They remained there for a while, till she told Manus of the special task she had for him. There was a huge beast in a quarter of her kingdom that was desolating the place. Should a man or creature come within seven miles of this beast, it would suck them in. It could swallow a team of six horses, and plough and the ploughman.

'It is prophesied that you are the man to destroy this beast; and as you have the Red-haired Man, your mother's brother, with you, there will be no fear for you.'

They took with them swords and knives; and the bitch-hound followed them. When they were at a distance of seven miles from the beast, they were drawn and sucked into its belly. Inside they drew their knives. They went one on each side of it, in order to make a hole through its side, and the hound kept tearing at the entrails, till they came out on each side of the beast, dirty, ghastly-looking wretches.

They returned home, and the nurse washed and bathed them. She gave them warm water for their feet, a soft bed under their thighs; and in the morning they woke fresh and healed.

THE SON OF THE KING OF IRELAND

HE KING of Ireland had an only son whose favourite pastime was hunting. One day he was hunting, and killed a black raven. He took the raven up in his hand and looked at it. The blood was coming from its head where the shot had entered it, and he said to himself:

'I will only marry a woman whose hair is as black as the raven's wings, and whose lips are as red as the raven's blood.'

When he went home that evening, his father said to him:

'Had you good sport today?'

'I had not. I killed only a raven. Now I am resolved to marry only a woman whose hair is as black as the raven's wings and whose lips are as red as the raven's blood.'

'It is not so easy to find the like of her,' said his father.

'I will travel the world to find her.'

'It is foolish of you to do such a thing,' said his father.

'Be that as it may, I shall go at any rate,' said the son.

He then bade his father farewell, and left. As he went on his way, making enquiry, he was told that the youngest of the three daughters of the King of the Great World was such a one. On his way he arrived at a smithy where the Smith was working. He knocked on the door; the Smith opened it and said:

'Come in, you will be a lucky man.'

'How do you know that I shall be lucky?'

'I will tell you,' said the Smith. 'I was working, making a large needle. It defied me to put an eye in it till you knocked at the door, but when you knocked

I managed to make the eye. Be seated, and tell me your news. Where have you come from, and who are you?'

'I am the son of the King of Ireland,' said the young man.

'Where are you going?'

'I will tell you,' said he. 'I have heard of the youngest daughter of the King of the Great World, and I am going in quest of her, that I may get a glimpse of her, and maybe speak to her father to see if he will give her to me in marriage.'

'Oh,' said the Smith, 'everyone knows that the son of the King of Ireland wishes to marry the daughter of the King of the Great World. I have already told you that you will be lucky. The needle I am making is for the King of the Great World. You can cross the river tomorrow with his people. I will ask them to ferry you. Remain with me tonight, and you will not lack food or bed.'

The young man spent the night comfortably with the Smith. Next day, the King of the Great World sent his boat across the river to fetch the needle. The Smith asked the crew to take the young man back with them, and they agreed.

They ferried the young man across the river and went to the house of the King of the Great World and delivered the needle. When the king saw the son of the King of Ireland, he knew that he did not belong to his country, and asked what he wanted. The young man said that he had come to ask for one of his daughters in marriage.

'Who are you and where do you come from?' said the king. 'You must be of noble birth if you have come to ask for my daughter.'

'I am the son of the King of Ireland.'

'You shall get one of my daughters, but you have three things to do first.'

'I will try to do them if you will tell me what I have to do.'

'I have a byre,' said the King of the Great World, 'which is filthy. You must clean it so well that a gold ball will run smoothly from one end to the other.'

The king took the Prince of Ireland to the byre and showed it to him. He began to clean it, but twice as much dirt gathered in it as he put out. He kept working at it, but toil as he did, he could not clean the byre. He began to wish he had not asked for the daughter of the King of the Great World. About midday, the king's three daughters, who were out for a walk, passed that way, and the eldest of them said to him:

'You are harassed, son of the King of Ireland?'

'Yes, I am,' said he.

'If I thought that it was for me that you came, I would clean the byre for you,' said she.

The second daughter said the same, but the youngest daughter said:

'Whether or not it was for me you came, I will clean the byre, son of the King of Ireland.' She then said: 'Clean, clean, crooked graip, put out a shovel!'

In no time, the byre was cleaned so thoroughly that a gold ball ran smoothly from one end to the other. The king's three daughters returned home, and left the son of the King of Ireland at the byre.

That same day the king came to the byre, and said:

'Son of the King of Ireland, is the byre clean?'

'It is!' said he.

'I am very much pleased with you for making it so clean.'

'May I marry your daughter now?' said the son of the King of Ireland.

'You have more to do,' said the King of the Great World. 'Tomorrow you must thatch the byre with bird feathers. The stem of each feather shall point inwards, and the point of each feather shall point outwards. A slender silk thread will keep the thatch on the roof of the byre.'

'Will you give me the feathers?'

'No,' said the king, 'you must gather them yourself.'

Next day, the lad gathered feathers on the shore, but whenever he gathered a handful, the wind blew them away. He said to himself: 'I wish I had never come to ask for the hand of the daughter of the King of the Great World.'

At midday the three daughters of the King of the Great World passed by, and the eldest of them said:

'Son of the King of Ireland, you are harassing yourself, trying to thatch the byre. If it was for me that you had come, I'd thatch it for you.' And the middle one said the same, but the young one said:

'Whether it was for me or not that you came, son of the King of Ireland, I will thatch it for you.'

She put her hand in her pocket, drew out a whistle, and blew it. The birds came and shook themselves over the byre, and soon it was thatched with feathers. The stem of each feather pointed inwards and its tip outwards. A slender silk thread kept the covering on the roof.

The king's daughters returned home, and left him at the byre. Later that day, the king came, and said to him:

'Son of the King of Ireland, I see you have thatched the byre. I am much obliged to you but I am not pleased with your teacher.'

'Will you now give me the hand of your daughter?' said the son of the King of Ireland.

'You will not get her today. You have more to do tomorrow.' And the king returned home.

Next morning the king said to him:

'I have five swans, and you must look after them. If you allow them to get away, you will be hanged, but if you keep them safely, you shall marry my daughter.'

The son of the King of Ireland went to herd the swans, but they defied him, and ran from him. In his plight, he sat down and said to himself: 'It is a pity I left my father's house to seek a woman. Everything has prospered for me till now, but this task is impossible.'

About midday, the three daughters of the king came that way, and the eldest of them said:

'The swans have run away from you, son of the King of Ireland!'

'Yes, and they have flown out to sea.'

'Well, if I thought it was for me that you had come, I would find them for you.'

The middle daughter said the same, but the young one said:

'Whether it was for me or not that you came, I will find the swans for you.' And she blew her whistle, and the swans returned.

The three daughters went home, but as the King of Ireland's son was looking after the swans, the King of the Great World came and said:

'I see that you have managed to keep the swans, son of the King of Ireland.'

'I have,' said he. 'Shall I be allowed to marry your daughter now?'

'No,' said the king, 'you have one small thing to do yet, and when you have done it, you shall marry her.'

They returned together to the palace, then the King of the Great World said:

'I am going to fish tomorrow, and you must clean and boil the fish that I catch.'

Next day the king caught a fish and gave it to the son of the King of Ireland to clean and boil.

'I am going to sleep for a while,' said the king, 'and you must have the fish cleaned and boiled by the time I wake.'

He began to clean the fish, but as he cleaned off the scales, twice as many came on. When the daughters came by, the eldest said to him:

'If I thought it was for me that you came, I would clean the fish for you,' and the second daughter said the same.

But the young one said:

'Whether it was for me or not that you came, I will clean the fish for you.'

She cleaned it, and it was put on the fire to cook. Then she took the king's son aside and said:

'You and I must take flight before my father wakens.'

They took two horses from the king's stables, and they fled together. The young daughter told the son of the King of Ireland that her father would kill them both if he caught them.

When the king awoke, he asked where his youngest daughter and the son of the King of Ireland were. He was told that they had fled together.

The young couple rode as fast as their horses would carry them. The king rode after them and tried to overtake them. Hearing a noise behind them, the king's daughter said to the young prince:

'Look to see if there is anything in your horse's ear.'

'I see in it a small piece of thorn tree,' said he.

'Throw it behind you,' she said.

He did so, and the little bit of thorn formed a great forest seven miles long and three miles wide. The son of the King of Ireland and the princess were on one side and the King of the Great World was on the other. The forest was so thick the king could not get through it. He had to return home to fetch an axe and hack down a way through.

He did this, and his daughter and the young prince saw the king pursuing them again. Being tired they had rested for a while; the king had had time to catch up with them. When they saw him coming, they set off again. Just as he was drawing near, the princess said to the young prince:

'See what you can find in the horse's ear.'

'There is a small stone in it,' said he.

'Throw it behind you,' said she. He did so, and the stone turned into a high rock, seven miles long and one mile high.

The king was at the foot of the rock, and they were on the top of it. They looked over the edge of the rock to see how he fared. The king looked up and when he saw he could make nothing of the situation, he returned home, while they continued their journey to Ireland.

They crossed the sea to Ireland, and they were but a short distance from the King of Ireland's palace, when the young princess said:

'I'll not go to the palace for a while. When you return home your dog will be leaping up to you with joy. Try to keep it from you, for if your dog touches your face, you will forget that you ever saw me.'

Then they bade each other farewell, and she went to stay with the Smith of that place. Meanwhile, the young prince was greeted by his dog at the palace gate, and before it could be stopped, the dog leapt up and licked his face, and he forgot the princess and all that had happened in the Wide World.

Having brought men's clothes with her, she put them on, and went to the Smith and asked him if he needed a servant. He said he did, for his servant had left the previous day. The new servant began to learn the Smith's trade and made excellent progress, and everyone remarked what a fine-looking lad he was. 'He' was working with the Smith for a year. The Smith had never had a servant so apt at learning, and good in every way.

Word came that the son of the King of Ireland was to marry the daughter of the King of Farafohuinn. Among those invited to the wedding was the Smith, and he insisted that his servant accompanied him. The 'servant' said to the Smith:

'There is something I have to make in the smithy that I want to take to the wedding. Will you allow me the use of the smithy tonight?'

The Smith consented, and the 'servant' made a gold hen and a silver cock. They both went to the wedding, and before leaving the 'servant' took grains of wheat in her pockets.

When they arrived at the palace, there was a roomful of people who had arrived before them. Many of them knew the Smith and welcomed him. They asked him if he could suggest some amusement to pass the time.

'I cannot,' said he, 'but perhaps my servant here will offer us diversion?'

The 'servant' agreed, and 'he' then put the gold hen and the silver cock out on the floor, and threw three grains of wheat to them. The cock picked up two of them and the hen got but one.

'Gok! Gok!' said the hen.

'What is the matter with you?' said the cock.

'Do you remember the day I cleaned the byre for you?' said the hen.

The company roared with laughter at this. The Smith's 'servant' threw out another three grains. The cock picked up two of them, and the hen got but one.

'Gok! Gok!' said the hen.

'What is the matter with you?' said the cock.

'If you remembered the day I thatched the byre for you with birds' feathers, the stem of each feather being inwards and the tip pointing outwards, and a slender silk thread keeping the cover on the roof, you would not eat two grains while I had but one.'

The king's son looked at the Smith's 'servant', and said:

'See if you have any more grains of wheat to throw to them.'

He had at once remembered how he had fared when he went to ask for the daughter of the King of the Great World, and he thought to himself that if he got another proof he would be assured. Then the 'servant' threw out more grains and the cock picked up two and the hen got but one.

'Gok! Gok!' said the hen.

'What is the matter with you?' said the cock.

'Do you remember the day when I found the swans for you? If you did, you would not eat two grains while I had but one!'

The king's son, realising how things were, went over to the 'servant' and put his arms around her, saying:

'Dearest of women, it is you!' and he opened the shirt of the 'servant' in the presence of the company and showed them her breasts.

Without further delay, she was taken to another room and given a woman's dress. When she was dressed, a gold chain was put about her neck, a gold ring was put on her finger, and a gold bracelet was given to her.

The son of the King of Ireland said to the daughter of the King of Farafohuinn:

'I have found again the woman that I went in quest of, and I can marry none but her, for I passed through many trials on her account. If you choose to stay, you may and will be allowed to join in all the wedding celebrations; but if you do not so choose, you may go, for you have no hold on me.'

She, whom he had arranged to marry, took this treatment as an affront, and was deeply offended, and she went away.

The son of the King of Ireland and the daughter of the King of the Great World were married.

The King of Riddles and the Bare-stripping Hangman

Part I

ONCE there was a King of Ireland who had been twice married, and had a son by each of his wives. The name of the first son was Cormac, and the name of the second was Alastir.

The king was very fond of Cormac, and always took him to the Hunting-hill.

Now the king had a hen-wife, who went on a certain day, with a sad and sorrowful countenance, to the queen, who asked what was troubling her.

'Great it is and not little, Queen of Misery,' said the hen-wife.

'What does that mean?'

'That the king is so fond of Cormac, son of his first wife. He will leave his kingdom to him, and your son will be penniless.'

'If that is the king's pleasure, it can't be helped.'

'Nevertheless it need not happen. If you will give me what I ask, I will make your son king.'

'What reward will you ask for doing that?'

'Not much,' said the hen-wife. 'Just as much meal as will thicken the contents of a little black jar, and as much butter as will make it thin, and my two ear-holes full of wool, and meat the breadth of one of my haunches.'

'How much meal will thicken the contents of your little black jar?'

'Fourteen chalders.'

'How much butter to make it thin?'

'As much as your seven sheep-pens will produce in seven years.'

'And what now is the breadth of one of your haunches?'

'As much as your seven byres will have produced at the end of seven years.'

'That is a great deal, hen-wife,' said the queen.

'Yes, but little in comparison with the third of Ireland.'

'It is,' said the queen, 'and you shall have it. But what plan do you have to make my son king?'

'Cormac was yesterday complaining that he was not well. Now, when the hunters come home, tell the king that Cormac must stay at home tomorrow, and that Alastir will go to the Hunting-hill in his place. I'll make a drink for Cormac. You shall give it to him after the others have gone, and he will not prevent your son from becoming king.'

This pleased the queen, and she promised to do as the hen-wife told her. The women thought that no one was listening while they were devising mischief, but Alastir was eavesdropping behind the door. He was very angry because he and Cormac were as fond of each other as two brothers ever were. He was considering what to do, and decided to tell Cormac about the women's intentions as soon as he came home.

At evening, Cormac returned. He was pretty tired, and not feeling better than in the morning. Alastir told him everything that had happened between his mother and the hen-wife. Cormac was afraid, and asked Alastir what he should do.

'Have courage,' said Alastir. 'I'll devise a scheme to get out of their way, and we'll not trouble them any more. Tomorrow I'll go with my father to the Hunting-hill, and I'll not go far when I'll say I must return home because I don't like going to the hill. Before I arrive, my mother will give you the drink. You will take hold of the cup but, for heaven's sake, don't taste a drop, and do not let it near your mouth. Lift the cup as though you were going to drink, then run out, holding it in your hand. I shall have two of the fastest horses in the stable waiting, and we will go away.'

And that is what they did.

Next day, Alastir went only a short distance with the king, when he refused to go any further, and returned home. He knew when Cormac would get the drink, and made the horses ready as he had promised. Scarcely had he saddled them, when Cormac ran out quickly, the cup in his hand. Alastir cried to him:

'Leap into your saddle and stick to what you have!'

Cormac did this, and they galloped off as fast as their horses would carry them. They kept going without stop or rest, until their horses were exhausted. Then they dismounted and sat down to rest.

'Show me the cup,' said Alastir to Cormac. He took the cup from his brother's hand, and taking a little stick, said:

'Now we shall see what is in the cup!' He dipped the stick into it, and put a drop in an ear of each horse.

'What are you doing that for?' said Cormac.

'Wait a little and you shall see,' said Alastir.

In a short time the horses began to go round dizzily, and before long they fell dead to the ground.

'Just think, Cormac, what would have happened to you if you had drunk the poison.'

'I would have been dead now!' said Cormac.

While they were talking, four ravens came and settled on the carcases of the horses, and they began to peck the eyes out of the horses. When they had eaten the eyes, they flew into the air. But they went only a short distance, then they uttered piercing screams and fell dead to the ground.

'What do you think of the drink now, Cormac?'

'If I had drunk it, I'd not be here,' said Cormac.

Alastir rose and, having put the four ravens in a napkin, he and his brother went on their journey. Alastir was in front, because he knew in advance what was going to happen. They kept going till they came to a small town. Alastir went into a kitchen in the town, and told the cook to dress the ravens as well as he usually prepared birds, but not to put finger or hand near his mouth till he had prepared them and washed his hands well.

'What does that mean?' asked the cook. 'I never before prepared food that I might not taste.'

'Do not taste and do not eat one bit of these, otherwise you shall not get them at all.'

The cook promised to do as he was told. After he had dressed the ravens and received his payment, Alastir wrapped the ravens in his napkin, and he and Cormac departed again on their journey. On the way, Alastir said:

'There's a large wood before us where twenty-four robbers are hiding. They never allow a man to pass them without killing him, and they will not let us pass if they can help it.'

'What shall we do?' said Cormac.

'Leave that to me,' said Alastir.

As they were going through the wood, they noticed a pretty little place above the road they were walking on, where the robbers were lying on their backs, basking in the sun. The two lads kept going, but as they passed the place where the robbers lay, two of the robbers cried:

'Who are these two impertinent fellows who dare to pass this way without asking our permission?'

And they went to meet the strangers, and threatened to strike their heads off.

'Oh, well,' said Alastir, 'there's no help for it, but we are both tired and hungry, and if you allow us to eat a bite of food before you put us to death, we'll be much obliged to you.'

'If you have food, take it quickly,' said the robbers.

'We have food,' said Alastir, 'and you can have some of it if you like.'

Then he opened the napkin, and divided the ravens into twenty-six pieces, a piece for each man in the company.

'Now,' said he, 'you must wait until you are all served, then you must begin to eat together, for if some of you eat your share first, you'll fight the rest for their share, and wound and kill each other.'

At this the robbers gave a loud mocking laugh, but they agreed to do as they were told. When they were all served, Alastir lifted up his head, and cried:

'Eat now!'

They did so, and praised the food. But it was not long before, one after another, they sat down. Every one that sat, fell asleep, and out of that sleep he was never to wake. At last they were all in the sleep of death.

'Now,' said Alastir, 'that is over, and the way before us is clear as far as the castle of the King of Riddles. Cormac, you shall travel as the King of Ireland, and I will travel as your servant. If you are told to do anything, say it is the servant that does it in the country you come from. When we reach the castle of the King of Riddles, you will have to pose a riddle or solve a riddle. If you do not, your head will be placed on a stake on the wall, beside the door. Many people like us have reached the castle before now but, as they could not pose a riddle nor solve a riddle, their heads were placed on the stakes on the wall. There is one stake still empty. Your head will be placed on it, if neither you nor I can pose a riddle or solve it tonight.'

They reached the castle. The King of Riddles gave them a great welcome, for he thought they had come to ask for his daughter, like all those who had preceded them. They were there but a short time when food was placed before them, but before they began to take it, the King of Riddles said:

'King of Ireland, pose a riddle or solve a riddle.'

'In the country that I come from,' said Cormac, 'it is the servant that does that.'

The servant came, and the King of Riddles said:

'Servant of the King of Ireland, pose or solve a riddle.'

'One killed two, two killed four, and four killed twenty-four, and two escaped. What does that mean?' said the servant.

The King of Riddles could not solve this, and he said to the servant:

'Go away now, and you shall have the answer to your riddle tomorrow.'

After dinner, they all spent the rest of the night until bedtime, telling interesting tales. Then the king sent for his daughter and her twelve maidens. He told them that the first to solve the riddle would marry his son and get half his kingdom. He then turned to his daughter and told her that if she solved the riddle, she would get her choice of a lover and half the kingdom.

The maidens wondered how they could solve the riddle. At last they agreed to put the servant in the coldest room in the castle, where there were holes in the wall, letting in the wind and the rain. They would put the master in the best room. Then they would tell the servant that he would get a room as good as his master's if he told them the answer to the riddle. And this is what they did.

The servant was not long in bed when he heard the door opening. He turned on his pillow and saw a beautiful young maiden standing there. She said:

'Are you sleeping, servant of the King of Ireland?'

'I am not,' said he. 'These are not sleeping quarters, with the wind and cold under me, and the wind and rain over me. Far will I carry the name of this castle when I go away!'

'You shall get as good a bed as your master if you will tell me the solution of the riddle you set.'

But he told her nothing, and she went back to the others without it. Then they came, one after another, but what had happened to the first maiden happened to them all. As soon as the last maiden went out, the servant went to the master's room, and the master came to the servant's room. He was there but a short time when the king's daughter entered, and said:

'Are you asleep, servant of the King of Ireland?'

'There is not sleep for me, for these are not sleeping quarters, with wind and cold under me, and wind and rain over me. Far will I carry the name of this house when I go away!'

'Well, you shall get as good a bed as your master if you will tell me the answer to the riddle.'

But he would not tell her and she went away.

Next morning, the king asked the maidens if they had got the solution of the riddle. They said they had not. Then he asked his daughter if she had got it, and she said she had not. When they sat down to breakfast, the King of Riddles said:

'King of Ireland, pose a riddle or solve a riddle.'

'As I told you last night, it is my servant who is accustomed to do that for me.' And the servant came.

'Servant of the King of Ireland, pose a riddle or solve one,' said the king.

'I have not got the answer to the first riddle I posed you,' said the servant.

'You insolent fellow. You put a riddle or solve a riddle now, otherwise your head will be struck off and placed on a stake in the wall.'

'I will put a riddle for you then,' said the servant.

And he put a riddle he had composed on the things that had happened to him in his room the night before, and the king solved it of course, so he did not lose his head.

In the end the King of Riddles gave his daughter to the King of Ireland, who was Cormac, and Alastir ceased to play the part of the servant, and he stayed with them, passing his time hunting and fishing.

The King of Riddles and the Bare-stripping Hangman

Part II

ONE day, while he was fishing, Alastir heard a splash in the sea, at the foot of a rock. A large dog-otter sprang out of the water, seized him by his ankles, and swam out to sea with him. And he did not see a blink of sky or earth till he was left above the reach of the tide in the prettiest bay he had ever seen, with smooth white sand from the margin of the waves to the edge of the green grass.

Alastir was now in Lochlann.

In a short time the dog-otter returned, with a freshwater salmon in his mouth. He left the salmon at Alastir's feet, and said to him:

'When you are going on any long journey, or when any hardship is coming on you, take a bite of this fish beforehand. Make a bothy here, and stay in it till you see me again, and until you get more instructions from me.'

Alastir put up the bothy that night. He then boiled a piece of the salmon, and after eating it, he felt stronger than ever.

Next morning he rose and went out, before breakfast, to the end of his bothy. He stood, and saw the great white-buttocked deer coming straight towards him, and the white red-eared hound after him, chasing him keenly. As the deer approached, the hound caught hold of the deer; and as he went past, the hound gave a bark, and sprang at the neck of the deer, and left him dead at Alastir's feet.

'Now,' said the hound to Alastir, 'you were faithful to your brother, and you shall receive your reward. When you are going on any long journey, or when any hardship is coming upon you, you shall eat beforehand a bite of the freshwater salmon, and a bite of this deer, and from anything else you see or hear, no further injury shall befall you. And if that should fail you will be told what to do.' Then the white red-eared hound wished him success and departed.

Alastir took the deer to his bothy, and left it beside the salmon. He made ready his breakfast, and ate a piece of salmon and a piece of deer. He then went out and, looking into the distance, he saw a large man, with the appearance of a king, and twelve Champions with him. They came straight to the place where he was. And the king said to him:

'How had you the courage and the boldness to come and kill my large white-buttocked deer?'

'The deer came of its own accord. I had need of food, so I killed it.'

'Well,' said the king, 'since you killed my deer, you must fight with my Champions until you fall or they do.'

'I am alone, king,' said Alastir, 'and you are many, also I have no sword.'

'You shall not be without a sword,' said the king. 'You shall have my sword, and if you take your life out of peril with it, it shall be your own.'

'I will try,' said Alastir, 'but I ask you as a favour that you will allow me to eat a bite of food before I begin.'

'You shall have that,' said the king, as he reached for his sword.

Alastir went into his bothy, and ate a bite of the fish and a bite of the deer. When he had done that, he thrust the king's sword into the carcass of the deer, and it went through as easily as through water.

'The success of this thrust be with each stroke,' said he. He felt that he himself was in great courage and in full strength, and he got ready for the fight.

The king said that he would get the advantage of the Fian – and fight one man at a time. One of the Champions was sent out to him. But they were not long at swordplay, when the Champion of the king fell, heavily wounded, on the ground. Alastir shouted to the next man to come on. He came, but in a short time he fell wounded on the ground like the first man. The same thing happened to the third man.

When the king saw his three Champions dropping blood and dying, he said to Alastir:

'Whatever is your native country, you are a Champion.'

Alastir then called to the others to come on quickly if he had to fight them all. But the king put a stop to the contest. He turned to Alastir and said to him:

'You have won your sword with victory, and you shall have it. Come with me and I will make you better off than you are here.'

Then Alastir asked the king, as a kindness, to leave the bothy standing just as it was, since he did not know if he must return to it. He got his request, and went away with the king.

On the way the king was under a heavy sadness for the loss of his three Champions; but at last he consoled himself that the one he had found was as good as the three he had lost. They kept going forward, through the wood, over heath, and over moss, until they arrived at a fine castle, the like of which Alastir had never seen before. The king told him to go in with him. The Champions went their own way, and Alastir entered with the king.

Food and drink were put before Alastir, and the king told him to eat and drink. He replied that he would not eat a bite of the food nor drink a drop of the drink until the king told the reason why he had been brought to this place. The king understood that he had a Champion in Alastir, and said that he would tell him.

'I had four daughters. Three of them were taken from me by the big giant who stays in the Black Corrie of the Ben Brock. The giant came at first at the going down of the sun, and took away the first of my daughters in my own presence, and in the presence of my Champions, and I saw her no more. I sent my Champions after the giant, and they followed him to his castle. But when they reached it, as a sudden blast of east wind would strip bracken in the winter, the giant swept off their heads. Only one escaped to tell me the tale of distress. At the end of seven years, the giant came again and, as it happened the first time, so it happened that time; he took my second daughter. And at the end of another seven years he came again, and took the third daughter with him. My Champions resolved to have revenge on him, and to bring my daughters home to me. They went away in full armour to watch the castle of the Black Corrie of the Ben Breck. After they had watched it during three rounds of the sun, they still did not see the giant. At last they were growing heavy for want of sleep and weak for want of food, and they therefore resolved to go to the castle and see what was within. They found the way to the den of the giant, and saw that he was in a heavy sleep. They said to each other that this was the time for them to have revenge for the king's daughter, and to take off the head of the giant. They sprang at him, and struck off his head with their swords.

No sooner had they done this than a great golden eagle stooped down, struck the first Champion in the face, and knocked him down. The golden eagle did the same to the next man, and when the rest saw this they fled. But scarcely had they got through the castle gate than they saw the giant coming after them, his head on his shoulders as before. When they saw him, the Champions scattered, and those who escaped made no stay until they arrived here. But those that the giant caught, he bared to the skin, and hanged on hooks against the turrets of the castle.

Now, the fourth of my daughters was about a day and a year of age when the others were stolen from me. And anyone who will bring to me the black brood-mare which is on the ben, on which a halter never was fitted, will get my daughter and half my kingdom.'

'Good is your offer, king,' said Alastir. 'He is a sorry fellow who would not make his utmost endeavour to earn it.'

'I knew that you were a Champion,' said the king, 'and if you will do this for me, you shall get your promised reward, and much more. On the morning of the next day, you will reach my stable, and get your choice of a bridle.'

On the next morning, Alastir reached the stable, and found many men and Champions before him, who were going to try to catch the black brood-mare, as he himself was, for the sake of winning the king's daughter as a reward. The stable was opened, and each one selected a bridle for himself.

They then went to the mountain to catch the black brood-mare. They were travelling through glens, over bens, and through hollows until they caught sight of her. Alastir tried to get before her, but as soon as she saw him, she ascended the face of the ben, sending water out of the stones and fire out of the streams, fleeing from him. They followed after her until the darkening of night came on them, and then they turned home without her.

When they reached the castle, they told the king what had happened. He told them that another day was coming, and that another sun was to go round, and that the man who brought home the black brood-mare at the end of a tether, would get his daughter and half the kingdom. When they heard this, every man and every Champion made ready to go up the ben before sunrise on the following day.

When the next morning came, each one of them set off in the full belief that it was with himself the victory would be on his return.

They reached the ben. Some of them were going on their bellies through the hollows, some creeping along the beds of streams, others were peeping over ridges, and taking advantage of every gap to see if they could catch sight of the black brood-mare.

At last they saw her on the sunny side of the Glen-of-the-Sun. Each man made ready, as well as he could, to catch her. But no better fate befell them on that day than on the day before, for she was sending water out of the stones and fire out of the streams, fleeing before them. At the going-down of the sun they were further from her than they were in the morning. They returned home wearily, hungrily, sadly.

When they reached the castle, the king sent out his gillie-in-attendance, to ask with whom the victory was. The gillie sent back word that they had seen her, but that they had not got within stone-cast of her. Then the king sent word that the morrow was the third day of their trial, and that he would be as good as his promise to any of them who brought home to him, at the end of a rein, the black brood-mare. When they heard this, each running Champion and each fighting Champion was under heavy anxiety, for they could not do more than they had already done. But they resolved that they would try once more to catch her.

After the supper was over, Alastir, as he was going through the castle, met the sorceress of the king.

'Son of the King of Ireland,' said she, 'you are wearied, sad and under a heavy stupor.' Alastir said that he was. 'You did not take the advice of your friends. Tonight you must go back to your own bothy, and you must take a bite of the salmon and a bite of the deer. But before you go, you must go to the king and tell him that tomorrow is the last day you have for catching the black brood-mare, and that you will not go after her unless you get your choice of a bridle before you depart. He will then go with you, and when you reach the stable you will see a door on your right hand, and you must tell him to open that door so that you can take your choice of a bridle. He will open the door for you, and you will see hanging from the wall, an old bridle that has not been worn by horse or mare for twenty-seven years, and you will take it with you. When you reach the mountain, you must give the others the slip, and go after the black brood-mare. As soon as you catch sight of her, you must shake the bridle towards her, and she will come with a neigh and put her head into the bridle. You must then leap on her back, and ride her home to the king.'

Alastir left the sorceress as pleased as he was the day the dog-otter left him ashore in the land of Lochlann.

On the third day, the Champions got ready, and went away to the mountain to catch the black brood-mare. When they arrived they took advantage of every cover, till they thought they were as near to her as they could get. But Alastir gave them the slip, and left them. He did not stop until he got ahead of the black brood-mare. She was coming, bearing a terrible appearance, driving water out of stones and fire out of the streams with the speed of her running. Then Alastir lifted the bridle and shook it towards her. As soon as she heard the jingling of the bridle, she stood, and made a hard neigh, which Mac-talla of the rocks (echo) answered four miles round. She laid her two ears along the back of her head, came at the gallop, and thrust her head into the bridle. Then Alastir leapt on her back, and rode her home to the king.

When the Champions saw the stranger riding away with the black brood-mare, all their cheerfulness and hope left them, and they returned home.

At night the king came out to meet them, and when he saw that it was the stranger who had the victory, he went over to him, went on his two knees to do him honour, and said:

'I thought that you were indeed a Champion, and you have proved it at last. Now, ask for any cattle, person, jewel or value, which is in my kingdom, and you shall get it, along with the reward I promised, in return for this deed you have done.'

The king made a great feast that night. But before the feast was over, word came to the king from the big giant of the Black Rock in the Ben Breck, that he would come for the fourth daughter at the end of a day and a year from that night.

This message made the king ill-humoured and anxious. He turned to the Champions, and told them that he was sorry he could not fulfil what he had promised unless they themselves would find out where the soul of that Bare-stripping Hangman of a Giant was hid, and kill him.

'My Champions have already struck off his head, but he put it on again, and he was as alive as ever he was. He defied them, and said that in spite of them, he would take all my daughters. Now he is coming at the end of a day and a year from this night, and the man of you who will put him out of life shall have my daughter and all my kingdom.'

All the Champions were full of anxiety because they did not know how they could kill the Bare-stripping Hangman of a Giant. But when they separated, the sorceress met Alastir, and said to him:

'Son of the King of Ireland, I hope you have received your reward tonight.'

He then told her everything that had happened and how the condition on which the king's daughter was to be found was more difficult now than it was before.

The sorceress had been lying back on the ground, and she rose up quickly to a sitting position. She took hold of her hair, gave a loud laugh, and said:

'Son of the King of Ireland, success will always be with you, if you take my advice.'

'I will do anything you ask of me, for I have found you true so far, and I have full confidence in you,' said Alastir.

'Well,' said the sorceress, 'from the spot on which you're now standing, go away in full armour, and remember not to part with the king's sword until you get a better one. Go first to your bothy, and eat a bite of salmon, and a bite of deer. Come out of your bothy, and set your face towards the rocky path of the Ben Buie (Yellow Mountain), and do not look behind you. Do not step back from any difficulty or hardship which may meet you until you reach the great castle, at the end of the mountain path. There you will see a woman looking out of the high window of the castle.'

The sorceress now took a writing from her bosom, and said:

'When you see the woman, you will know her. Tell her that you have a writing for her. She will then come and open the door to you, and tell you what you have to do after that. You may now set off on your journey. The blessing of the king be with you, the blessing of his daughter is with you, and you have my blessing. Now, whatsoever the woman asks you to do, be sure that you do it.'

Alastir took courage, and went to his bothy. On the next morning, before sunrise, he departed on his journey through the rocky mountain path of Ben Buie. He kept going far long and full long until the path grew so full of fissures and sharp pointed rocks, that he had to crawl on his belly to get over them. At last the jagged rocks gave way to a great chasm between steep precipices which were as deep under him as they were high above him. Then he saw the path running on one side of one of the precipices on so narrow a ledge that there was not the breadth of a foot-sole to it. Then he felt afraid that he was astray, and was about to return. But a buzzard came flying over his head, and cried to him:

'Son of the King of Ireland, remember the advice of the sorceress.'

At once Alastir remembered his promise, and decided that he would go forward as long as breath was in him. He was then hanging from cliff to cliff, and leaping from ledge to ledge, until the path gradually grew better. At last he got on to the smooth surface. He went on as fast as he could go, over the rocks, for the evening was coming and the castle was still not to be seen. The ascent was so steep, he could not make great speed. But he won to the top at last. He told himself that he would not take long now, and ran as fast as he could down the hillside. He was thinking that, when he got to the foot of the brae, every hardship would be over, but when he reached it they were, to all appearance, only beginning. Instead of the castle, he saw a great Red Lake before him. He looked about to see any way of getting over the lake, but he saw only rocky precipices, and only a bird on the wing could go over them. He was in a dilemma, whether he should return or go forward, when he heard the buzzard crying over his head:

'Son of the King of Ireland, don't be afraid, nor apprehensive of any difficulty or hardship that will meet you.'

When he heard this, Alastir took courage, and kept going forward on the path into the lake. At first he wondered why he was not sinking into the lake, but in a short time he saw that the road on which he was walking was scarcely covered with water. He kept straight on the path until he arrived at the other side of the lake. As soon as he got his feet on dry land, he lifted his head, and saw a beautiful green field before him, and a great castle at the end of the field. Twilight had come, so he hastened towards the castle.

When he reached the castle, he saw a woman looking out of one of the windows. He cried that he had a writing for her. She came down quickly, and opened the door to him. He handed her a letter. She took it and told him to wait until she had read what was in it. As soon as she read the letter she bounded towards him, seized his hand in both of hers, and kissed it. She took him in, and asked him which way he had come. He said he had come by the rocky path of Ben Buie.

'If that is so,' said she, 'you have need of meat and of drink.'

She set meat and drink before him and told him to be quick, because he had a great deal to do.

As soon as he had finished eating and drinking, she took him to the armoury; and told him to lift the sword that was over against the wall. He tried that, but he could not put wind between it and the earth. She opened a press which was on the side of the house, and took out of it a little bottle of balsam. She drew out a cup of gold, and put a little drop out of the bottle into it, and said to him:

'Drink it!'

He did that. He again seized the sword, and he could lift it with both hands. She gave him another little drop, and then he could lift the sword with one hand. She gave him a third drop, and no sooner did he drink it than he felt stronger than he ever was. He seized the sword, and worked with it as lightly and as airily as he could work with the king's sword.

'Now,' she said to him, 'there is a big giant having two heads on him, staying in this castle, and he is coming home in a short time. Come with me, and I will set you standing on the porch, where you will get the opportunity to strike him when he stoops to enter under the lintel. Be sure that you strike him well, and strike the two heads off him, for if you send but one head off him, he will take hold of that one and kill you with it, as he did many others before you.'

Alastir left without delay, and stood on the porch as she had told him. He was not long there when he saw the giant coming. When he reached the door, he bent his heads, and gave a grunt. Alastir took advantage of him, and struck him with all his might. With one stroke he threw off one head and half of the other head. Then the giant gave dreadful leaps and screams, but before he found time to turn round, Alastir struck the other half of the head off him, and the giant fell, a dead carcass on the earth.

The woman came out, and said to him:

'Well done, Son of the King of Ireland. Success is with you.'

He then asked her who she was. She replied that she was the eldest daughter of the King of Ben Buie.

'You are going away to seek the soul of the Bare-stripping Hangman to save my youngest sister from him. Come in and I will send you on your journey before the sun will rise tomorrow.'

He went in, she washed his feet, and he went to bed.

Before the red cock crowed, and before the sun rose on dwelling, or on mountain, she was on foot, and had breakfast waiting for him. After he had risen and had his breakfast, she took a letter from her bosom, and handed it to him, saying:

'Keep this carefully until you reach the great castle of the eight turrets, and you shall give it to the woman you will see looking out of one of the roof windows of the castle.'

She gave a pull on her own little bottle of balsam, and on her cup of gold, and gave him a drink. She then put him on the head of the way, she wished a blessing to accompany him, and said she would remain in that place until he returned. He left the king's sword in the castle, and went away with the giant's sword.

The path on which he was walking was smoother than the one on which he had travelled the day before. He got on well, but the distance was so long that night began to come on him before he came in sight of the castle. About the greying of the evening, he saw the turrets of the castle far from him. He took courage and hardened his step, and though it was a long distance from him, he was not long in reaching it.

There were such high walls about the castle that he was not seeing how he could enter. But he lifted his head, saw a woman looking out at a window, and cried that he had a letter for her. She came down and opened a large iron door in the wall. After she had read the letter, she took him by the hand and brought him in.

She then looked at his sword, and asked him where he had found it. He told her that he got it from the woman of the castle where he was the previous night. There was another great sword standing against the wall, and she told him to see if he could lift it. With difficulty he put wind between it and the earth.

'No man that came before you did even that much,' said she. She gave him a drink out of her little bottle of balsam in a cup of gold, and then he could play the sword with both hands. She gave him the next drink, and he could play the giant's sword as nimbly as he could play the sword of the king.

'Now,' said she, 'you have no time to lose. The Great Giant of the Three Heads, Three Humps, and Three Knobs is staying here, and he will come home in a moment. Come with me and I will put you in a place where you can strike him.'

He went with her, and she set him standing on a bank, at the opening of the great iron door in the wall. Then she said:

'When the giant stoops to come under the lintel, be sure to strike him before he lifts his heads, and to send the three heads off him with the first stroke, for if he gets time to rise he will tear you asunder, as he did those that came before you.'

The giant came, and stooped under the lintel, but before he got through the door, Alastir struck him with all his might, and sent two of his heads off and half the third. The giant gave a leap, and one of his humps struck the lintel and was put out of place. Then he fell, and before he had time to rise and give the next leap, Alastir struck him the second time, and sent the other half of the third head off him. With a great, melancholy groan, the giant fell, a dead carcass on the ground.

The woman came out then, and said:

'Well done, Son of the King of Ireland. The blessing of my father and of my sister is with you, and you shall have my blessing now.'

Then he asked her who she was. She said she was the second daughter of the King of Ben Buie.

'You are going away to seek the soul of the Bare-stripping Hangman, so that you may save my youngest sister from him. If you come alive out of the next castle you reach, you need not be afraid of anything you may meet, for everything will succeed with you to the end of the journey. But you have no time to lose.'

Then she took him in, and served him with meat and drink, and put him to bed.

After he had had his breakfast next morning, she gave him a drink out of her little bottle of balsam in a cup of gold. She then put her hand in her bosom and took out a letter, and said to him:

'You shall give this to the woman whom you will see standing in the doorway of the castle to which you will come.'

He went away, having with him the great sword with which he had struck off the giant's heads. He got on smoothly until he arrived at the next castle, a great shapeless mass of a place, without window or turret. He saw the woman standing in the doorway, and cried that he had a letter for her. She seized the letter, and after she had read it, grasped him by the hand, and took him in.

She washed his hands and feet with a mixture of water and milk. She looked at his sword, and asked him where he had got that blade. He replied that he had found it in the castle in which he had stayed the previous night.

'Since you have gone thus far, your sword will serve you, and you shall not part with it as long as breath is in you, till you reach the end of your journey. The Great Fiery Dragon of the Seven Serpent Heads and the Venomous Sting is staying in this castle. She will come at sunrise tomorrow, and you must meet her outside, for if she gets inside, neither you nor I will be seen alive any more.' She then sent him to sleep in a warm comfortable bed.

She herself remained awake, and when the time came, she wakened him. She gave him his breakfast, and after breakfast, a drink out of her little bottle of balsam in her cup of gold. He then grasped his sword, and went outside.

Scarcely had he got over the threshold of the door when he felt the dragon coming. He made ready for her, and, as soon as she came, a hard contest began between them. He was defending himself from the seven heads, while she was wounding him with a deep sting at the end of her tail. They fought to the time of the going down of the sun. Then she said to him:

'Your bed is yours tonight, but meet me before sunrise tomorrow.'

The dragon went on her way, and he went inside the castle. The woman washed his sores, put balsam to every wound on his body and sent him to bed.

When he woke next morning, he felt that he was as whole and sound as ever he was. After he had had his breakfast and a drink of the balsam, he took his sword and went to meet the dragon. They fought from morning to evening, he defending himself from the seven heads, and she wounding him with the sting in her tail. At the going down of the sun, they stopped. She went her way, and he returned to the castle.

The woman served him this night as she did on the night before. When he woke on the third morning, he was as whole and sound as he ever was. After he had had his breakfast and a drink of the balsam, he grasped his sword, and went to meet the dragon.

On this morning he heard her coming with terrible screaming. But he thought that since he had withstood her the two days before, he would try her again this day.

The monster came and they went at each other. She was shooting stings out of all seven mouths at him, and he was defending himself with his sword. About the greying of the evening, he was growing weak, but, if he was, he understood that she also was losing her strength. This gave him courage, and he boldly closed up with her. At the going down of the sun she gave up, and stretched herself on the ground.

'Now you have vanquished me,' said she, 'but the advantage was with you. At night you were warm and comfortable at the fireside of my castle. But if I had had half an hour's warmth of that fire, you would have returned no more than those who came before you.'

Alastir now drew his sword, and with seven strokes, struck the seven heads off the dragon. But at the seventh stroke, she gave her tail a flip, and struck him in the side. He fell as if he were dead, and neither saw nor felt anything further until he awoke about midnight.

The woman was washing and healing his wounds. When she had done that, she put him to bed. The next morning, she went to him and asked him how he was. He answered that he felt strong and sound.

'That is good,' said she, 'for the greater part of your trials is now over and past.'

When he arose and had had his breakfast, she said to him:

'You have killed the Great Giant of the Two Heads in the castle at the end of the rocky path of Ben Buie, and you have killed the Great Giant of the Three Heads, Three Humps, and Three Knobs in the castle of the eight turrets, and you have killed the Fiery Dragon of the Seven Serpent-Heads and of the Venomous Sting in this gloomy castle. Only one of those who came before you, on the journey on which you are going, got thus far. He came over the rocky path of Ben Buie, and over the path of the Red Lake and nearly drowned. He got through the broken ground, past the first two castles, but he could not go past this castle without going through it. The Fiery Dragon met him at the door, and killed him. But you have come on the right path, and success was with you thus far. I will not keep you longer, for you have many things to do. You have but a day and a year for killing the Bare-stripping Hangman, and if you have not finished your task before then, he will take away my fourth sister as he took us. I will go with you, and put you on the head of the way. You shall neither stop nor rest until you reach the Great Barn of the Seven Stoops of the Seven Bends and of the Seven Couples. You shall see, under the barn on the Yellow Knoll of the Sun, a really old man cutting divots with a turf spade. You shall tell him the business you are on, and he will tell you what you must say and do after that. You shall take advice from everyone that will give it to you, faithfully. The blessing of the king is with you, the blessing of the sorceress is with you, and the blessing of Sunbeam my sister is with you, the blessing of Light-of-Shade my sister is with you, and you have my blessing. Be going on your journey, and everything will be right when you return.

Then he went away, and travelled onwards long and full long. When he began to grow weary, he remembered his achievements and his victory. This lightened his mind, and he went on his way reassured. While in the midst of his thoughts, he came to the head of a very pretty glen. He said to himself: 'It must be that I am not far from the Great Barn of the Seven Couples.' As soon as he let the words out of his mouth, he saw the barn only a little way before him, and the prettiest knoll he had ever seen, shining like gold in the sun, at the bottom of the glen, and the very man of the oldest appearance he had ever seen, cutting divots with a turf-spade on one side of the knoll.

He took his way to where the man was, and gave him the salutation of the day. The man answered him briskly and vigorously, much younger in his talk than in his appearance, and he asked Alastir where he came from.

'I came from the castle of the King of Lochlann, through the rocky path of Ben Buie, through the castle at the end of the path, where I killed the Great Giant of the Two Heads, through the Great Castle of the Eight Turrets, where I killed the Great Giant of the Three Heads, Three Humps, and Three Knobs, through the Gloomy Castle of the Fiery Dragon of the Seven Serpent Heads and of the Venomous Sting, and from there as far as here, to see if you would tell me where I can find the soul of the Bare-stripping Hangman.'

The Old Man looked him in the face, and said:

'Let me see your sword, Hero.'

Alastir drew his sword out of the scabbard, and handed it to him. The Old Man took the sword between his two fingers, and put it between him and the light. Then he handed it back, and said:

'Let me see you flourishing the sword, Hero.'

Alastir seized the sword, and gave a back sweep and a front sweep with it, as lightly as though it were a deer-knife in his fist. The Old Man bounded towards him, took him by the hand, and said:

'Hero, you have come the way you said. I cannot tell you where the soul of the Bare-stripping Hangman is now, for it fled from the place where it was four days ago. But it may be that my father will tell you.'

'Oh, is your father alive, and may I see him?'

'Oh, he is alive, and you can see him. He is over there, casting the divot.'

Alastir went over to the man and asked him if he could tell where the soul of the Bare-stripping Hangman was hidden. The man answered:

'I cannot, for it fled from this place where it was two days ago. But it may be that my father will tell you.'

'Oov, oov, sir, can I see your father, or is he able to speak to me, for he must be very old?'

'Oh, you can see him, and he can speak to you. There he is, laying the divot.'

Alastir went over to the man laying the divot, and asked him if he could tell him where the soul of the Bare-stripping Hangman was hidden. He answered:

'I cannot, for it fled the place where it was yesterday. But go to my father and he will tell you where you can find it.'

'What sort of man is your father? Can I see him, and can he speak to me?'

'You shall see him and he will speak to you, and tell you what you have to do.'

'But where shall I find him?'

'He is in that little clump of moss behind the crooked stick. But I myself must go with you. When you are speaking to him, you must take great care not to go within hand's length of him, for if he gets hold of a bit of your body, he will bruise you like a grain of barley under a quern-stone. Before you leave him he will ask to hold your hand. If you give it to him, he will bruise it until it will be as small as a crumb of black pudding. But here is a wedge of oak. You shall give it to him when he asks for your hand.'

The man handed Alastir a stout piece of the head of a caber, then they went into the house where the Old Man was. The divot-layer took down an armful of moss from behind the crooked stick and laid it on the hearthstone. He took his father out of the little clump of moss, and placed him on the flagstone.

'What is your need of me now, son?' said the father. 'It is a long time since you came to see me.' The son answered:

'There is a Young Champion here who is seeking to know where the soul of the Bare-stripping Hangman is hidden.'

'Son of King Cormac of Ireland, which way have you come thus far?' inquired the Man of the Little Clump of Moss.

Alastir told him every step he had taken from the day he left his father's house, and everything that had happened to him up to that day.

'Truthfully you have told me everything, Son of the King of Ireland. Your father burned the hen-wife, and your mother is under sorrow for you. Her prayer and her blessing follow you, the blessing of the young King of Riddles follows you, the blessing of the young Queen of Riddles follows you, the blessing of the King of Lochlann follows you, the blessing and the victory of the sorceress follow you, and my blessing will follow you. You were faithful to your brother, and every man and beast that shall meet you, will be faithful to you. And, brave Hero, give me a shake of your hand, and I will tell you where you shall find the soul of the Bare-stripping Hangman.'

The Old Man stretched out his hand, and Alastir stretched out the wedge of oak to him. He seized the wedge, gave it a bruising and a shaking and made pulp of it. When he let it go, he said:

'Son of the King of Ireland, hard is your hand, and it would need to be thus far. You are tired, thirsty and hungry. You are worthy of meat and drink, and you shall get both. After your supper you shall go to bed, and at sunrise tomorrow you will be ready for the journey. Keep going forward without turning, without stopping, without looking behind you, till you reach the thick-foliaged grove of trees. You will see there the Swift-footed Hind of the Cliffs, near which neither dog nor man ever got. Catch her, open her, and find a salmon in her stomach. Open the salmon, and in its belly you will find the Green Duck of the Smooth Feathers. In the belly of the duck, you will find an egg, and you must catch the egg and break it before it touches the ground. For if it ever touches the ground, you will never, after that, see king or men. But though your hand is hard it will not break the egg without my help.'

And he handed a jar to Alastir, and said: 'There is ointment for you. As soon as you reach the thick-foliaged grove of the trees, you must put the ointment on your hands, rub it over every bit of your skin that happens to be naked, or which you may think blood of hind, scale of salmon, feather of duck or eggshell will touch. Accept hospitality from every man or beast that offers it to you, without asking. And you yourself will know what to do after that. Catch this ointment now, and take it with you, and be ready for the journey as I told you.'

Alastir knew it was not safe to stretch out his hand for the little jar. So he stretched out his sword, and said:

'Put the little jar on the point of my finger.'

The Old Man did that, and grasped the sword in his hand, and squeezed it till it was as round as a stick. Then he said:

'You will accomplish your task. Return the way you came! Take the King of Lochlann's daughters out of the castles in which they are imprisoned, and take them with you! Then take them to the castle of Ben Breck, where you will find the great giant stretched dead on the floor! Cut off his head and feet, as far as the knees, and take them with you to the castle of the King of Lochlann! When you arrive at the castle, light a great fire, and when it is in the heat of its burning, you will throw the parts of the giant on top of the fire! As soon as they singe in the flame, they will change into as handsome a young man as you ever saw. He is the brother of the King of Lochlann, who was stolen from his mother, when he was a child, by the Fiery Dragon. She kept him under spells, doing every mischief she could to the king, until your arrival. Now, do as I tell you, and my blessing will accompany you.'

The next day Alastir went on his journey. He kept going forward far long and full long. The evening was coming on him, the calm still clouds of day were departing, and the gloomy dark clouds of night were approaching, the little nestling, folding, yellow-tipped birds were going to rest at the roots of the bushes, in the tops of the tree tufts, and in the snuggest, sheltered little holms they could find for themselves. At last Alastir was growing tired, and weak with hunger. He gave a look before him, and whom did he see but the Dog of the Great Headland. When they met each other, the kind dog gave him a salutation and hearty welcome, and asked where he was going. Alastir told him that he was seeking the soul of the Bare-stripping Hangman. The dog said:

'The night is coming, and you are tired, come with me and I will give you the best hospitality I can tonight.'

They reached the dog's lair, and it was a dry, comfortable place with abundance of fire, venison of deer, hinds and roes. He got enough to eat and a warm bed, with skins of stags under him, and the skins of hinds and roes over him.

Next morning he got his breakfast, which was the same as his supper. When he was going away, the kind dog said to him:

'Any time you need a strong tooth that will not yield its hold, or a fast strong foot that will travel on the rocky top of mountain, or run on the floor of the glen, to do you service, think of me, and I will be at your side.'

He gave the kind dog thanks, and departed on his journey. He kept going forward far long and full long, until he was growing tired and evening was coming on. He gave a look before him, and whom did he see coming to meet him but the Brown Otter of the Stream of Guidance.

When they met, the otter gave him a cheery salutation and asked him where he was going. Alastir told him.

'The night is coming and you are very wearied,' said the otter. 'Come with me and you shall get the best hospitality I can give.'

Alastir went with the otter to his cairn. There was a warm, comfortable place, with abundance of fire, and enough of salmon and grilse. He had a good supper, and as easy a bed as he had slept on, of the smooth bent of the freshwater lakes.

Next morning his breakfast was of the same sort he had had for his supper the night before. When he was going away, the otter said:

'Any time a strong tail to swim under water, or stem a current or rapid, can be of service to you, think of me, and I will be at your side.' Alastir thanked the kindly otter, and departed.

He travelled on, far long and full long, until he was growing tired and night was coming. He looked about him, and whom did he see perched on a stone but the Great Falcon of the Rock of Cliffs. When they met, the falcon asked him where he was going, and Alastir told him.

'The night is coming and you are tired and hungry,' said the falcon. 'You had better stay with me tonight and I will give you the best hospitality I can.'

So he went with the falcon to his sheltered cliff. It was a dry, comfortable place, where he got an abundance of the flesh of every kind of birds, and a bed of feathers. Next morning, after he had had his breakfast, the falcon said to him:

'Any time a strong, supple wing, that can travel through air and over mountain, can be of service to you, think of me and I will be at your side.'

Alastir did not go far when he saw the thick-foliaged grove of trees. He reached the grove, but was barely in it when the Swift-footed Hind of the Cliffs sprang out and ran up the mountain. He chased her, but the faster he went the farther she was from him. When he had exhausted himself pursuing her, he thought of the dog, and said: 'Would not the Dog of the Great Headland be useful here now?' No sooner had the words left his mouth than the dog was at his side. He told the dog that he was exhausted following the hind, and that he was farther from her than he had been when he began to pursue her.

The dog went after her, and he went after the dog, till they reached the little Green Lake. Then the dog caught the hind, and left her at Alastir's feet. It was then that Alastir remembered the ointment. He poured it quickly on his hands, and rubbed it on every bit of his skin that might come in contact with the hind's blood. He then tackled the hind, and opened her. But if he did so, it was not without a fight, for her hoofs were so sharp and her feet so strong, that if it had not been for the ointment, she would have torn him asunder. When he opened the hind's stomach, the salmon leaped out of it into the little Green Lake.

He chased the salmon round the lake, but when he was at one bank the salmon would be at the other. At last he remembered the Brown Otter of the Stream of Guidance, and at once the otter was beside him. He told the otter that the salmon was in the little lake, and that he could not get hold of it. The otter sprang out quickly into the water, and in a short time came back with the salmon, to lay it at Alastir's feet. Alastir seized the salmon, but as soon as he made a hole in its belly, the Duck of the Smooth Feathers and Green Back, sprang out, flew to the other side of the little Green Lake, and lay down there. He went after her; but when he had nearly reached her, she rose and flew back to the side he had left. When he saw that he could not catch her, he thought of the Great Falcon of the Rock of the Cliffs, and at once the falcon was at his side. He told him how the duck had got away, and that he could not catch her. The falcon sprang quickly after the duck, and in an instant came with her and left her at Alastir's feet.

Alastir remembered that if the egg should touch the ground, all would be lost. He therefore opened the duck very cautiously, and as soon as he saw the egg, he seized it quickly in his hand, but the egg gave a bounce out of his fist, and shot the three heights of a man into the air. But before it struck the earth, Alastir caught it, squeezed it between his two hands and two knees, and crushed it into fragments.

Alastir had now finished everything he had to do. He therefore returned home the way he came. He found the path as smooth and safe as it had formerly been full of obstacles and dangers. In a short time he reached the gloomy castle of the Fiery Serpent. The woman met him at the door, and cried:

'Darling of all men of the world! You have conquered, and you shall receive your reward.'

She went with him, and in a short time they reached the great castle of the eight turrets. Light-of-Shade met them at the door, and went with them. Then they reached the great castle at the end of the rocky path, and found Sunbeam waiting for them. She went with them, and they reached the castle of the great giant of Ben Breck, and found him stretched dead on the ground. Alastir seized his own great sword and took the head, and the feet as far as the knees, off the great giant. Then he tied them up and took them with him.

'Now,' said Sunbeam, 'tonight is the night when the great giant was to come for my youngest sister, and my father is in heavy sorrow, because he is sure that you have been killed, when you did not return. He has all his men assembled to meet the giant when he comes. But his sorrow will be turned to cheerfulness, and his sadness to laughter. When he comes to meet us, you must tell him all that has happened to you since the day you departed to this very night.'

When they drew near to the castle, they saw a great crowd of men awaiting the coming of the giant. The king and all those in the castle were sad and sorrowful for the maiden that was to be taken from them. But in the midst of their grief, the king looked out and saw Alastir coming with three women in his company, and the head, legs and feet of the giant slung over his shoulder. He hastened to meet them, seized Alastir in his arms and kissed him.

'Darling of all men of the world! I knew victory would be with you, and I will be as good as my promise to you. But since you have brought home all my daughters, you shall have your choice of them, from the oldest one to the youngest.'

'Well,' said Alastir, 'she whom I went to save from the Bare-stripping Hangman is my choice.'

When each of the others heard this, she was sorry he did not choose herself. But since he had won the victory, and done so much for them, they all agreed that he should have the one he chose.

The king asked Alastir what he was going to do with the head and feet of the giant.

'Before I eat food or take a drink, you shall see that,' said Alastir.

He then got fuel, and made a large fire, and when the fire was in the heat of its burning, he threw the head and the feet into the flames. As soon as the hair of the head was singed and the skin of the feet burned, the very handsomest young man they had ever seen sprang out of the fire.

'Oh, the son of my father and mother, who was stolen in his childhood!' cried the king, hastening over and embracing the young man in his arms.

When they had saluted each other, they all went into the castle.

The king resolved that Alastir and his daughter should be married that very night. But when Alastir heard this, he said:

'King of Lochlann, your offer is good enough. But I will not marry your daughter, nor will I accept a bit of your kingdom until you send for the young King of Riddles and the young Queen of Riddles to come to the wedding.'

The king was full of anxiety, for he did not know in which direction he should send for them. Then he remembered the sorceress. He went to her and told her about Alastir's request.

'Get everything else ready,' said the sorceress, 'and I will have the King of Riddles and his queen here before sunrise tomorrow.'

And what she said proved true. The first look the king gave next morning in the direction of the sea, he saw two coracles coming to the shore. Out of one, came Cormac, the King of Riddles and his queen, and out of the other came the sorceress.

Alastir hastened to meet them, and what an affectionate welcome they gave each other! The king came to meet them with most cordial salutations. They all went to the castle, and the marriage was consummated. After the wedding was over, they made a great feast that lasted a year and a day. At the end of that time, Cormac and his queen returned to their own place, and Alastir and his wife went with them.

Cormac remained in the castle of the King of Riddles, but Alastir returned to his father's place. When his mother saw him she gave him a great welcome, and his father greatly rejoiced when he heard that his eldest son, Cormac, was now the young King of Riddles.

The King of Ireland now made another feast for Alastir and his bride and for all that were about him.

And I got nothing but butter on a live coal, porridge in a basket, and paper shoes. They sent me for water from the stream, and the paper shoes came to an END.

MAGHACH COLGAR

FINN MacCoul was in Ireland, and the King of Lochlann in Lochlann. The King of Lochlann sent his son, Maghach Colgar, to Finn to be educated. The King of Sealg sent his son, Innsridh MacRigh nan Sealg. The two boys stayed in Ireland with Finn, who taught them all he knew.

One day, there came a message from the king in Lochlann that he was dying and that his son, Maghach Colgar, must return home to prepare for his own crowning in Lochlann. After Maghach had gone, the chase failed, and the Fianna did not know what they should do.

Maghach heard of this and wrote a letter to Finn, saying:

'I hear that the chase has failed you in Ireland. I have broughs at sea and on shore, with provisions for a year and a day in each of them, with meat and drink, finer than you can imagine. Come here, you and your men of the Fianna. Provisions for a year and a day are waiting for you.'

Finn received the letter, opened it, and read it to the Fianna.

'Here is a letter from my foster-son, Maghach Colgar, in Lochlann, saying that he has many broughs at sea and on shore, with provisions for a year and a day in each of them. It is best for us to go.'

'Who shall we leave to look after the darlings and little sons of Ireland?' said Fiachaire, the third son of Finn.

'I'll stay,' said Diarmid, son of Finn's sister.

'I'll stay,' said Innsridh MacRigh nan Sealg, Finn's foster-son.

'I'll stay,' said Cath Conan MacMhic Con.

'We will all stay,' said the four of them.

'You are going, my father,' said Fiachaire, 'and it is well, but how shall we get news of you in Lochlann?'

'I shall strike the Hammer of the Fianna in Lochlann, and you will hear it in Ireland, and know by the sound of the blow I strike how I fare.'

Finn and his men went to Lochlann, and Maghach Colgar, son of the king of Lochlann, met them.

'Hail to you, foster-father,' he said to Finn.

'Hail to yourself, foster-son!' said Finn.

'I heard that the chase had failed in Ireland. I could not let you die without meat. I've many broughs at sea and on shore, with food for a year and a day in every one of them. Which will you choose?'

'It is on shore that I used to be always, so I'll take the one on shore,' said Finn.

He and his men went to one of the broughs. There was a door for every day in the year on the house, and every kind of food and drink within it. They all sat down on the chairs, and every man of them took from the table a knife and fork. They sat there and looked about them. There in the round, half-ruined brough, was a hole in the roof, glazed over with ice. They tried to rise from their chairs, to examine the hole, but they could not move. They were stuck to their seats and the chairs were stuck to the earth. There seemed no way they could escape from the place.

At the time that Fiachaire and Innsridh were returning from the chase, they heard the hammer of the Fianna being struck in Lochlann.

'My foster-father has wandered the world, and now he is in mortal danger,' said Fiachaire.

So Fiachaire and Innsridh went from Ireland, and when they reached Lochlann, they found the brough where Finn and his men were trapped. They knocked at a door, and Finn said:

'Who is there?'

'Fiachaire and Innsridh,' they said. 'What is wrong? Who are the enemy?'

'There are two hundred score Greeks, with their great leader, Iall, at their head. They are coming to get my head for their great feast tomorrow. You must defeat them at the place of battle,' said Finn.

Fiachaire MacFinn and Innsridh MacRigh nan Sealg went to the place of battle, and there they met the great warrior, Iall, at the head of the host of Greeks.

'Where are you going?' said Fiachaire.

'We are seeking the head of Finn MacCoul, to be ours at our feast tomorrow!'

Then Fiachaire closed in on one side of the Greeks, and Innsridh, son of the king of the Sealg, closed in on the other side of the Greeks, till their gloves clashed one against the other, until the enemy was slain. Then they returned to the brough where Finn was. And Finn asked:

'Who fought the hideous fight on the place of battle today?'

'Fiachaire, your son, with Innsridh, son of the king of the Sealg. We fought the Greeks.'

'Remember that place of battle,' said Finn. 'Yonder are now three hundred score of Greeks, seeking my head tomorrow.'

Fiachaire and Innsridh went to the place of battle, and met a great host of Greeks coming towards them.

'Where are you going?' said Fiachaire.

'To seek the head of Finn MacCoul, to be ours at our great feast tomorrow,' said Iall, who led them.

Fiachaire closed in on the enemy at one end, and Innsridh closed in at the other end till their gloves met and clashed one against the other, and all the enemy was slain. Then they returned to the brough where Finn was, and knocked on a door.

'Who is there?' said Finn.

'Fiachaire, your son, and Innsridh, son of the king of Sealg. We fought a hideous fight with three hundred score Greeks today.'

'Remember the place of battle,' said Finn, 'for there are now four hundred score more Greeks, with a great warrior at their head seeking my head for their feast tomorrow.'

Fiachaire and Innsridh went to meet the Greeks and their great leader.

'Where are you going?' Fiachaire asked them.

'We go to seek the head of Finn MacCoul, to be ours at our feast tomorrow,' they said.

Then Fiachaire and Innsridh fought the Greeks till they had killed every man of them, and their two gloves clashed one against the other. Then they returned to the brough and the Fianna. They knocked on a door.

'Who is there?' asked Finn.

'Fiachaire, your son, and Innsridh, son of the king of Sealg, your foster-son, who fought the hideous fight with so many of the Greeks today.'

'Remember the place of battle,' said Finn, 'for there are twice as many men still there, with a good and heedless warrior at their head, coming to get my head, to be theirs at the great feast tomorrow.'

They reached the place of battle, but there was not a man to be seen.

'I will not believe there is no food left in the place of such large bands of men,' said Fiachaire.'I am very hungry. We ate but a morsel since we left Ireland. You go and look for food, Innsridh. See if you can get some scraps of bread, and cheese, and meat, and bring it to us. I will stay and keep watch, in case the enemy should come unexpectedly.'

'I don't know the place, and I don't know the way,' said Innsridh.'You go and I'll stay.'

Fiachaire went and Innsridh stayed, and the Greeks came, and he asked them where they were going.

'We're going to seek the head of Finn MacCoul,' they said.

Then Innsridh began to slay them till not one of them was left alive.

'What good does it do you, if you slay my men, and I kill you?' said their warrior chief. And he and Innsridh began to fight.

They made a crag of a bog and a bog of a crag, and the place where they would sink up to their knees, they sank up to their eyes. Then the great warrior chief gave a sweep with his sword, and cut off the head of Innsridh, son of the king of the Sealg. He met Fiachaire, and held up Innsridh's head for him to see.

'What have you there?' said Fiachaire.

'The head of Finn MacCoul.'

'Give it to me,' said Fiachaire.

The head was handed to him, and he kissed the mouth and the back of the head, then he swung the head back, then forward, and struck it down on to the great warrior's own head, and made one head of two, as the warrior fell dead in the ground before him. Then he returned to the brough where Finn was, and knocked on a door.

'Who is there?' asked Finn.

'Fiachaire, your son!'

'With whom did you share the hideous fight at the place of battle today?'

'With Innsridh, your foster-son, and with the Greeks.'

'How is my foster-son?'

'He is dead. He killed the Greeks, and their great warrior chief killed him. Then I killed the great warrior chief.'

'There is still Maghach Colgar, son of the king of Lochlann, and the great band of Greeks with him.'

So Fiachaire went to the place of battle, and Maghach Colgar called to him:

'Is that you, Fiachaire MacFinn?'

'It is.'

'Bring me your father's head, and I will give you free passage throughout Ireland.'

'My father gave you schooling and teaching, and all the Drach (magic) he knew. Yet you would now take the head off him. You shall not get my father's head, until you have mine first!'

'You have killed my people,' said Maghach, 'now I shall kill you.'

And they began to attack each other. They made a crag of a bog, and a bog of a crag, and the place where they would sink to their knees, they sank up to their eyes. One time Maghach's spear struck Fiachaire, he gave a roar. This roar was heard in Ireland, and it was heard by Diarmid as he returned from the hunt.

'Fiachaire has travelled the universe and the world,' said Diarmid, 'and the spear of Maghach has struck him!'

'Cast your spear and hit the foe,' said Conan, who was with Diarmid.

'If I cast my spear I may kill my friend.'

'If it were a yellow-haired woman, well would you aim at her.'

'Wailing be on you! Urge me no longer!'

And he shook the spear under the shield.

'Who would come on me from behind in the evening?' said Maghach in Lochlann, 'and not come on me from the front in the morning?'

'Tis I who would come on you,' said Diarmid in Ireland, 'early or late, and at noon!'

'What good is that to you,' said Maghach, 'for I will take off the head of Fiachaire before you can reach Lochlann.'

'If you take his head off him,' said Diarmid, 'I shall take off your head when I reach you.'

Before Diarmid reached Lochlann, Maghach took the head off Fiachaire. So Diarmid took off Maghach's head and took it to Finn, who was still in the brough and who said:

'Who is there?'

'It is Diarmid, your sister's son, who fought a hideous fight with Maghach, son of the king of Lochlann, who had killed Fiachaire, who had killed all the Greeks. I killed Maghach, and here is his head.'

'Though Maghach killed Fiachaire, why did you kill Maghach, and not let him keep his life? But remember the battle-field, and the Greeks who are still there to be fought.'

'Cath Conan, would you rather come with me or stay here?' said Diarmid.

'I'd rather go with you,' said Cath Conan.

They went and when they reached the place of battle, no man came to meet them. So they sat down and Cath Conan fell asleep, waiting for the Greeks to come. But it was not long before they came, bursting through the doors of the brough. There was a door for every day in the year on every brough, so they burst forth all together about the head of Diarmid. And Diarmid fought them, and the sound of the swords and the men woke Cath Conan, who began thrusting his sword at Diarmid's leg.

Diarmid felt something tickling his leg and looked down and saw Cath Conan poking with his sword.

'Wailing be on you, Cath Conan!' he said. 'Leave me in peace and hit the foe. You'd be better to thrust your sword into an old boot than cram it into my leg!'

Together they killed every man at the place of battle. Then they thought of Finn and all those in the brough, who were without food, and they filled their napkins and pouches with food left by the enemy they had slain, and returned to the brough. They knocked and Finn called:

'Who is there?'

'Diarmid, your sister's son and Cath Conan.'

'And the Greeks?'

'Every man of them is dead.'

'Oh, come and bring a deliverance of food,' said Finn.

'Though I have the food, how can I get it to you all in there, stuck as you are to your chairs?'

Indeed, he had no way of giving them the food, except through the hole above them in the brough. So he let the food down to them.

'How can we free you from there?' said Diarmid.

'There is a solution, but it's hard to get,' said Finn, 'and it's not every man that could get it, in fact it is not to be got at all.'

'Tell me what it is, and I will get it,' said Diarmid.

'I know that you would subdue the world to get it. Perhaps I should not tell you, yet it is the only thing that will release us.'

'Tell me all the same, so that I can get it.'

'The three daughters of King Gil, live in a castle in the middle of a ford, without any servant or any living person but themselves. Now, you must get them and wring every drop of blood from them till they are as white as linen. And their blood must be gathered into cups.'

Diarmid went, and as he went he wore holes in his shoes, and the soles of his feet were black. He went on and on till the white clouds of day were going and the black clouds of night coming, and still he had found no place to rest in. He reached the ford, put the small end of his spear under his chest, and cut a leap. He was in the castle that night. Next day, he took the three daughters of King Gil, two of them over one shoulder and one over the other shoulder. He put the small end of his spear under his chest, and at the first leap he was on the shore.

He took the three girls to the brough, and he wrung every drop of blood that was in each of them, from the tips of their fingers and toes, into cups, till they were as white as linen. Then he spread a black cloth over the three girls, took the cups of blood to the hole in the brough, until they were all freed except one they called Conan. As Diarmid reached Conan, the blood was finished – there was not enough to free Conan, who cried:

'Are you going to leave me like this, Diarmid?'

'Wailing be on you, Conan, the blood is finished!'

'If I were a fine yellow-haired woman, you'd have freed me!'

'I will free you, if only your skin sticks to your flesh.'

And Diarmid caught Conan by the hand and pulled him loose, but his skin stuck to the seat and the soles of his feet to the earth. Now that they were all free, they remembered the three daughters of King Gil, and they said:

'It would be well now if the children of the good king were alive, instead they should be buried under the earth.'

But when they went to where the maidens were, they found them alive, laughing and fondling each other. So Diarmid took two on one shoulder and the other one on his other shoulder, and carried them back to their castle where he had found them.

Then he and the Fianna went home to Ireland.

The Smith's Rock in the Isle of Skye

THERE was a report that the Fian were asleep on a rock on the Isle of Skye, and if anyone would dare to enter the cave in the rock, and blow the Wooden Crier, which was beside Finn, three times, the Fian would rise alive and well.

A Smith, who lived on the island, heard this report, and resolved to go and try to enter the cave. He reached the cave, but found the entrance barred by a locked door. He made a detailed note of the keyhole, then returned to his smithy and made a key to fit the hole.

The Smith went back to the rock. As soon as he turned the key he had made, in the lock, the door opened. He saw a great wide space before him, and on the floor lay a band of enormous men. They seemed to be dead, and one man, bigger than the rest, lay in their midst, with a huge hollow baton of wood beside him. The Smith saw that this was Finn and his Wooden Crier. It was so large, he was sure he would not be able to lift it, much less blow it.

He stood for a time looking at the enormous whistle. At last, he told himself that, as he had come so far, he would at least try. Carefully, he took hold of the Wooden Crier with both hands. With great difficulty, he managed to raise it, end up, to his mouth. He blew it with all his might. So loud was the sound it made, that the Smith thought the rock, and all that were in it, would come down on top of him.

The enormous men who lay on the floor, shook from the tops of their heads to the soles of their feet. The Smith gave another blast on the Wooden Crier, and with a spring, they turned on their elbows. Their fingers were like prongs of

wooden graips, and their arms like bog oak beams. Their size and their terrible appearance put the Smith in such fear, that he threw the Wooden Crier from him, and ran out of the cave. The men inside were crying after him:

> 'Worse have you left us than you found us!
> Worse have you left us than you found us!
> Worse have you left us than you found us!'

The Smith did not look back till he got outside the cave, and had slammed the door. He turned the key in the lock, drew it from the keyhole, and threw it into the loch which was near the rock. This loch is still called the Loch of the Smith's Rock, or Lochan Chreag a'Ghobha.

Notes on the Stories

The Naming of Finn'

From *Waifs and Strays of Celtic Tradition*, Vol. IV.

This story of Finn, as collected by J.G. Campbell, is made up from six versions – the essence of which is similar, with certain constant details repeated in all of them. The oldest version, according to Campbell, is *The Boyish Exploits of Finn*, translated from a fifteenth-century manuscript by O'Donovan, but that is part of the vast Irish work on Finn that I have not used at all.

The *tooth of knowledge* occurs in many stories, but none explain its origin. Perhaps the finger of Finn has the 'knowledge' because it touched the burnt salmon, a magical as well as royal fish in Celtic mythology.

How Finn Kept the Children of the Big Hero of the Ship

From *Waifs and Strays of Celtic Tradition*, Vol. II.

There are other versions of this tale and one is called *How Finn Found Bran* (Vol. IV, p.204) but they are fragmentary by comparison.

Pups are mentioned in other tales, e.g. *The Daughter of the King Under-The-Waves*, and it demonstrates how important hounds were from very early times to the hunter.

The theft of newly born children at midnight occurs in many folk tales. It must be a natural fear among primitive people even if it was not a reality.

Those who have climbed the hills of Scotland, Wales and Ireland, will understand the term *at the back of the wind* – the sheltered side of a knoll on the hill, which allows the wind to blow over one's head.

Travelling and straying in the *bespelling run* seems to have been an old curse – to have to travel forever, like the *Wandering Jew*. In this story, it is merely a threat.

THE HERDING OF CRUACHAN

From *Waifs and Strays of Celtic Tradition*, Vol. II.
The Cruachan of the story is not the mountain in Argyllshire, as some think. It was the Roscommon Cruachan near Belanagare, Ireland, the ancient palace of the kings of Connaught.

The Life Centre of the giant (sometimes called the life-index), hidden in an egg, occurs in the folk tales of many countries, including Russia. To reach it and destroy it always requires the aid of animals and birds, and a fish. Always it must be destroyed at one blow.

THE FIANN

From *Popular Tales of the West Highlands*, Vol. II.
Danan, the people of Scandinavia, Northerners. *Ord Fianna*, Finn's magical hammer, which would summon his friends from the four quarters of the earth to help him in a moment of mortal danger. Sometimes linked with the *Wooden Crier*, a whistle with the same powers.

FINN'S JOURNEY TO LOCHLANN

From *Waifs and Strays of Celtic Tradition*, Vol. III.

HOW FINN WENT TO THE COUNTRY OF THE BIG MEN

From *Waifs and Strays of Celtic Tradition*, Vol. III.
Here again are the helpful companions or servants – otherwise the story is different to most of the others.

FINN AND HIS MEN

From *Waifs and Strays of Celtic Tradition*, Vol. IV.
There is no account of the dog-fight except one verse in 'The Fight between Bran and the Black Dog'.

A *Leash* of dogs is fifty dogs.

THE FIGHT BETWEEN BRAN AND THE BLACK DOG

From *Waifs and Strays of Celtic Tradition*, Vol. IV.

THE LAD OF THE SKIN COVERINGS

From *Waifs and Strays of Celtic Tradition*, Vol. III.

There are many versions of this story. The other well-known one is *The Bent Grey Lad*, collected and translated by Mac Innes, in Vol. II of this series. The skin coverings were clothes made of sheep or goat skins. All these stories about the Lad have similar themes.

The Cup, the four-sided Cup of the Fianna, called a cup of victory, also a cup of healing, was coveted by the Norsemen, who made frequent attempts to get hold of it.

The *Avasks* are thought to be symbolic of the clouds of darkness, which threaten to extinguish the sun and the twilight. In this strange story, Finn of the Yellow Hair is supposed to be the sun, and the Yellow-haired Lad, the dawn, overcast with fleecy clouds, or this is what the Rev. J. Macdougall suggests. Certainly the story is full of symbols, and Macdougall suggests it is 'a mythological one from beginning to end'.

THE DAY OF THE BATTLE OF THE SHEAVES IN THE HOLLOW OF TIREE

From *Waifs and Strays of Celtic Tradition*, Vol. IV.

FINN'S RANSOM

From *Waifs and Strays of Celtic Tradition*, Vol. IV.

The Gaelic word 'eirig' has been translated by J. G. Campbell as 'ransom' – I am sure it could be more exact.

The little man, the Swaddler, is in Gaelic the *Lapanach*, which may be the origin of the name *Laplander*. The Lapps are very short, muscular and strong – not unlike the impression one gets of the Swaddler.

THE DAUGHTER OF THE KING UNDER THE WAVES

From *Popular Tales of the West Highlands*, Vol. III.

The idea of a land under the sea is widely spread in the mythology of many peoples. It seems to have been visited without any difficulty. *The little russet man* who helps Diarmid across the river reminds one of Charon, the ferryman, who has to be paid. The West Highlands and Islands have a great many ferries, and of course, fords.

Leoån Creeåch, Son of the King of Ireland, and Kaytav, Son of the King of Colla

From *Waifs and Strays of Celtic Tradition*, Vol. II.

The apple-throwing incident occurs in several Celtic tales. Slaying by casting an apple is found in the older Irish Celtic tales; Cuchullain slays Con Mac Dalath in this way.

A King of Scotland

From *Waifs and Strays of Celtic Tradition*, Vol. II.

In the original, this is called *A King of Albainn*, but *A King of Scotland* seems a more direct English translation.

Murdoch Mac Brian is what the Big Lad calls himself, and in the early version of the story he probably was this famous prince, of ancient Ireland.

It is interesting that the Hero is condemned for grieving for his dead father, which will bring him bad luck – a belief found in Norse stories.

Heads on spikes: the Celts were head hunters in earliest times – seen in the pillars of stone, with heads carved on them, or niches for skulls. The Celts were known for their veneration of the human head and their practice of taking the heads of their slain enemies and preserving them as trophies.

How Finn Was in the House of the Yellow Field

From *Waifs and Strays of Celtic Tradition*, Vol. III.

The House of the Yellow Field was so called after the battlefield on the banks of the Shannon. It was also called the *Rowan-tree Dwelling*, because its walls were made from rows of wooden posts driven into the ground, and interwoven with wattles of the rowan tree. It was built by the three kings of Insh Tilly, wicked magicians or Druids, who were in alliance with Miodhach. The house was enchanted, and so formed a trap into which Finn and his men were taken.

Caoilte, who appears in several stories, had the swiftest feet in the Fianna. *'When at full speed his shoulders rose so high, he looked as though he had three heads, and then he could outstrip the swift March wind!'*

Cuchulin, the third in the race to *'Lochlan'* (which in this case meant the banks of the river Shannon), was the Hero of Ulster, as Finn was the Hero of Leinster.

Kyle Rhea

From *Popular Tales of the West Highlands*, Vol. III
This may be the modern strait, Kyle-Rhea, between the Isle of Skye and the mainland, but this is also said to get its name as Kyle-Righ or King's Strait, so named from a visit or expedition of King Hâkon of Norway in 1263. The strait in the story seems to be nearer to Ardnamurchan. Dates and places are seldom exact in these tales however.

Finn's Questions

From *Popular Tales of the West Highlands*, Vol. III.

Diarmid and Gráinne

From *Popular Tales of the West Highlands*, Vol. III
The scene of this story is supposed to be set on the ridge between Oban and Loch Awe. Lon Mac Liobhain is said to be the dark smith of Droutheim, Isle of Mull.

The Fair Gruagach, Son of the King of Ireland

From *Popular Tales of the West Highlands*, Vol. II.
Macalpine's *Gaelic/English Dictionary* says the *Gruagach* means 'a damsel, household goddess, having beautiful long hair'. The 'long hair' gives the clue to the meaning in this story, for at the time of the Fian, long hair was only worn by special people – wizards, druids, or gods in disguise. Also fair hair was associated with the rays of the sun. Finn was said to have fair hair, and so, I suppose, did many of their enemies, the Scandinavians or Lochlanners, as they were then called.

The *Lady with the Green Kirtle* and the *carlin*, or old hag, were both able to perform magical feats which the Fian could not equal, and seem to have the qualities of the *Fates*.

The transformation of a man into animal, bird or fish is also common to the Norse and Russians. In the Highlands, it is still called 'shape-shifting'. Again the wife of the *Tree Lion* in her magic castle, and the leaping man in disguise, who carries the wooer, appear in the tales of Norse and Northern European mythology. The *Tree Lion*, according to J.F. Campbell, is a griffin.

The *Spell Run* or spell put on the Gruagach by the Lady of the Green Mantle is given in full. Although it sounds like nonsense, it is, after all, an incantation, which I am sure is much more impressive in Gaelic.

CONAL

From *Popular Tales of the West Highlands*, Vol. II.

J.F. Campbell writes:' The story loses part of its merit when translated into English. The Gaelic describes the battles with a succession of words which convey, by their sound and rhythm alone, the idea of the fight which they describe... By the constant repetition of the sounds: dejee, gash, gach etc., suggest the singing, cracking, clashing and hacking of blades, and the rhythm, which varies continually, and must be heard to be understood, does the same.' I can well imagine that this is correct, and it can be said also of the runs and bespelling incantations. Gaelic is a wonderfully expressive language. Listening to a modern Gaelic poet like Sorley Maclean, one can experience the meaning even if one cannot understand it literally. It is also one of the few ancient languages that has survived to this day, when it is still spoken as the mother tongue of several thousand people, and is taught in some schools (indeed, in a few, the children are taught all subjects in their mother tongue, Gaelic). Best of all there are still modern and young poets composing their poetry in that language.

THE TALE OF YOUNG MANUS, SON OF THE KING OF LOCHLANN

From *Waifs and Strays of Celtic Tradition*, Vol. II.

The sea-faring run, which occurs in a number of the stories, may sound fanciful, but anyone who has sailed around the Hebrides will confirm the fantastic colours of the sea at sunrise and sunset. Also in an account made by the young men and their captain, Tim Severin, who recently sailed their leather boat from Ireland to Nova Scotia, to celebrate St Brendan's crossing of the Atlantic, there are descriptions that remind us of the sea-faring runs.

There are many tales about Manus. It is not clear who he really was but he is always described as the son of the King of Lochlann, so he was probably a Scandinavian – certainly from the north-east.

THE SON OF THE KING OF IRELAND

From *Waifs and Strays of Celtic Tradition*, Vol. II.

This tale has many similes, especially in northern folk tradition. The black feathers of the raven and the red blood conjure up an idea of beauty throughout. The three tasks are also familiar. More surprising are the similarities of the obstacles thrown in the path of the pursuing parent – small objects transformed into massive barriers, like a range of mountains, a forest etc., which we recognise from the folk tales of Lowland Scotland, Scandinavia and Russia, but these incidents also occur in some ancient tales of China and India. Have they travelled or are they natural solutions to wishful thinking of the problems of people everywhere? Folk tales certainly seem to highlight the fundamental and basic factors we share in common, as well as our superficial and national differences.

Farafohuinn seems to be a made up name – probably it just means 'faraway'.

THE KING OF RIDDLES AND THE BARE-STRIPPING HANGMAN

From *Waifs and Strays of Celtic Tradition*, Vol. III.

The hen-wife is represented here in her usual role of mischief-maker. Her demands sound ridiculous, but they were granted because greed will always grant such requests. A *chalder* is equal to sixteen bolls, or sacks.

Although he is the son of the wicked second queen, Alastir is certainly the hero of this story from beginning to end. He also has 'virtues' and second sight, not that this shows him how to escape from danger; for this he must use his wits, as is the case with most seers. It is because he is younger than Cormac that he agrees to act as the 'servant', while Cormac calls himself the 'Son of the King of

Ireland', while at the castle of the King of Riddles. But when Cormac marries the daughter of the King of Riddles, Alastir continues his quest on his own, aided by the dog-otter, who befriends him as a reward for his faithfulness to his stepbrother, Cormac.

The *rocky path of Ben Buie*, or the Yellow Mountains, appears in many stories, and maybe in some of our dreams.

The *balsam*, or *healing ointment*, also is mentioned in many stories, and reminds us of the 'Elecampane' of the old Mummers' play, *The jar that held the ointment* – in this case the ointment was used to render a body invulnerable.

As for the *Bare-stripping Hangman*, he gets his name from his custom of stripping his victims naked before hanging them on a nail!

Maghach Colgar

From *Popular Tales of the West Highlands*, Vol. II.

The Smith's Rock in the Isle of Skye

From *Waifs and Strays of Celtic Tradition*, Vol. III.

This legend is identified with several places in the Highlands. Wooden graips are long-pronged graips or forks of wood, used for lifting bracken, seaweed etc.

LIST OF SOURCES

Popular Tales of the West Highlands
Collector and translator, J.F. Campbell of Islay.
Published by Alexander Gardener of Paisley and London, 1890–1892.

Volume II

The Fian: p. 85, No. 29 (told by Alex. M'Donald, Barra, 1859)
Conall: p. 148, No. 35 (told by Alex. MacNeill, fisherman, Barra)
The Fair Gruagach: p. 424, No. 51 (Alex. MacNeill, Barra)

Volume III

Finn's Questions: p. 46, No. 59 (Donald MacPhie, smith, Barra)
Diarmid and Gráinne: p. 49, No. 60 (Alex. Macalister, Barra)
Kyle Rhea: p. 120, No. 67 (Alex. Carmichael, excise officer, Islay)
Daughter of the King Under the Waves: p. 421, No. 86 (Roderick MacLean, tailor, Barra)

Waifs and Strays of Celtic Tradition
Argyllshire Series
Collected and translated from the Gaelic by D. MacInnes.
Published by the Folk Lore Society, London, 1890, and by Alfred Nutt and David Nutt, London, 1891.

Number II

The Son of the King of Ireland: p. 2, No. 1
A King of Scotland: p. 68, No. 3

The Herding of Cruagachan: p. 94, No. 4

The Tale of Young Manus: p. 338, No. 10

Leoän Creeäch, Son of the King of Ireland: p. 376, No. 11

Number III

Collected and translated by J. MacDougall.

How Finn Kept the Children of the Big Young Hero of the Ship: p. 1, No. 1

Finn's Journey to Lochlann: p. 17, No. 2

The Lad of the Skin Coverings: p. 27, No. 3

How Finn Was in the House of the Yellow Field: p. 56, No. 4

The Smith's Rock in the Isle of Skye: p. 73, No. 5

The King of Riddles and the Bare-stripping Hangman: p. 76, No. 6

Number IV

Collected and translated from the Gaelic by J.G. Campbell.

The First Story of Finn: p. 16

The Day of the Battle of the Sheaves: p. 172

Finn MacCoul in the Kingdom of the Big Men: p. 175

Finn and his Men: p. 197

Finn's Ransom: p. 239

Numbering of Duvan's Men: p. 258

A Celtic Miscellany
Translations from Celtic Literature

By Kenneth Hurlstone Jackson.

Published by Routledge & Kegan Paul, 1951.

The Hill of Howth: p. 71, No. 20

OTHER BOOKS TO READ AND LOOK AT:

Proinsias Mac Cana, *Celtic Mythology*, Hamlyn, 1970.

John Sharkey, *Celtic Mysteries*, Thames and Hudson, 1975.

Anne Ross, *Pagan Celtic Britain*, London and Columbia, 1967.

CLUES

CLUES TO PEOPLE

Caoilte: The son of Ronan and a relative of Finn. He was the swiftest runner in the Fianna. 'At full speed his shoulders rose so high, he looked as though he had three heads, and then he would outstrip the March wind' (J. Macdougall). He was said to have a fairy mistress, who gave him an enchanted belt which increased his powers of endurance, and a ring that made him victorious. He was as heroic as he was swift-footed, and he was also one of the chief bards of the Fianna.

Conan: One of the most prominent and best-drawn characters among the Fianna. He has been compared to Homeric *Thersites*. He appears to be spiteful, cowardly and boastful. He was the brother of Goll, and belonged to the Clann Maoirne. His surname was supposed to be Maol because he was 'crop-eared', but in *The House of the Yellow Field*, he is left to free himself from the hearth to which he has been stuck, and in his effort to tear himself away, leaves the skin and hair from the back of his head, and so acquires the nickname Conan Maol, or Bald Conan. He is disgraced when he is unable to wrestle with the king's daughter, but his fatal mistake and end comes in the story of *Kyle Rhea*, when he tries to smoke the wives of the Fian out of their house after they had been suspected unjustly of unfaithfulness, and he had been directed to keep watch over them. Altogether an unpleasant character, for getting himself and others into trouble. Ridiculed by the Fianna, but feared on account of his venomous tongue, he was always his own worst enemy.

Cuchulin: Cuchulin was the Hero of Ulster, as Finn was that of Leinster. He was supposed to have lived in the first century of the Christian era, but appears in the third. He does not appear often in the stories about the Fianna.

Cumhal: A leader of the Irish warriors, and the father of Finn, who was killed by trickery by the Lochlanners.

Diarmid: Diarmid Donn (the auburn-haired) was one of the best-loved members of the Fianna, and a nephew of Finn. He was said to be extremely handsome and attractive to women. He had a beauty spot on his face, so fatal in its power of attraction that he had to hide it.

Finn MacCoul: Finn MacCoul, whose name is more correctly spelt in Gaelic *Fionn MacCumhaill*, was son of Cumhal, the great Irish warrior chief and legendary hero. The oldest version of his origins is *The Boyish Exploits of Finn*, translated from a fifteenth-century manuscript by O'Donovan, and printed by Kuno Meyer. His character is clearly drawn in the legends and tales about him in this book, and it is said that he rests with the other members of his Fian in the Smith's Rock.

Gráinne: The daughter of the Earl of Ulster, and Finn's bride. She fell in love with Diarmid and eloped with him.

Manus: The son of the King of Lochlann who came to Ireland to carry off Finn's wife and Bran, his hound. He was defeated, was not killed but returned later to trick the Fianna into unprepared combat and attack by the Lochlanners while the Fianna were feasting, without success. The tale about Manus in this collection gives an earlier and very different account of him.

Ossian: Ossian was Finn's son, and legend says that his mother was a deer, only because Ossian wrote a song with the line: 'If you are my mother, and art a deer'.

He is the finest bard of the Fianna, and his name has provoked more discussion and recognition than any other poet of the Celtic race. He outlived all other members of the Fianna, and joined Saint Patrick, who married his daughter, who treated him very badly in his old age. His poems were said to have been written out by Saint Patrick, who eventually burnt them when he learned that they were mere inventions. James Macpherson claimed that he had found fragments of the manuscripts of Ossian's poems. He 'translated' and published what he claimed to have 'found'. See *Macpherson* under M below.

CLUES TO MEANING

Balsam: The little jar of balsam, or reviving ointment, used to bring the dead to life, occurs in many stories. It is an ancient custom found in most primitive tribes and survived, in mime, in the old Mummers' plays, where it was often used by the character called the Doctor.

Ben: Mountain, summit.

Bothie: Rough cottage or hut to house labourers.

Brough: A broch, round tower or fort, with inner and outer walls of dry-stone, and small chambers for human habitation and a central space for animals. Peculiar to Orkney, and the outer islands and coastal districts of Scotland and Ireland. In these tales, they are often called 'houses'.

Carle: Old man.

Carlin: Old woman, hag; sometimes a witch.

Chalder: A measure of grain, about eight-quarters.

Cruachan: Name of the site of the ancient kings of Connaught, now Rath-croghan, central Co. Roscommon.

Dogs, Hounds: Hounds were obviously of great importance to the Fianna as hunters, as indeed they still are. It was natural for the hunters to have their favourite dog, who was not only a working companion, but a dear friend. They seem to have been Deer Hounds, and bitches were especially precious.

Bran was the name of Finn's special dog, and how he acquired him is told in the story of *How Finn Kept the Children of the Big Hero of the Ship*. Bran, Finn's favourite dog, had a magical and venomous claw, which he used in extreme circumstances. He also had a gold chain, which also incidentally saves Finn's life.

The Grey Dog, Bran's brother, was given to a chief of the Lochlanners, who got him from the Young Hero, in exchange for the latter's life. The Grey Dog went mad when he lost his first master and was allowed to run wild in the Great Glen by the Lochlann chief. He was recovered from the Great Glen by Finn, with the aid of Bran's gold chain.

The Black Dog occurs in many Gaelic tales, seemingly sinister in most cases, and in these tales there is a fight between Bran and the Black Dog, who is killed by Bran.

A leash of dogs means a group of fifty dogs. In some tales Conan is the keeper of the dogs.

Fianna: Bands of warriors and hunters, made up from two clans, and Finn MacCoul was leader and chief over them both. According to one account there were 9,000 perfect heroes in the Fianna, and their tasks were to protect their country from invaders from the east and north, and also to protect women from giants. The many tales of their exploits are as much due to the excellence of their bards as to their success in heroic deeds. A single band of the Fianna was called a Fian, and Finn had his special Fian, or group of warriors, who were also close friends.

Foghaid: Finn's enchanted whistle – sometimes called the *Wooden Crier* – which could be heard by any member of the Fianna, when blown under great stress.

Foster-brothers: Fostering was an important feature of ancient Celtic society, and persisted in Gaelic Scotland until the eighteenth century. The sons and daughters of lesser nobles were sent at an early age to be brought up in the households of more powerful nobles, and were only returned to their natural parents when the boys were of military age, and the girls were ready for marriage. In the early Celtic tradition, the bond between foster-brothers was very strong, and in some instances almost sacred. So also was the bond between foster-children and foster-parents, which was lifelong. The Romans noted that this was peculiar to the Celts who, at the same time, considered it a disgrace for a son to sit next to his natural father in public. It is doubtful if this was the custom among the ordinary Celts, however, who are not mentioned much in early accounts, and were probably considered to be slaves by the warriors and 'heroes'.

Gillie: Boy attendant. Nowadays, a manservant serving the gentry in country pursuits – shooting, fishing, etc.

Glaive: Spear, lance.

Graip: Dung-fork, formerly made of wood.

Green Isle: Celtic paradise, like Avalon of the Ancient Britons. Unlike Avalon, it was not the resting place of the dead heroes or warriors such as the Fianna, who went to their rest in dark caverns.

Heads: The ancient Celts took the heads of their vanquished enemies as trophies of victory. The practice had a profound religious and superstitious role in their life. The heads were displayed on spikes outside their broughs and castles, and at the entrances of their sanctuaries. Niches have been found in the pillars for heads, at these entrances. Later, heads carved in stone were added, rather the way stonemasons carved heads of their neighbours on the pillars and entrances of our old medieval churches and cathedrals.

Hill of Howth: A peninsula on the north side of Dublin Bay, Ireland.

House of the Yellow Field: This was called after the fields on the banks of the Shannon, on which it was built.

Kirtle: Woman's gown, or outer petticoat.

Knight: Different to the romantic title, rather a chief or horseman.

Lady of the Green Kirtle: Part goddess, part fairy. Green was the colour of fairy clothes.

Lochlann: Name given to the lands north-east of Scotland, including North Germany, between the Rhine and the Elbe, also Denmark, Norway and Iceland – but generally Scandinavia.

Mac an Luin: Finn's sword, which was made especially for him, and whose cut was so sharp and sure that no trace of the victim was left on its blade. It is said that Finn himself was slain by his Mac an Luin, and that no other sword could have slain him.

Macpherson: James Macpherson (1736-96), born at Ruthven, Perthshire, published *Fingal, An Ancient Epic Poem in Six Books, together with several other poems, composed by Ossian, son of Fingal*, translated from the Gaelic by James Macpherson, and published in 1761 by Bucket and De Hondt, Strand, London. He was only 25 when he produced this work, which was encouraged by the *literati* of Edinburgh, and was part of the new romantic movement, which in itself was a reaction against the rationalism and classicism of the eighteenth century. For true assessment of this strange work, read *Sources of Macpherson's Ossian* by Professor Derek Thomson.

Press: Cupboard.

Runs: Runs are series of formal description. There are Bespelling runs, Boat-beaching runs, Resting and Travelling runs, Saluting runs, etc.

Salmon: This royal fish was considered a repository of 'Other World' wisdom.

Scholars: Older schoolboys, studying with monks – probably what would now be called students – college boys.

Shinty: An old game, still played in Scotland and Ireland, rather like hockey, played with clubs of wood, resembling golf clubs, and a ball, or knot of wood. In Shinty there are two goals, called 'hails', and the object of each side is to drive the ball beyond their opponents' goal/hail.

Smalls: The two wrists, ankles, and knees, which were tied together after capture by an enemy.

Son's grief: It was a Celtic and Scandinavian tradition and superstition that to grieve too much for a dead father was unlucky for a son, and brought disaster to him. (Hamlet?)

Swans: Consistently regarded as a sign of purity, with sexual associations. A disguise for lovers.

Sword: Of great significance in all Celtic legends.

Sword of Light: The bright, mystic emblem of the sun. In old stone carvings, this sword points to the left, or the north.

Tara: Traditionally the capital of ancient Ireland – about twenty miles north of Dublin County in Co. Meath.

Wandering Lads: These Lads appear in so many tales, always with the same request to be of service to the Hero. As soon as they had negotiated and agreed on a wage, they assumed a power over the Hero, their master, that suggests their role had more significance than that of a casual servant. They devised quests, which had to be undertaken, in return for the services often forced on the Hero.

Worlds/Earth: Uttermost World, World Under the Waves – in Celtic mythology, a plurality of worlds occur, as in all northern mythology. For descriptions of the earth, as the 'red quarters' or 'brown quarters', I can find no explanation – they are probably poetic.

Year and a Day: This seems to be a formal measure of time in all northern folk tales, as is seven years and a day. One can guess at that 'extra day' and connect it with the extra day of our 'leap year'. I must admit that I do not know.

Note: I hope Gaelic speakers will forgive the simplified spelling of names like *Finn MacCoul*. It is sometimes used by J.F. Campbell, but my reason is that the simple spelling conveys the sound which, to non-Gaelic speakers, *Fionn Mac-Cumhall* does not.